UNFORESEEN

NICK PIROG

www.nickthriller.com

Author's Note

I wrote this book in 2003 when I was 22 years old. It's raw and unpolished, but it is my baby. If you haven't read anything by me before, you might want to start with *Gray Matter* or *3 a.m.* then come back and read this one later. That being said, I am still very proud of this book and hope you enjoy it.

Happy reading,

Nick

Chapter 1

The topmost of the Penobscot Bay lighthouse was barely visible, the morning sun reflecting off its watchful eye. I cranked out the sails and picked up a paltry breeze, doing precisely the opposite of what I'd intended, heading the boat farther out into the vast Atlantic. I snatched up the book on sailing I'd bought, *Sailing for Dummies*, and skimmed the table of contents for "How the Hell to Get Back to Shore." But evidently, my copy was missing that chapter.

There was an enlightening page about fetching and after reading it twice, I determined I would have been better off going with the *Sailing for Idiots* line. The only fetching in my future would be for a ride back to land.

I slipped into the captain's chair—a red nylon lawn chair—and found a section more up my alley entitled, "Getting Your Feet Wet." There was a series of sketches with attached labels and after careful debate, the Michelob bottle and I decided we had ourselves a schooner. According to the book, "The schooner is a traditional rig with two or more masts, the front mast (foremost) being shorter than the main mast."

I peered up to check if the front mast, *foremost*, was indeed shorter than the main mast, but I didn't know which end of the boat was the front. Thus the boat audit was a complete failure. Why couldn't everything on the boat have labels on it like in the book? I made a mental note to buy some sticky notes on the way home.

The sun had recently escaped the ocean's horizon and there were a few far off fishing boats. I pulled the binoculars up from around my neck and focused them on the nearest ship. The ship was charcoal for the most part, close to a hundred feet long, and came fully loaded with three tattered men. The rest of the boats were too far away to make out their names and I couldn't help wondering if one of them was the *Maine Catch.* I still owed the crew a round of beers for saving my ass. That, however, was a completely different yarn altogether.

I set the binoculars down, took a long swig of beer, leaving an inch reserve in the darkly tinted brown bottle, and picked up the second piece of reading material I'd brought along. It was a hardback novel entitled *Eight in October.* The much-anticipated book was a true-crime thriller based on a string of murders that occurred throughout Maine in October of the past year.

I turned the book over in my hands. The majority of the cover was monopolized by one of Maine's eminent firs, each of the tree's leaves visually changing from emerald green to saffron yellow and finally to cranberry red, giving off the impression of an iridescent autumn in overdrive. From each of the leaves fell a droplet of blood, forming a puddle at the base of the tree.

I peeled opened the front cover gingerly as if the words might fall out if I hastened. I found the dedication page and regarded the dedication: To the eight women who lost their lives.

I didn't read the names. I didn't have to. I knew them all by heart.

~

I clapped the book shut and had the fleeting thought to chuck *Eight in October* into the pickled abyss. The book belonged beneath the sediment at the ocean's floor. The last thing this community needed was a fifteen-ounce relic from a fifteen-day nightmare. I was pissed off at the author, some swine named Alex Tooms, who had decided to turn a buck at the mercy of these eight women. I was curious as to this Tooms' countenance, but it seems he didn't have the fiber to put his picture on the book jacket. This decision may have been impacted by the letter I sent him detailing the collection of ways I planned to end his life should I ever recognize him in public. If my letter had swayed his decision, the point was moot; the prick had a book signing coming up on October 1st, or more notably, on the anniversary of the first woman's murder.

What a classy guy. I hope someone writes a book about how he was beaten to death with his own book at his own book signing.

I'd buy it.

I put the book down. Baby steps.

At this rate I'd get through the book in a touch under a decade. I grabbed another beer from the cooler and decided while I was there I might as well grab two. Did I mention the cooler came with the chair and is, by default, attached to the chair? Well it is.

I knocked back the two beers and chased them down with egg salad. With my stomach content and the alcohol finding its way into my bloodstream, I decided to take another crack at the book. It was almost noon and I was behind on my three-word-a-minute quota. I found the first page and began reading:

> *Autumn in Maine is like nowhere else. The leaves fall from the trees a harvest gold and trickle to the ground a deep cherry. The lobster catch is at its peak, fishermen's cages teeming with the vermilion crustaceans. The sun wakes a nation, crawling across the Atlantic a refulgent auburn. Last October, Maine was blanketed in red. Not by the leaves, not by the lobsters, not by the sunrise, but by the blood of eight young women. Truly, last autumn in Maine was like nowhere else.*

I peeled the label off the beer bottle, smoothing it out like a crisp dollar bill, and thought about the last sentence, *Truly, last autumn in Maine was like nowhere else.*

I had to credit Mr. Tooms: he may lack all levels of morality, but his writing did capture the solemnity of the period. It was around this time last year when the first woman was found. I'd been living in Philly at the time and the murder had earned a small write-up on page eighteen of *The Philadelphia Inquirer*. I remember this distinctly because it was the first time anything from Maine made the paper.

Maine's papers were a different story. In a state with the lowest crime rate in the country, finding a woman in thirty pieces was front page news. One of the lesser papers, the *Waterville Tribune*, ran an article written by none other than investigative journalist Alex Tooms. The paper was on the verge of bankruptcy and had nothing to lose by running Tooms' vivid and grotesquely accurate accounts of the murders. The newspaper sold more copies in October than it had the entire nine months prior.

After the massacre ended—or, as I like to say, *went on medical leave*—this Tooms character had publishers throwing themselves at him, as to say, gold bars. The book already climbed to number five on the *New York Times* Best Sellers list and nearly every person I'd talked to had either read it, was in the process of reading it, or was reading it for the second time. My sister even said it wasn't half bad. I'd been calling her Judas all week.

I was interested in how Tooms described the body of the first victim, and after skimming five pages I found what I was looking for:

> *Called "The County" by most New Englanders, Aroostook covers 6,453 square miles and grows more potatoes than any other county in the United States. Sitting amidst two of these square miles was a small, functionally spartan farmhouse. By noon on October 2nd, the once tame farmhouse had been transformed into the largest crime scene in Maine's 350 years of existence.*
>
> *Bangor Chief Medical Examiner, Dr. Caitlin Dodds, described the scene simply as, "Sickening. Just sickening. It was truly Johnny Appleseed meets Jack the Ripper."*
>
> *The victim's body was scattered throughout a half acre radius, severed into more than thirty definitive pieces. The most disheartening revelation came when the victim's abdomen was unearthed. The blond haired, blue-eyed, medical examiner said, "It was immediately evident the victim was pregnant, except the baby, or fetus, was absent."*
>
> *Less than thirty feet away was the victim's unborn child.*

I tossed the book against the railing of the boat and it came to rest in teepee-like fashion. This was the explicit reason I didn't want to read the book in the first place. Now I had the image of an unborn baby lying in a field in my mind.

I grabbed another sandwich (bologna and cheese) and concentrated on a less depressing image, specifically, Dr. Caitlin Dodds. I think there was an unwritten rule that if you were a woman in law enforcement you had to be unattractive, stiff, and named Mel. Dr. Caitlin Dodds was the exception to this rule—she was a stunner.

I closed my eyes and fell asleep with the good doctor on my mind.

Chapter 2

When I opened my eyes, I was blinded by the sun directly overhead. There wasn't a cloud in the sky and the daystar seemed to take up half the seamless cerulean. We were in the midst of one of Maine's renowned Indian summers and the temperature was around seventy.

I took a deep breath of the crisp ocean air, which was reminiscent of eating a saltine between gasps on an oxygen tank, and gazed across Mother Atlantic. There wasn't much for waves on her this morning and it was hard to believe I was bobbing along in the second largest body of water on the planet. An osprey flew nearby and did his dive-bomb-fish-retrieval thing, and I couldn't help feeling sympathy pangs for the little silver guy in the osprey's beak. One second he's swimming downstream to visit his brother; the next second he's Superman, only to be super dead. Poor little fella.

I kicked off my khaki shorts, boxer briefs, and docksides then checked to see if there were any other boats in the vicinity before walking the plank au naturel. The Atlantic was freezing but a good freezing, the kind you get in water above fifty degrees but below fifty-one. If you want to get technical, I wasn't in the Atlantic per se; I was in the Penobscot Bay which, forty miles east, invariably becomes the Atlantic Ocean.

The bay retained its summer heat a wee bit longer than, say, the English Channel, and I was frigid not freezing. I trod water and watched the predominantly white hull of the *Backstern* bob up and down with the current.

If you're wondering about the name, my sister, Lacy, aptly

named the boat after her pug Baxter. Alas, the *Backstern* was moving but it was coming toward me. So no worries, right? Wrong. My entire body had turned into one comprehensive cramp. Now this could have been rooted in my not waiting a half hour after eating. Perhaps the five beers I'd guzzled in the last hour had something to do with it. There's also a slim chance it was related to the two chunks of lead that had gone zipping through my flesh nearly a year ago. Most likely it was a combination of all three.

I turned over onto my back and went into the dead man's float, praying I wouldn't substantiate the term's connotation. Some form of sea life brushed my side and immediately I was more frightened of my pecker becoming some fish's lunch than drowning at sea.

Once safely back on the boat, I couldn't help but notice if something had eaten Paddington, it would still be hungry.

The dusty, white sands of the shoreline were visible for the first time, but I still had three hours or so until I washed up. I plucked *Eight in October* off the boat deck and sank into the captain's chair.

The third woman's murder especially interested me, and I found what I was looking for on Page 59:

> *When the body of Amber Osgood was found on the afternoon of October 5th, the buck was passed from the Bangor Police Department to the United States Federal Bureau of Investigation. The FBI sent a task force to Maine to head up the investigation. The task force was comprised of agents Todd Gregory and Wade Gleason, both from the FBI Violent Crime Unit, and FBI consultant Thomas Prescott.*
>
> *Todd Gregory, 27, was a third-year man at the FBI and regarded as the top young agent in his field. Gregory was short, strikingly handsome with hazel eyes, dark brown hair, and olive skin.*
>
> *Wade Gleason, 47, had been a staple in the FBI community for more than twenty years. Gleason had worked more than two hundred serial homicide cases and was considered worldwide to be the best in the business. The soft-spoken African-American was tall, athletically built, and known simply as "Glease" by peers.*

> *Rounding out the team was FBI consultant Thomas Prescott. Prescott, 33, a "retired" homicide detective, was ruggedly handsome with unruly brown hair, slate blue-gray eyes, and renowned for his irascible wit, erratic behavior, and confrontational style.*

I threw the book over the side of the boat. Erratic behavior, my ass. Who the fuck did this jerk think he was? First things first, I was *handsome,* not ruggedly handsome. And second, my confrontational style stemmed from the fact I was working with three morons. All right, two morons. Wade Gleason was one smart cookie and he'd kick the shit out of his own mother if she overcooked his steak. But Todd Gregory and Caitlin Dodds were about as useful as a twelve-dollar bill.

As for that little pipsqueak Gregory, he was so pretty most of the male cops I knew had a thing for him, and not just the gay ones. I'd been flipping through *People* magazine at the supermarket in June or July when I came across his pretty little face in their "50 Most Beautiful People" issue. Evidently, it violates Maine state law to light a magazine on fire in a public place because I was arrested and forced to pay a small fine.

I peered over the edge of the boat, but *Eight in October* was nowhere to be found. Rats. Now I would have to spend another twenty-seven dollars on a tasteless book I'd find no solace in reading.

I grabbed a beer from the cooler and sucked down all twelve ounces, then lying back I let my mind wander to the day I first met the task force.

Chapter 3

I opened the door of the large Philadelphia apartment to the distinct ring of my cell phone. I extracted my cell from under the middle, olive drab, sofa cushion and flipped it open

"Prescott."

"Is this Detective Prescott?" came a harsh deluge.

"That's *ex*-detective Prescott." At least according to the three documents I had to sign, initial, and lick.

The voice softened a bit. "Right. This is Charles Mangrove. I got your number from Dwight Stully."

Dwight Stully had been my chief at the Seattle Police Department and was still my main contact with the world of law enforcement. The name Mangrove sounded familiar and I hoped I was talking to the long-lost, twice-removed, third cousin of the Mangrove I suspected. "Any relation to the Charles Mangrove who happens to be Deputy Director of the FBI?"

"One and the same. One and the same."

Oh boy.

Charles continued, "Listen, I'm calling in regards to these killings up in Maine. Are you familiar with them?"

I only knew of two killings, but from my experience, "them" was an overtone for three or more. If I were smart, I would have hung up the phone. But I wasn't smart. Cunning, yes. Deft, sure. Competent, probably. But smart? Well, the jury was still out on that one. I said, "Sure, the two gals who got hacked to shit. What's this have to do with the FBI?"

"You mean three gals. This morning they found a third. She was killed on an island off the coast of Maine called Campobello. Campobello is Canadian territory."

"So why isn't the Royal Caribbean Mariachi Band taking over?"

"You mean the Royal Canadian Mounted Police?"

I guess Charles took my silence as some sort of nod and persevered, "Actually, it's Interpol's jurisdiction."

I was confused, but I was used to being confused when working with the FBI. "You skipped the part about how it landed in the hands of the Far Below-average Intelligence Agency."

He laughed. "Dwight told me you were a smart ass."

Cunning ass. Get it straight. "Yeah, well, it keeps people on their toes, and it keeps me from killing myself. Send old Dwight my regards next time you see him."

"Will do. I'll tell you how the case landed in our lap. Interpol has their hands tied with about fifteen hundred terrorist threats and doesn't give a rat's ass about a brother who hacked up his sister and a couple other girls. They think they're pawning this off on us, but we need the publicity."

The big picture was starting to come into focus and it wasn't a Picasso. "And you're calling me to get my tailor's number?"

"Right. Listen, we want to hire you to augment the investigation. Glease told me a little about you and it seems to fit with what I've heard: you're a prick, but you're a smart fucking prick."

Cunning fucking prick. Say it with me.

I asked Chuck, "Is that who I'll be working with?"

"Yep. You'll be working directly under him."

I didn't like working under anyone, but if I had to, there were worse people to work under than Wade Gleason. "Who else is on the team?"

"Guy named Todd Gregory. Young guy. Graduated number one from Georgetown a couple years ago."

"Sounds like my bio ten years ago and look how I turned out."

He laughed again and said, "You'll have FBI status and the government will pay you a healthy stipend."

"First off, I don't want FBI status. I have a reputation to uphold. And secondly, what exactly is the government's idea of a healthy stipend?"

"Five hundred dollars a day plus expenses."

Five hundred magoombas a day. Their balls must be deeper in the meat grinder than I thought. I said, "You can call me an FBI consultant."

"Deal. You have a fax?"

I rattled off my fax number and Charles said, "I'm sending you the information packet and autopsy reports the Bangor Police Department forwarded me from the first two murders."

Sure he was. I would get about a fifth of what the Bangor Police Department sent the FBI. The Feds are an odd bunch. They recruit you to help them out, then go to great lengths to ensure you don't know jack squat. I'd always hated when the suits came in and stripped a case from me. I inquired, "Who had the baton before it was passed to you idiots?"

He laughed again. Wow, three for three. If only my dates went as well. Charles said, "I talked with the Bangor medical examiner, some lady named Dodds. She was understandably upset when she found out we were stripping the case. We could use a feminine eye and her forensic background will be incomparable, so we decided to keep her on as part of the task force. Part of our new image."

New image, my ass. I cut to the chase, literally. "When does my flight leave?"

~

It was raining and my doorman, an old black gent named Hale, and I huddled under the apartment building's long balustrade. Ten minutes later, Hale had successfully hailed me a cab. I can just picture Hale's reaction to the results of his job aptitude test when they told him his occupational dreams were limited to doorman or weatherman. Nevertheless, Hale threw my bag in the trunk and wished me a safe trip.

The cabby delivered me to Philadelphia International in less than ten minutes and I rewarded him with a crisp fifty. He seemed quite appreciative and I was wished a safe trip yet again. The woman at the American Airline's desk asked to see my driver's license, handed me a ticket, and I was wished a safe trip for a third time. I checked my back for a sign that read "Going on Unsafe Trip" but it must have fallen off.

I walked to the terminal and handed my ticket to a computer with light brown hair and a large mainframe. The computer directed me through black curtains to a nicely cushioned window seat.

Holy fucking hand baskets, the Federal boys shelled out for first class. If it wasn't an off day in my rotation, I would have shit my pants.

I'd flown first-class on one other occasion and I remember noticing they kept the best looking flight attendants up here and the gargoyles in coach. A twenty-something knockout with dark brown hair and hazel eyes appeared from thin air and asked if I would enjoy a preflight cocktail.

A preflight cocktail? I never knew such a thing existed. I ordered a whiskey sour and my flight attendant theory placated, I extracted the fax documents from my attaché case.

My drink came and I flirted shamelessly with the stewardess (her name was August but she was born in November, talk about irony) until she broke away to do the preflight announcements. A few minutes later we were in the air and Manhattan was just a postage stamp on a postcard. August jumped on the intercom and informed us we were cruising at an altitude of 31,000 feet. I was going to inform her I was cruising at 31,000 feet, 8 ½ inches, but I didn't feel like getting sent to coach.

The flight was only about an hour and fifteen minutes and I needed to get cracking if I were going to know my one-fifth backwards and forwards. I read all twenty fax pages and noticed the autopsy photos were mysteriously MIA. I'd been on the case for all of one hour and twelve minutes and the Feds were already flaking out on me. They probably figured sending me first class would cancel out their lack of geniality. Dickheads.

The gist of the reports was as follows: two women had been raped, beaten, turned into jigsaw puzzles, and their eyes taken as door prizes. The most intriguing nugget was the first victim, Ingrid Grayer, had been pregnant and the DNA showed the father was the brother, Tristen Grayer. Tristen was the prime suspect, whom the *New York Times* had dubbed "The Mainiac." There was a small write-up on him, which would have been more poignant had it read, "We have no information at this time."

The plane landed and I walked out into the Bangor International Airport corridor, realizing I'd left the fax documents in the seat pocket in front of me. Whoops, looks like someone had their leisure reading for the next flight.

There wasn't much I could do at this juncture, so I bought a book by Michael Crichton called *Timeline* that I'd heard had been made into a bad movie. I found the airport bar, Arriv*Ale's*, and retreated to a far corner. Fortunately, the bar's service was better than the bar's name, and within ninety seconds I had an Irish coffee in front of me and a club sandwich on the way. I read about fifteen pages of the Crichton novel, which I didn't understand because I was one of the few people on the planet without a Ph.D. in quantum physics, and polished off the club.

I'd just started over on page one when two guys appeared over my left shoulder. They were both clad in dark suits with black ties and I had the eerie feeling I was on the set of *Men in Black III.*

If I had two words to describe each of the people before me they would be: short & pretty and tall & black. I'd actually worked with tall & black on a couple cases prior to this one, and we hadn't hated each other, which is a rarity with me. I can be a touch annoying.

I stood up and extended my hand, "How's it going, Glease? Been what, a year and a half?"

Wade Gleason smiled, revealing teeth almost too white, and said, "How can I forget? You lost a hundred dollars to me in a game of one-on-one. My wife wanted to thank you personally for a lovely night on the town. Speaking of which, you and that Jennifer girl ever get hitched?"

"Nope. She left me for a Dalmatian two weeks before the big day." A lie but not far off.

It appeared as though Wade had no intention of introducing me to short & pretty and I asked, "Who's your caddie?"

Wade did a poor job of suppressing a smile and introduced the two of us. Todd Gregory was no taller than five-three and would probably get carded when he tried to vote come this November. I shook Todd's petite and presumably freshly manicured hand and said, "What'd you do, slip the bouncer a fifty?"

His smile muscles were clearly atrophied as he made no reaction to my jest and said dryly, "You're funny. I heard you were funny."

I looked at Glease and threw him my best *You've got to be shitting me. Is this guy for real*? look, and said, "You've got to be shitting me. Is this guy for real?"

~

The three of us settled into a black Caprice, only driven by mobsters and FBI agents, and I was disappointed when the driver said his name was Tim and not Fagioli.

I was trying to get a feel for how much involvement I would have in this case and said, "So let me get this chain of command straight. It goes Director Mangrove, then you." I pointed at Gleason in the front seat. "Then me." I pointed to myself. "Then Fagioli." I pointed at the driver. "Then that guy." I pointed to a bum sleeping on an airport bench. "Then his babysitter." I pointed at Gregory to my right.

Gregory didn't laugh and I was beginning to wonder if he was hearing impaired. Gleason said, "Actually it goes him, then me, then you."

Gregory stared out the window, letting the implications of the news sink in. It was difficult to talk with my black Armani dress shoes touching my tonsils, but I somehow managed, "You mean to tell me this little shit is Special Agent in Charge?"

"It's part of our new image."

"I can't believe this sack is SAC. Glease, you've been the Denzel of the suits for twenty years and now they got you working for Michael J. Fox's little brother. How in the hell are you okay with that?"

Gregory turned his gaze from the window and said, "If Wade is Denzel Washington and I'm Michael J. Fox. Then who exactly does that make you?"

I wanted to say, "I'm Brad Pitt, you fucking idiot," but I wasn't that big of a badass so I said, "I'm Stephen Baldwin."

Glease couldn't contain himself and erupted in laughter. I added to my buddy Todd, "And I said you were Michael J. Fox's little brother, not Michael J. Fox."

~

I spent the next hour and twenty minutes ogling the continuous landscape called Maine. Red firs, yellow maples, green spruces, orange you name it. It made every snapshot my eyes had taken in the past seem black and white. When God painted the world, Maine would be the area where he dabbed his brush to rid the excess paint. Layers of greens, swimming with yellows, sleeping on reds, hiding from oranges.

Another thing I noticed was as you move north along the coast it was as if you were traveling into the past, America circa 1960. (It appeared the state of Maine was a couple decades behind its 49 counterparts. Well, 47. I imagine the Dakotas are much the same.) Electrical cables ran for miles along the country highway and I had the quiet feeling the car was racing the current, and possibly time.

We stopped at what appeared to be a station of sorts and after reflecting back on my conversation with Director Mangrove, "Campobello is Canadian territory," I deduced it was a border crossing.

See that? One part cocky bastard, two parts astute detective.

I opened the car door and realized how darkly tinted the windows had been. The sky was not overcast, but a perfect cobalt blue. Glease grabbed his attaché case from the trunk and the two of us made our way to the small group congregating near a sign reading "Roosevelt Bridge."

There were three people in the group. A short, fat, balding man who'd obviously gotten the short end of the stick. Todd Gregory, who had a stick up his ass. And a blonde bombshell, who looked in desperate need of a stick.

Glease and I nudged our way into the circle and it turned out the bald man was not George Costanza but a Canadian Mountie named Francis. Francis was wearing a neatly pressed red suit a couple sizes too small and the three hairs left on his scalp had somehow formed themselves into a cowlick. We shook hands and he didn't say "Eh" or "Hoser," and I was skeptical if he was really Canadian.

The blonde bombshell was more like a blond nuclear bombshell. She was gorgeous, her eyes the same cobalt blue as the sky, set in a soft, angelic face. She had on a white V-neck blouse, a tan blazer, a matching knee-length skirt, and black stilettos. She looked like she'd just stepped off Wall Street and I was shocked to learn she was the Fed's contact at the Bangor Police Department. The delectable Dr. Caitlin Dodds.

We were all introduced and I was hoping Dr. Caitlin was thinking *Dr. Caitlin Prescott, not bad, not bad at all*, but she looked more like the type to make me adopt her last name.

There wasn't much for small talk and after each of us signed a form we broke huddle and headed back to the cars. I hesitated for a couple seconds, gazing across the Atlantic trying to make out where the thin bridge ended and this so-called island began. There was an ulterior motive for my hesitation which paid off when I fell into stride behind the good doctor. To say the view was spectacular would be an understatement, her professional skirt unable to shroud the well-maintained, grade-A caboose housed beneath the fabric.

Thomas Dodds, I could deal with that.

~

No one was allowed at the crime scene until the Feds arrived, which is a terribly stupid policy and everyone was pissed off. Well, except the Feds. And me. And Francis, the quasi-Canadian Mountie, didn't seem all that upset. So I guess that left Caitlin. Dr. Caitlin Dodds was pissed off.

I made a point to get in the same car as Dr. Dodds who greeted me with a grunt when I had her slide over in the backseat. No one else filed in, and within ten seconds it was clear why: Dr. Caitlin Dodds was a monstrous bitch.

The car started onto the bridge and after staring at me for a couple awkward seconds, the doctress barked, "What? Your suit get lost at the cleaners?"

I've always had the uncanny ability to give off the impression I'm lying whenever I'm telling the truth, and vice versa, so I said, "I'm not FBI."

"Yeah right, you're not FBI like I'm not on my fricking period." She rummaged through her purse and extracted what I can only assume was a tampon.

I attempted to roll out of the car and plunge myself into the Atlantic, but my door wouldn't open. Blasted federal perks. I turned around and saw what I'd thought was a tampon was, in actuality, a pack of Mentos. Now there would be a good commercial. The Freshmaker.

After popping a Mentos—she neglected to offer me one—Dr. Dodds unbuttoned her blazer and revealed she'd been concealing three deadly weapons. While all were thirty-eights and all were equally special, only one was a Smith & Wesson.

I made my way up the eighteen inches to her eyes, and she said, "Sorry, I'll try to de-bitch. I'm just a little wound up right now. I thought these killings were over. Then this morning I get word they found another woman. Then to top it off, they tell me I'm not allowed to do anything because she was found in Canada and the case is being turned over to you imbeciles."

I liked this girl, she hated the Feds almost as much as I did. I cocked my head at the car speeding alongside ours and said, "You mean those imbeciles."

Caitlin sat quietly, no doubt trying to get a read on the asshole with the lavender shirt and tan tweed jacket sitting beside her. Finally she asked, "What are you?"

I repositioned myself on the black leather, "I'm the government's idea of a safety net."

"Safety net? Please explain."

"If I break this case my name is never mentioned and the FBI gets another slot on the bedpost. However, if the case breaks them, my name shows up all over the place and I get slaughtered on the bedpost."

She began buttoning her blazer and said, "It's notch on the bedpost, not slot on the bedpost. Maybe you would have gotten it right if you hadn't been using my tits as a teleprompter."

I knew I'd stared at them one second too long. "Sorry, won't happen again. But you have to admit, it's one hell of a teleprompter."

She tried to look offended but it's hard when the sides of your mouth are turned up in a grin. I guess she thought it was in her best interest to change the subject and said, "Why'd you agree to come up here if you knew this in the first place?"

Making a concerted effort not to let my eyes drift to her boobies, I said, "I could care less if they pin all the blame on me. Hell, I'd take the blame for the JFK assassination if it'd keep these FBI types from bringing it up after one Sex on the Beach. I'm here for one reason and one reason only—I kill killers."

I think the last three words hit deep because she turned her gaze to the window. A suffering thirty seconds passed, each rivet in the bridge rumbling louder than the last, when Caitlin turned and said, "Let me get this straight. You had drinks with an FBI guy and he ordered a Sex on the Beach. What a bunch of pansies."

Be still my heart.

Chapter 4

I finished off the bottom third of a now warm beer and lifted my 160-pound frame from the captain's chair. I still hadn't regained the weight I'd lost and I could actually see the egg salad and bologna vying for position at the gates to my large intestine.

I cranked the steering wheel to the left as I approached the Bayside Harbor, making sure to stay clear of the large ten-foot tires denoting the marina entrance. Funny story: about two months ago I'd taken to the high seas, making sure to pack enough food and beer to last a week (just in case I repeated my *Maine Catch* disaster). But you know what? Sailing is boring. Let me rephrase that: sailing looks like a blast. *Not-sailing*, the term I came up with for what I do on the water, is boring. Next thing I knew, a week's supply of food and drink were gone, I was five pounds heavier and drunk as a skunk.

When I woke up, I was naked except for a pair of socks, which still baffles me because I started the day in bare feet and sandals, and my boat was in the middle of a marsh swamp. Lucky for me, some acne-faced fifteen-year-old was fishing nearby and agreed to sail the boat back to the Bayside Harbor if I gave him a cool hundred up front. When we were about a hundred yards from the harbor, the little shit had the balls to ask me for another hundred. I told him to go jump off a bridge, whereby, he jumped off the boat.

Long story short, I cut a check for two grand to the owner of a 22-foot whaler. After the quote "whaler incident," it'd been common practice for the local kids to line up on the pier each Saturday waiting for my boat to enter the marina. The kids would dive in the water and try to be the first to climb aboard, thus receiving a crisp five-dollar bill from the marina manager on the successful dockage of my vessel.

As I passed through the tire entrance roughly at three miles per hour, I made out close to fifteen kids meandering on the small wooden pier. There was one runt I rooted for each time whose name was Kellon. He was a foot smaller than the other boys and looked like he still belonged on his momma's tit.

Kellon was the only one to notice my boat penetrate the harbor and stealthily entered the water. He had about a twenty-second head start before any of the other kids took notice and dove in. He was within ten feet, splashing up so much water he was hardly visible, when he was overtaken by a couple of the elder boys.

I ran to the edge of the boat and shouted, "Come on, Kellon! Come on, buddy! You can do it. Show these kids who owns this friggin' town."

The elders were pulling themselves over the side when they kept *accidentally* falling back in. When Kellon finally reached the hull, I leaned over the edge and snatched him from the surf. Then I stood him on the railing and whispered in his ear, "Tell the big kids who owns this town."

He took a deep breath and yelled at the top of his lungs, "Kellon owes dis fwiggin' town."

Now, I didn't like kids much, but if I said I wasn't looking for a place to stow him, I'd be lying. He was about three beer bottles tall, with brown eyes the size of half dollars, and missing his four front teeth. With him on the railing, I was only a couple inches taller than him and before I knew it, the guy was wrapped around my neck like a koala.

From previous conversations, I knew Kellon was seven, had a bit of a lisp, and boats were his favorite thing in the "wool-wide-wuld."

I let him go to work and watched in silence as he jimmied the sails and expertly navigated the boat to my designated slip. It was common knowledge that slot 23B belonged to Thomas Prescott, aka, Captain Dipshit.

The marina manager was Kellon's dad, and instead of giving Kellon a Franklin, he gave him a Dr. Pepper. What a lame-o. Plus, the kid needed Ritalin, not caffeine.

I took out my wallet to pay him, but unless Kellon took plastic, he was shit out of luck.

I hauled the cooler and chair out of the boat and Kellon insisted on carrying the cooler to the car for me. When everything was tucked away in the trunk of my Range Rover I asked him, "What's your second favorite thing in the whole wide world?"

He stared at the ground deep in thought, then brown eyes bulging, yelled, "Kwytes!"

Then a kite it was.

~

I screeched out of the dirt parking lot and onto a long expanse of leaf-checkered road, Maine once again impressing me with the wide spectrum of colors at its disposal.

I'd grown up near the Puget Sound which is beautiful in its own right, but it couldn't compete with the majesty of Maine. The road in front of me wrapped around a jutting mountain before straightening out, and I floored the gas, putting all 320 of the Range Rover's horses to work.

There was a front coming in over the Atlantic, and the ocean and sky were beginning to mesh into gray. I squealed around an inlet and thanked God I was off the water. If I were inept when the conditions were perfect, I could only imagine how quickly I would find a way to die if the waves reached two feet. Speaking of the waves, they were beginning to pick up in their intensity, smashing against the rock banks, turning frothy milk white then vanishing between the cracks.

I grabbed my cell phone from the glove compartment and the display screen showed I had three new messages. The first message was from my sister's boyfriend, Conner, reminding me of our rowing engagement the following morning. The second was Lacy relaying she wasn't "hip to cooking" and that I should pick up something on the way home. The final message blindsided me and I slammed on the brakes, the Range Rover fishtailing twice before coming to rest courtesy of Maine's many miles of coastal guardrail.

I replayed the message. It was Caitlin. She was wondering how I was doing and wanted to get together for dinner. I hadn't talked to Caitlin in over a month. I wondered what had prompted the call. Possibly the anniversary of the first murder. Perhaps my sitting in my car outside her house last night for close to five hours. It could be any number of things.

Unable to banish Caitlin's message from thought, I nearly missed the exit for the town of Belfast. I navigated through the small coastal town and saw the bustling of September coming to an end. People were packing up for the winter and businesses were liquidating merchandise. The 25% OFF signs of a week ago had been swapped out for 50% OFF, and in another week those would be replaced with YOU NAME THE PRICE.

I stopped at an Italian restaurant called Angelini's and read the sign in the window: "Last day October 10th, see you in May." (Maine literally closed down from mid-October to late May. Technically speaking, the population of Maine plummeted from 537 to somewhere around 300.)

I ordered two meatball sandwiches from Angelini and inquired if there were any bookstores nearby. He directed me to a store in the same complex and said he could have two fresh sandwiches ready for me in about ten minutes if I wanted to check out the store.

The Bookrack was owned by a fifty-something gal named Margery. Margery had coke bottle lenses held within light pink frames and her white hair was styled soft serve vanilla making her look closer to eighty than sixty. Margery told me she didn't have any copies of *Eight in October* at the "pres-ant mom-ant," but was expecting another shipment in the next couple days.

These mom-and-pop stores are all the same and I told Margery that if she could somehow find it in her heart to rummage up a copy of *Eight in October* I would buy at least two other hardback novels. Five minutes later, I left the Bookrack with a bag containing Michael Crichton's latest novel *I got a 1550 on my SATs! What'd you get, stupid?*, *Sailing for Idiots*, and *Eight in October*.

Back in the car, I took Route 1 northbound to the town of Surry. I passed the legendary Lighthouse Museum (historical side note: The Lighthouse Museum houses the largest collection of lighthouse lenses in the world) and turned onto a small street leading to the Surry Woods. The houses in Surry Woods are separated by miles of oaks, maples, and firs, and if you're going out to your mailbox, you should think about packing a lunch.

I drove for a half mile, went down a steep hill, found the dirt entrance to 14 Surry Woods Drive, wound eastward for a short par three, and parked in an immense leaf-strewn yard.

My sister and I moved into the large, three-story Colonial about ten months ago, Christmas Eve to be exact. The house was built in the late 1950s but had been completely restored in the last couple years. The majority of the house was comprised of copper brick and the trim was a ghastly pea green I'd had on my to-do list for, well, the last ten months. I'd had a run in with the house a year ago and fallen in love with the location. Ten miles of woods to the north, south, and west. Three thousand miles of ocean directly east. 14 Surry Woods Drive was literally one of the few places in the world where dense woods visibly met white, sandy beach.

The previous owners gave me a good deal on the house for bringing their daughter's killer to justice. Who was I to argue?

~

Walking around the car, I took a gander at my front bumper. The collision with the guardrail was more serious than I'd let on and the bumper looked a little loose. Okay, it was hanging on by a thread.

I marched the seven stones to the front door and was reaching for the doorknob when the flap to the doggie door flew open and something shot through my legs. Unless Baxter stood still it was impossible to discern if he was a dog, a cat, a hamster, or a racquetball. I mean I love dogs but not dogs that are smaller than cats. That goes against everything God intended. I once saw Baxter get beat up by a rabbit. I'm not kidding you. A little white rabbit beat the piss out of him. He wouldn't leave the house for a month.

I walked through the front door and set the cooler on the kitchen counter, then remembered the sandwiches. I went back out to the car and grabbed the Angelini's off the passenger seat and noticed that Baxter, at some point, had jumped into the car and fallen fast asleep on the driver's seat.

Did I mention Baxter was narcoleptic?

He could fall into the deepest of sleeps at a whim. It took the vet four visits before they diagnosed him with the sleeping disorder.

I nudged the pug with my hand, watched him stir, and then he vanished in a puff of smoke. I'd come to the conclusion that Baxter was half pug, half poltergeist. He was a pugtergeist.

When I walked back into the kitchen, Lacy was emptying the contents of my cooler into the refrigerator, her dark brown hair visible over the top of the refrigerator door. Her voice boomed from behind the stainless steel, "How were the sandwiches?"

"Great. I ate the egg salad and the bologna."

"You didn't eat the turkey?" Lacy was world famous for her turkey sandwiches and she stood up, her right hand heavy on her hip. She smiled, "Good. We can eat them tomorrow when you take me painting."

Painting? Oh, right. "What time do you want to get going?"

"I want to see the sunset." She laughed. "Well, not see, literally."

I laughed with her. Lacy was taking her blindness in stride. If you weren't the wiser, you'd never suspect Lacy's almost-teal eyes served only for decoration. Lacy had Multiple Sclerosis and her current acute exacerbation, better known as an attack, relapse, or flare, was temporary blindness. According to the doctor, Lacy's condition was due to an inflammation of her optic nerve. He said this usually clears in four to twelve weeks. It'd been eight weeks since the lights went out for Lace. I prayed every night she would open her eyes and the world would be staring back.

I replied to her painting question, "Sounds good. By the way, I'm rowing with your boy toy in the morning."

"That's what I heard. I'm glad you and Conner still hang out even though you and Caitlin broke up."

Conner was Caitlin's little brother. Caitlin and I had been the ones to hook up the two of them. "Speaking of Caitlin, she left a message on my phone this afternoon. She wants to get together for dinner. I've been brainstorming excuses for the last hour."

"Tell her you went blind, it always works for me." She snickered at her own wit and said, "Just kidding. I was the one who told her to call you."

"What do you mean you 'told her to call me?'"

"I had lunch with her this afternoon and we talked about you guys. It's usually an off-limits topic, but I could see how lonely she was. She really misses you. And God knows you're too stubborn to call her. Even though you're just as lonely, I might add. The two of you were good. Don't let another one get away because you're an idiot."

Speaking of which, I wondered if they had *Relationships for Idiots*. I made a mental note to ask Margery next time I was at The Bookrack.

Lacy and I grabbed our sandwiches and retired to the living room. The Italian leather couches, oak entertainment center spanning the wall, and plate glass coffee table came with the house for an extra ten grand. Lacy flopped down on one of the tan couches and picked up the remote. If I were a Mariners' fan, Lacy was a diehard. She'd forced me to buy some digital cable package where you get every baseball game on the planet (there was even a channel where you could watch little Asian boys play pickle).

Lacy found the Mariners' playoff game—they were down 5-4 in the seventh—and took a third of her sandwich down in one bite. She smiled, revealing one of Angelini's mammoth meatballs bulging from each cheek.

I couldn't help myself and said, "Conner has trained you well."

~

Lacy said she was going to bed and I watched her negotiate the stairs flawlessly. I, on the other hand, retreated to the back deck for some leisure reading. I wasn't cold, but I had goose bumps on my arms and threw a couple logs in the outdoor fireplace. (I'd chided Lacy when she'd first purchased the novelty, but it had come to be my favorite addition to the house.)

The waves washing up thirty yards behind me played lead orchestra to the Surry Breakwater lighthouse's baritone foghorn.

I cracked open my second copy of *Eight in October*, the white pages glistened in the moonlight, and I had the eerie feeling the moon was trying to read over my shoulder. I was a half paragraph into Tooms' description of the third victim when *Eight in October* reunited with his long lost cousins in the outdoor fireplace. The heart of the book erupted in flames, shimmering the deck in a flaxen glow. I laid back in the chaise lounge, my goose bumps a distant memory.

Chapter 5

I woke up as a couple jaundice-riddled fingers of light began to extend from the horizon. The Surry Breakwater lighthouse floated in the fog, its strident warning coming in thirty second intervals.

I ambled down the deck stairs to the beachfront and did a hundred sit-ups followed by a hundred push-ups, then set off at a brisk trot down the shoreline. The gull-to-sand-grain ratio went from roughly one-to-eight to one-to-none in a matter of twelve seconds. If you've never seen a maladroit seagull, you're one of the lucky ones. It's almost painful to watch these birds expend so much energy simply to hover. It was the aviary equivalent of only paying the interest on your credit card bill. But enough about birds.

My right quadriceps tightened after a quarter mile and I stopped to knead the muscle with my hands. My right quadriceps was visibly smaller than its left counterpart, and my fingers subconsciously found the bullet's entry and exit wounds. Both scars were roughly the size of a nickel, and it looked and felt like the tissue was made of cork.

When I set off again, the sun had officially broken the horizon, its rays slowly riding the waves toward shore. It took me twenty minutes to cover the distance to Owl's Head peninsula, smack the sign with my open palm, and turn around. I covered the distance back in about half the time, sprinting the final three bellows of the foghorn before collapsing in a heap on the white sand.

I glanced into the bay and saw Lacy treading water about thirty yards out. Lacy had been an All State swimmer in high school and had been attending Temple on a swimming scholarship when she was diagnosed with MS. With the onset of her temporary blindness, she began treading water daily for forty-five minutes to keep fit. She must have heard my sandy collapse and screamed, "Conner called ten minutes ago. He said that if you aren't there in the next ten minutes, he's hiring a lawyer then killing you."

~

The Verona Rowing Club was a large red brick structure surrounded by high terra-cotta walls. There was a group of four women milling around the club entrance, all peeking in my direction as I approached. I wasn't sure if it was fame or infamy that brought about the stares. Either way, it was unpleasant, and I picked up the pace as I made my way past them. In hindsight, I wouldn't have walked like I was squeezing a quarter between my butt cheeks, but hindsight's twenty-twenty. Get it?

As I made my way through the front entrance to the outdoor lockers I could make out Conner stretching on the other side of the bridge, an oar over his shoulders, bent over at the waist. I grabbed my rowing shoes from the locker and ran the last hundred yards up and over the bridge.

Conner caught my final strides and straightened. He had his shirt off and his initials, CED, tattooed across his ripped abdominals. I must have been a sight because his initials were vibrating wickedly.

He said, "What? Rowing isn't enough of a workout, you have to get a ten mile jog in beforehand? You look like you just escaped your own grave for Christ's sake."

I would have laughed, had I not been throwing up. Conner tossed me an orange Gatorade, "Holy shit. You aren't gonna die out there are you, old-timer?"

I rinsed out my mouth and killed off the entire contents of the Gatorade. "Call me 'old-timer' again and you can start calling that oar Bubba. You got that, Ellis?"

Connor bit the inside of his right cheek, something he did every time someone called him by his middle name. And about the threat, it was empty. Conner was like Godzilla and I was a fleeing three-foot-five Asian, yelling ill-timed English outbursts. Conner was twenty-seven, a couple inches taller than me, had blond hair, blue eyes, and a physique the likes of Batman's armor.

The women from the entrance had made their way outside and I noticed a brunette pointing me out to a newcomer. She was either saying "That's the guy who threw up all over the bridge" or "That's the guy who walks with his butt clenched like a queer" or "That's the guy from that *Eight in October* book."

All the options were equally painful and I was ready to shy away from the paparazzi. I cocked my head at the water insinuating it was time to ship out, and Conner slipped into the front slot of the shell as I hopped in to the back.

An artificial reef helped stop the Atlantic from invading the mile and a half expanse of still water, which at seven in the morning housed close to twenty scullers. This was the fifth time I'd rowed with Conner—albeit, the first since the publication of *Eight in October*—and we hit a steady rhythm early on.

We skimmed over the glass water and Conner said between strokes, "So what's it like being famous?"

Oh, and I forgot to mention, when you row with Conner, it's imperative you pass the time with idle chatter. I tried to conceal my wheezing lung and said, "What?"

He yelled over his shoulder, "I said, what it is like being famous?"

I'd heard him the first time, but I'd needed a few seconds to rest and to phrase my answer. "That book never should've been written. *(breath)* I didn't ask for this shit."

"What? To be recognized? To be famous? Did you see that lady pointing at you? You're a state treasure for Christ's sake. Did I say state treasure? Because I meant national treasure. Which magazine cover was your ugly mug on? *Time* or *People*?"

For the record, I was on both. I wisely ignored his question. "What about you? *(breath)* Don't tell me you haven't *(breath)* been getting your *(breath)* fair share of celebrity *(breath)* status."

Conner stopped mid-stroke and turned around. He was biting the inside of his cheek again, and said, "Tell me you're kidding. Didn't you read the book?"

I could feel my heartbeat pulsate in my right shoulder and I was thankful for the chance to rest. "Nope. I accidentally dropped one copy in the Atlantic, and another copy accidentally fell into my outdoor fireplace."

"And Lacy didn't tell you anything about me in regards to the book?"

"Nope. I told her if she even mentioned the book I'd rearrange all the furniture in the house." Which I'd gone ahead and done anyway. Lacy just recently stopped smashing her shins against the coffee table.

Conner's lips tightened, "That weasel Tooms didn't so much as mention my name. Can you believe that shit? I make the biggest break in the whole case. Hell, the only break in the case and Tooms doesn't even mention my name. That's bullshit, is all that is. Fucking bullshit."

He wasn't lying. Conner had been the one to stumble on the information leading us to the killer. Sorry—*supposed*—killer. I felt bad for the kid, I thought for certain his name would've surfaced once, if not multiple times throughout the book. In the back of my mind, I knew I was solely responsible for his name's absence. If I'd sat down with Tooms, I would have given all the credit to Conner. I grabbed his shoulder, "That is bullshit. You know I would have set him straight, but I don't think you, me, or anyone else deserves an iota of credit. It's not over."

"What do you mean it's not over? It's been a year, Thomas. Tristen Grayer is dead. D-E-A-D. Dead. You need to quit reading that *Pet Cemetery* shit—it's messing with your head."

I dug my paddle into the water and said, "I don't read Stephen King. I read Michael Crichton." I prefer to be confused shitless rather than scared shitless.

We spent the rest of the hour talking about how big a bastard Alex Tooms was and swapped retribution recipes should we ever get him alone. Hypothetically speaking, of course. Conner wanted to take him to some island, Matinicus or something, and torture him until he wrote a revised version of *Eight in October*. I wanted to potato peel his entire body, let him scab over, and *nearly* die of infection. I'd get him to a hospital before the wounds became gangrenous.

Yeah, I know, I'm a softy at heart.

Chapter 6

I somehow made it up the deck stairs, through the sliding glass door, and flopped face first onto one of the tan leather couches, the leather immediately bonding to my sweat-laden flesh. Lacy heard my wheezing resounding through the leather and let out one of her infamous cackles.

Through a fit of giggling she said, "I have the best visual of you right now, and if it's anywhere near what's really going on, you are one pathetic loser." She did a good Lloyd Christmas.

I shouted through a crack between two cushions, "Water! Drinky! Dying!"

Lacy needed to brush up on her caveman seeing as how the water was not poured down my throat, but down my back. My body went from being so hot to so cold so fast, I'm surprised I didn't have a seizure. After the initial shock, it wasn't half bad, that is until the water found its way down the crease of my back and into the mighty balloon knot.

I tilted my head up, stretching the leather's molecular boundaries, and yelled, "You are the devil!"

The faucet ran again, and seconds later a cold glass was placed in my hand. After a tremendous effort on my behalf and a fair portion of my skin pulled from the bone, I was on my back and without lifting my eyelids successfully guided the cold glass to my lips. I chugged.

The cold liquid moved down my esophagus into my stomach, rested for a microsecond, did a U-turn, started up my esophagus, exited my mouth, and came to rest on the tan leather sofa. My eyes opened at some point in the ordeal and were now transfixed on Lacy who, if you're curious, was on her back, legs kicking, tears streaming.

Something is definitely wrong when you are subjected to a practical joke at the expense of a *blindy*.

I actually found myself laughing when I yelled, "What in the hell did you give me?" I licked my lips, but my buds only detected the acidic bile from my purge. The sofa was speckled in white, and I said, "Don't tell me you fed me some of that soymilk crap."

Lacy had regained some control over herself and said, "Sorry, I couldn't help it. I didn't think it was going to work—" She started into another fit.

I stepped over her and said, "I hope you pee yourself."

~

When I woke up in the bathtub, the water was lukewarm. The hot bath and three Tylenol had tag-teamed my aching muscles, and I didn't feel too shabby.

I walked out of the bathroom and into the master bedroom sans towel, preferring to air dry. There wasn't much in the room other than a queen-size bed and an old beat-up dresser I'd bought at a neighborhood garage sale. Sitting atop the synthetic oak dresser was a picture of my parents. The picture was taken on their fiftieth birthday. Exactly two years later, on their collective fifty-second birthday, the two had been flying back from a Rolling Stones concert when my dad's company Lear went down.

Next to their picture was a picture of Conner, Lacy, Caitlin, and myself. The four of us had been together for close to nine months and they'd been some of the best months of my life. Deep down, I wasn't sure if I still loved Caitlin. I knew I didn't not love her, if that makes any sense. This reminded me I still had to call her and I picked up the bedside phone.

She picked up on the third ring and I said, "Hi, Cait."

Caitlin didn't respond for a couple seconds and I envisioned her shuffling for the appropriate cue card. She cleared her throat and said, "I was hoping you'd call. We should still be friends, if not friendly."

Yikes.

I wasn't sure how to respond to this and after consulting my list of Swiss replies I opted for, "Uh, how ya been?"

"Come on, Thomas, we haven't spoken for a month, and all you have to say is, 'Uh, how ya been?'" She did a good impression of me.

I wanted to say, "It's the only thing I've said so far," but I didn't want to put myself into a corner. I thought of a conversation with a woman as a boxing match and thus far—what, five seconds in—I'd already taken a quick jab and was being set up for a swift right hook. "Look, I'm sorry, but it's hard to stay friends with someone you love."

Oops. I quickly added the unequivocal, "—d."

This was the boxing equivalent of tying both hands behind my back and squirting lemon juice in my eyes.

I mouthed her next words with her, "Thomas, do you still love me?"

This was like *Mad-Libs*, all you had to do was fill in the blanks. I thought about the question while I wrote a *Mad-Lib* to myself on the back of an envelope: Thomas Prescott is *a(n) adjective, adverb noun* for getting himself in this *adjective* situation and should be forced to *verb, noun* for being such *a(n) adjective adverb noun.*

Caitlin waited patiently for my reply, which sadly was, "I don't know Cait. I just don't know."

I scribbled in the blanks and read what I'd written: Thomas Prescott is *a(n) ginormous, fucking asshole* for getting himself in this *~~confusing~~, ~~uncomfortable~~, fucked-up* situation and should be forced to *eat ~~shit~~, ~~an onion~~, glass* for being such *a(n) stupid fucking idiot.*

I was brainstorming for an adverb besides "fucking" when Caitlin said, "You don't know? Great, Thomas. That's just great. I guess I'll just wait my whole life until you figure that out. Grow up, you fucking coward." The line went dead.

I guess *fucking* was the only adverb.

~

I threw on a pair of khaki shorts and a charcoal University of Washington hooded sweatshirt. Lacy came into the room, handed me a glass of pink liquid, and said, "I made you a smoothie, to, you know, smooth things over."

I took the glass from her and, after careful inspection, took a sip. "Strawberry-banana, good choice. Consider yourself forgiven. Although, I should warn you, I will get you back and it's going to be like a thousand times worse."

I already had a plan and it was mean, almost deranged. Diabolical actually. I couldn't help it; I had to win at everything.

Lacy put on her inculpable face, "You wouldn't take advantage of a whittle, itty-bwitty, bwind girl, now would you?"

~

I grabbed Lacy's easel and paint bag and walked to the car. Lacy was in the passenger seat, Baxter asleep on her lap, the cooler at her feet.

We headed down the long drive, snaked through a couple backstreets, and five minutes later I was merging onto US 1 southbound.

Lacy asked what I intended to do about Caitlin and I told her I wasn't sure. We explored my options for the next twenty minutes, and we both decided it would be in my best interest if I called her back and set up dinner for later that evening.

I jumped on the Maine Turnpike, I-95, and after about five miles exited for Portland. At a population of 84,000, Portland is the most populated city in Maine. It would be a stretch to call it a *metropolis*. It was a *tropolis* at best. To be safe, we'll call it an *opolis*. *Olis*, it was an *olis*. It's an *is*.

There was a large marketplace to the right and I entered it, scanning the store fronts for a bookstore. I didn't see any bookstores, but I did see a kite shop, and I made a mental note to swing by before Saturday. We drove for about a half mile before coming to a Super-Duper-Ultra-Hyper-Mart.

There was one copy of *Eight in October* left, resting in the number three bestseller slot. Speaking of three, I couldn't believe I was buying the book for the third time. I was going to ask for a waterproof/fireproof copy, but they'd probably have to special order it.

I grabbed a case of beer and swiped the old Visa. Back at the car I handed the bag to Lacy. Rummaging through the bag, she found the book and said, "What's this?"

"You know very well what it is."

"I didn't think you were gonna read it."

"I finally broke down and bought it yesterday. Actually, I bought it twice yesterday."

She shook her head, "Then why did you just buy it now?"

"We'll my first two copies met an untimely demise." I recounted each book's respective demise.

"How far did you get?"

I knew what she was fishing for and said, "Conner told me."

She winced. "You should have seen him. He read the book out loud to me, and when he realized his name was never going to show up, he lost it. He scared me, Thomas. He started breaking stuff."

"Don't think too much of it, Lace. That Tooms guy really screwed him over. He'll get over it."

~

Lacy didn't know exactly how to get to the lighthouse and it was an excuse to use the Range Rover's navigational system for the first time.

I pushed the screen under the CD player and it instantly refreshed. I chose the audio option and the system became voice activated. It asked in a generic woman's voice, "Destination?"

I stammered, "Uh, lighthouse."

"There's seventy-five lighthouses in Maine, you idiot." Lacy remarked wisely.

I mentally added *Car Navigational Systems for Idiots* to my book list and reset the system. The woman's voice came on again, "Destination?"

I prodded Lacy with my arm and she said, "Portland Head Lighthouse."

For the next ten minutes the generic woman's voice shouted out commands every thirty seconds, and I finally had an idea what it was like to be married. Once safely in the lighthouse observatory parking lot, the woman shouted, "Put car in Park."

I put the car in park and she nagged, "Turn off ignition."

It took every ounce of self-control not to smash the screen with my fist. I made a mental reminder to call the company and have them change the voice to that of Bob Costas or Heidi Klum.

Lacy took two sandwiches from the cooler and handed me one. After a bite I asked, "What's so special about this particular house of light?"

She rolled her eyes. "I think it was the first lighthouse ever built that's still in existence. It's special to me because I've seen it in so many paintings I have a mental picture in my head and I'll be able to paint it."

"And you couldn't do that in our front yard because—?"

"Because I'm trying to lead a normal life. I refuse to paint a lighthouse landscape from our front yard. If I keep painting these things, I'll never forget them."

She tapped the side of her head, "I'll keep them up here forever."

"Lace, your vision will come back. One of these mornings you're gonna wake up and the lights will be back on. You'll see." I laughed at my unintentional pun. "I mean you'll see you'll see."

She held up her beer and said, "Cheers to that."

~

The Portland Head lighthouse was an all-white stucco frame and stood on a large inlet of reddish-brown rock. Lacy asked me two questions before she made her first brushstroke: roughly how many yards away was the lighthouse, and what was the diameter of the sun in inches?

I answered about two hundred yards and an inch and a quarter, respectively.

I set two beers down next to Lacy and found the gravel path leading to the lighthouse. As I neared the lighthouse the sound of crashing waves grew exponentially louder.

There was a large rock about thirty yards to the left of the lighthouse, which I started toward. When I finally reached the rock, I saw it was a bit larger than at first glance and chose his little brother to the left of him. I took a swig of beer and looked down at my lap—where, oddly enough—Baxter was fast asleep. I guess when you move at the speed of sound and weigh less than a nice T-bone you can sleep wherever you please.

After taking in the horizon for a dozen waves, I grabbed *Eight in October* and delved back into the massacre. I read close to eighty pages before my reading light plunged into the western mountains. In truth, the fourth murder was especially gory, and I took the liberty of stopping prematurely. But I did dog-ear the page on the off chance I ever built up the courage to revisit the scene. See, I already had nightmares of the guest bedroom. I didn't need them solidified.

Chapter 7

The girl's name was Ginny Farth. She was the fourth victim in two weeks. The call came in an hour ago, and we, the task force, were the first people to enter the crime scene of 14 Surry Woods Drive.

The guest bedroom was small, about fifteen by fifteen. Ginny was scattered roughly one body part per ten square feet. The guestroom walls were painted *Robin's Egg Blue*. The carpet was painted *Ginny Farth's Vital Fluid Red*.

Dr. Caitlin Dodds was clad in a white Bangor Medical Examiner parka, hovering over Ginny's decapitated head. The doctor lolled the brunette frayed orb to the side. She looked up at Gregory, Gleason, and myself and stated blandly, "The bastard took the eyes again."

The three of us nodded solemnly. Honestly, I would have been disconcerted if he hadn't taken the eyes. The eyes were the only constant in a sea of variables. There was no pattern to the killings. Only the eyes.

I'd seen enough. I walked out of the room, down the stairway, past a sliding glass door, and noticed a thin light moving through the blackness. I'd assumed we were in the middle of vast woods. So why was I looking at a lighthouse?

I slid the glass door open and walked out onto a long narrow deck then ambled down a half dozen stairs. Kicking off my shoes, I plopped down on the cold beach. The waves ran within a dozen feet of my outstretched toes and my shadow was forced to gargle every so often.

What the hell was going on? I couldn't get a read on this Tristen Grayer psychopath. Was he killing in lust? Macabre mutilations excite the lust murderer. For them, killing triggers a bizarre sexual fantasy that has developed in the dark recesses of their warped minds. But I couldn't get a bead on what Tristen's fantasy was. Was it rooted in the eyes? He'd left us nothing else to go on. We didn't even have a picture of the kid for crying out loud. The neighbor, Elby, had said Tristen was badly burned in a fire years earlier. Is that why he takes the eyes? Because he's disfigured and doesn't want the victim to see him? Had the contemptuous stares from his childhood prompted these women's deaths? And the sister. It had all started with her. Why had Tristen killed Ingrid? Because she was pregnant with his son? Because she didn't want to keep the baby? Had he raped her in the first place?

I heard footsteps on the deck and seconds later Dr. Caitlin Dodds plopped down next to me. I couldn't help but notice her usually striking features go soft under the moonlight. In a couple hours Caitlin would try to piece Ginny Farth back together, a chore I didn't turn green with envy for. Caitlin grabbed a handful of sand and tossed it on my bare feet.

I said, "Well, doctor, where do we go from here?"

She seemed miles away and it took four waves for my voice to hit her drum. She shook her head in disarray, "You're the expert. You tell me what the hell is going on here."

I shook my head. "I'm baffled. I've never seen anything like this. Usually with killings of this nature, the killer knows the killee. How Tristen, a hick farm boy from Potato Town crossed paths with Miss Richwood here, I don't have the faintest idea."

"So you don't secretly know how he's selecting his victims?"

I tried to hide a grin. "Yeah, I have it written on a sticky note in a safety deposit box."

"Which bank?"

"Swiss Miss in Manhattan."

She smirked. "Are you aware your bank also makes hot chocolate?"

"You got me. Sincerely, I don't have the slightest clue what this son of a bitch is up to. When he wants us to catch him, we will. Until then we're going to have to sit tight and count bodies."

She nodded to herself.

There was a clamoring of footsteps and Caitlin and I turned simultaneously to see Gleason and Gregory hovering over us. I looked at Gregory's small shadow and remarked, "Where's the rest of him?"

He didn't say anything and I prodded, "Don't tell me that's all of it?" I noticed his shadow flip me off.

Caitlin and I stood up and joined the two, our four shadows resembling a small mountain range on the beachfront. Gleason asked, "Where do we go from here?"

Gregory offered, "I think we should go talk with some of the neighbors and see if anyone saw anything odd this afternoon."

I turned to Gregory and stated, "Slow down there, Hot Toddy. The victim wasn't killed here today. She's been dead for at least a day, maybe two." I'd seen enough dead bodies in my day to know the difference between a freshy and a staley. Ginny Farth was a staley.

Gregory scoffed at this and turned to Caitlin for confirmation that I was an idiot and an asshole. She nodded and said, "He's right. I won't know for sure until I perform the autopsy, but she looks to have been dead for a period of at least thirty-six hours."

At this, I stuck my shadow's thumb up Todd's shadow's ass. Gleason tried to hide a grin with his hand and Caitlin camouflaged her snickering as a cough attack. Todd didn't seem to notice and I was set to get even more creative with my shadow antics when a young officer pitter-pattered down the deck stairs and approached our foursome. We all turned in unison as he nodded at Caitlin and said, "Are you Detective Dodds?"

The officer had on a tan uniform with the letters PCS inscribed on his name plate. I would later learn he was from the Penobscot County Sheriff's office.

Caitlin nodded, "That's me."

The officer cocked his head back toward the house and said, "There's a young cop here who claims he's your brother."

"Conner's here?"

"Yeah, that's his name." He paused, then added, "Uh, he has an important call for you."

Caitlin eyed him and said, "Well tell him to take a message and I'll call them back. Can't you see that I'm busy? That I'm trying to find the guy who chopped the girl in that house into thirty fricking pieces."

Even in the twilight it was evident the officer blushed. He went to turn on his heel, then seemed to get a second wind of courage. "It's just that if the guy really is your brother, then he's probably telling the truth about the other thing."

The entire group took a collective step forward and I asked, "What other thing?"

"The guy on the phone—" The officer's features slowly climbed into a wry smile. "Tristen Grayer."

~

The five of us did a steady trot up the beachfront, up the stairs, through the house, and out the front door. There were about seven cop cars littering the football field expanse of front yard and the officer pointed to a gentleman standing at the edge of the crime scene tape cordoning off the area. The young man looked to be in his early twenties, had broad shoulders, and short, almost buzzed blond hair. He was handsome if you like the tall, good looking type, and even from a distance of fifty feet I could distinguish that he shared two traits with his sister: azure eyes and zero patience.

He bowled over the thin cop attempting to restrain him and ambled toward our approaching group. The thin cop was in the process of going for his cuffs when Caitlin cut him off, "It's okay. He's my brother—and he's a cop."

Caitlin turned to Conner and asked, "Why are you in civilian clothes?"

He said, "I was on my way to the station when I got the call."

All eight eyes were trained on the cell phone Conner was holding in his right hand; the screen pressed hard against his thigh. Caitlin asked awkwardly, "Did he ask for me personally?"

"He called the station and asked to be transferred to you but they accidentally put him through to me."

Gregory asked, "What else did he say?"

"Nothing. He said he had a message for Detective Caitlin Dodds and demanded that I track her down. I told him to go to hell and that's when he told me who he was. I don't even know if he's still on the line."

Caitlin took a deep breath—as did the rest of us—and took the phone from Conner. She said, "Dr. Dodds. With whom am I speaking?"

She began walking in a small semi-circle and I was only able to hear snatches of the conversation, "How do I know it's really you? . .

. Okay, okay, that's enough . . . Stop! Please . . . About an hour ago . . . Thank you for being so thoughtful . . . Rot in hell you piece of shi—"

Gregory slipped the phone from Caitlin's grasp and stated perfunctorily, "Todd Gregory, Special Agent in Charge." Gregory whipped out a small booklet, which I can only imagine was titled *Serial Killer Phone Call Procedure Booklet,* and said, "Would you like to turn yourself in?"

I mentally gagged, then made eye contact with Caitlin. I walked over to her and asked, "You okay?"

She nodded and I asked, "What did he say?"

"He didn't think that we'd found Ginny yet. He was calling to tell us where to find her. Then he started telling me what he did to her. How she begged him to stop. How he got on top of her—" She shook her head silently and soon had her head buried in my chest. She caught herself, straightening, and stated, "We should really go listen in."

As we made our way back to the group, Gregory rifled through four or five pages of his booklet then read, "We can help you. What do you want from us?"

I'd had enough. I wrestled the phone from Gregory's runway model grip and pressed *End.* Gregory stammered, "What did you do that for? There are certain steps that need to be taken. I was following procedure—federal procedure."

I said calmly, "He'll call back."

Gregory plunged his face into his hands then glared at me incredulously. "No, he won't call back. This isn't a movie, you idiot. This is real life. And in real life when you hang up on a serial killer he doesn't call ba—"

Gregory's tantrum was interrupted by the distinct ring of a cell phone. I noticed Caitlin forcing a smile down as I depressed *Send* and put the phone to my ear. I cleared my throat and said, "Jack 'n the Box."

I looked at Gregory, who appeared to be in the middle of a deep breathing exercise trying to find his chi. Or maybe it was his nine millimeter.

Tristen did not find this amusing. "Who is this?"

"Can you hold on a sec? I have another call." I pulled my ringing cell phone from my pants pocket and answered it. It was Lacy. She wanted to know if I could take her to the doctor in the morning.

I told her of course I would and hung up. I coughed into my hand then returned to my buddy Tristen. "Sorry about that. You were saying."

He said the words slowly, "Who is this?"

"Thomas Prescott. But you can address me as King Tom, Thomas the Magnificent, or The Man Who is Going to Cut Off Your Dick and Shove it Down Your Throat."

I could hear him breathing heavily on the line. Then he said, "Thomas Prescott. I saw your name in the paper. Mr. Big Shot serial killer hunter." He paused then added, "So what do you think of my work so far?"

"I've seen better." For the record, I had not.

"I'm just getting warmed up."

I took a second to digest this which, oddly enough, felt like indigestion. I said, "Can I ask you a question?" I didn't wait for a response, "Why her? Why Ginny Farth?"

"She needed to suffer."

"Why? Why did she need to suffer?"

He said solemnly, "So *he* would suffer."

He? "Who's *he* you piece of shit?"

He didn't reply and I prodded, "Tristen? You there? Tristy?"

I looked at Gregory, Gleason, and Caitlin, then shrugged. I handed the phone to Gregory and said, "What does it say in your little manual to do when a serial killer hangs up on you?"

Chapter 8

It was closing in on nine when Lacy finally authorized an acceptable hanging locale for her resplendent painting. (The locale, if you must know, was the wall directly across from her bed. She wanted it to be the first image she saw when her sight came back. My idea.) As for the painting, it was exquisite. Lacy had a unique style, capturing the essence and mood of, well, Lacy. She painted the picture in her head; that was her signature. Even when she had her sight, she painted the image etched on her eyelids.

After Lacy and I finishing hanging her painting I called Caitlin. After a somewhat cordial conversation the two of us agreed on a dinner date for later that night. The restaurant was Austin's, an upscale place with great seafood and a decent steak, which just happened to be located in Hampden, smack-dab in the middle of point A, my house in Surry Woods, and point B, Caitlin's apartment in Bangor.

~

I pulled into Austin's parking lot ten minutes late. It was a Sunday night and I'd expected a full lot, but there were only two other cars. Oh, how the seasons are a changing. I parked next to Caitlin's red Pathfinder and couldn't help wondering how I'd managed this far without the assistance of alcohol.

Every restaurant in Maine smells the same, like they use lobster shit for insulation. Austin's differentiated itself from the competition by keeping its lights low and its wine list high. I bypassed the hostess and walked into the dining arena. The last time I'd eaten here it'd looked like a Def Leppard concert, now it looked like a deaf leper colony. The only people there were an old couple in a back corner booth who looked like they'd just finished having a legion fight and Caitlin at a table sipping a glass of lemon water.

If I thought I looked good, Caitlin looked gooder. She was wearing a teeny-weeny black dress that didn't leave much to the imagination. Her hair was up, a couple strands of dirty blonde dangling past her shivering blue eyes. She stood up when I approached. After a couple unpolished seconds we decided to embrace, or someone did, and I gave her a quick peck on the cheek.

She held my waist for a beat too long of the slow rhythmic brass, neither of us knowing how to proceed. With her heels on she was only an inch shorter than me, and I didn't trust myself so close to her blues. The two of us parted and we both sat. Meeting someone for the first time at a restaurant is awkward. Meeting someone you've loved, and possibly still love, is about three tiers above awkward. It's uncouth.

I mean, Caitlin and I have separate lives, we came in separate cars, and we would probably get separate checks. The key word here was separate, and as Caitlin stared at me from across the table, it hit me: I wanted us to be unseparate. *Deep, huh?*

Caitlin started, "You look good, Thomas."

I dittoed, then added, "Sorry I dropped off the face of the Earth. I'm not used to staying friends with women after the relationship has absolved itself."

"The relationship didn't absolve itself, you broke up with me." She scoffed, "Absolved itself. I'll absolve you."

I laughed, and she laughed, and the black tension cloud hanging over us went searching for other prey. (Within minutes we would invariably hear the elderly couple begin quibbling over the missing Geritol tablet.)

The wine came. The food came. And the wine came again. Caitlin and I were clicking and no one—not me, the waitress, or Miss Cleo herself—would have suspected the two of us had come in separate cars. I'd just finished telling her about finding Baxter on my lap that afternoon when the conversation inevitably turned to *us*.

Caitlin broached the subject, "Are you having as miserable a time as I am?"

I nodded. "I think we could be friends after all." It was a fishing comment, but I wasn't certain what exactly I was fishing for.

Either Caitlin liked the bait or she wanted out of the water altogether. She said, "I don't want to be friends. I want—"

She stopped and I could see tears start to form in her eyes. I knew I had the words to fix everything, for her, for me, and possibly forever, but I kept them to myself. She dabbed at her leaking eyes with her napkin and I said, "Caitlin, I still have feelings for you. I know how badly I hurt you and I couldn't live with myself if I did that to you again. But events are going to transpire in the next couple days, and I don't think it would be fair to either of us if we started things up right now."

"What events? Not this crap again. This is why you broke up with me in the first place. Because I didn't back you and your theory. If you felt betrayed because I gave my side of the story to Alex Tooms, I'm not sorry. This is your baggage, not mine. It was a terrible time, but I chose to get over it just like everyone else."

My systolic pressure rose ten points. "Caitlin, there are only two people who know what really happened that night. One of them is me and the other one is not you."

"Yes, but the other person is dead."

"No, someone is dead. The person I'm talking about may or may not be dead. I survived. He could have too."

Caitlin's frustration was evident in the lines on her face. "Thomas, you almost died. Hell, no one knows how you didn't. Two gunshot wounds, a tumble down the side of cliff, and drowning for twenty minutes in the Atlantic usually gets the job done."

This was like déjà vu; we'd had the same conversation the first time I'd ended things.

I stated, "The only issue I have is the one person who should believe me doesn't. The body that was found was not the man I shot."

She took a deep breath. "I did the autopsy, Thomas. There was no bullet wound. Cause of death was brain trauma from falling off the cliff. The skin they found underneath your fingernails was a perfect DNA match to Tristen's. Forensic science doesn't lie."

She did have a case, but it dissolved quickly under cross-examination. First, I'd shot my attacker in the knee, although this was a bit fuzzy seeing as I'd just woken up from a four-hundred and thirty hour nap, when this revelation first dawned on me. As for the skin underneath my fingernails, they never found a scratch on John Doe.

There was only one explanation that could justify this and it was so far-fetched I hadn't tried it on anyone, least of all Caitlin right now. She'd storm out of the restaurant after four words.

Caitlin decided it was in her best interest to change the subject, and I visualized her turning a huge topic dial from *Ridiculous Theory* to *Uncomfortable Silence* to *Sustained Uncomfortable Silence* and finally back to *Us*.

Yippee, my favorite.

Her eyes penetrated deep into mine like she was trying to count my rods and cones, then in a calm, controlled whisper, she said, "Will you accompany me to Lacy's MS benefit?"

Lacy was hosting a gallery opening for young painters, including herself, with all the proceeds going to the Multiple Sclerosis Society. It was next Friday and I wasn't sure walking in on the arm of Caitlin Dodds was in my best interest. But I rarely did anything in my best interest, so I said, "I'd love to."

Caitlin reached across the table and grabbed my hand then turned the knob to a point somewhere between *Tristen Grayer* and *Us*. She said, "I don't know what you think is going to happen tomorrow, but I don't want you to get your hopes up. Nothing is going to happen and, when it doesn't, I want you to get on with your life and I want to be part of it."

She stood, kissed me on the forehead, and exited Austin's. I guess we weren't getting separate checks after all.

Chapter 9

The book signing was at the Borders in Bangor at noon. I exited the highway at the Bangor exit and after a couple streets came to a large stretch of retail stores. At the end of two blocks was an immense gray brick Borders store. A banner on the side of the building notified people to "Come get your copy of *Eight in October* signed by author Alex Tooms, October 1st, 12:00 p.m.–3:00 p.m."

I checked my watch, it was two minutes after twelve and there was already a line wrapped halfway around the building. I was in the process of parking when I realized I'd left my copy of *Eight in October* on the kitchen table. I decided against the forty minute round trip to retrieve the book and expunged my wallet from the glove compartment. Let's see, how much had I spent on this insipid book? Four times twenty-seven equals—carry the one—one hundred and eight dollars.

Hell, if I kept this up, *Eight in October* would be the number one selling book of all time. Look out, *The Bible*.

As I made my way to the end of the line, I couldn't help notice the number of men far outweighed the number of women. Then I thought about it, women didn't read true-crime genre, they read Danielle Steel and those Nicholas peeter-puffers.

Inside the store, there were about a hundred or so people filing through a series of switchback rows. I stood on my tiptoes, trying to catch a glimpse of the guest of honor, but my view was blocked by a table stacked high with copies of *Eight in October*. The guy in front of me turned and asked, "Did you get a look at the pictures? Pretty gnarly shit, huh?"

"What pictures?" I inquired benignly.

He pulled a magazine from his back pocket. It was last November's issue of *Time* with the caption "The Maine Event" plastered on the front cover. On the left side of the cover was a picture of Tristen Grayer's disfigured corpse. Splitting the cover were the letters "vs." And the right half was a blown-up picture of yours truly in my University of Washington hoodie.

I held my breath. The man bypassed the cover and began rifling through the magazine's pages. Unconsciously he must have noticed something and ultimately made his way back to the front cover. He glanced from me to the cover, then did the act one more time for good measure, before asking, "That you?"

I assured him it was not *moi.*

He said, "Same face. Same sweatshirt. I think this is you."

"Well, it's not." I edged myself as far away as possible without losing my place in line.

The man whispered something to the guy in front of him, which was overheard by the people in front of them, and within a short two-minute span, everyone was craning their necks to get a look at the famed Thomas Prescott. A couple brave souls approached me and asked if I would sign their copy of *Eight in October.* I politely told them I would if I had a pen. They kept supplying me with pens but they kept snapping in half. It was weird. After the third pen, people stopped asking.

~

The line moved steadily and by 1:30 p.m. I was ten people from the front of the line. The stack of books was much smaller now, but it still obstructed any view of Alex Tooms. The anticipation was killing me, I wanted to see what this jerk looked like. He couldn't possibly be an attractive guy, could he? My brain had concocted an image of a half human, half Jaba-the-Hut-type thing. That's probably why they had the book wall erected, to hide the beast.

When it was finally my turn, I walked past the book curtain, took in a deep breath, and mentally shit my pants. Alex Tooms was a woman.

~

Alex, or make that Alexandria, had her eyes glued to the book she was writing in, yet I could still make out the majority of her features. She looked to be in her late twenties, a compact 5'6", mocha brown hair held back in a ponytail, and sleek olive skin. She was wearing faded blue jeans with a simple red tank top, and I wasn't sure if she had three older brothers or four. She sensed my presence and, without looking up from her present endeavor, said, "Do you need to buy a book?"

I heard myself say, "Yes, I need a book."

She pushed her project aside, grabbed a fresh copy, all the while with her head down, mind you, and said, "Who do you want it made out to?"

For as much as I was dreading this moment, it couldn't have played out any better. I licked my chops and said, "Thomas Prescott."

It was as if she was tied down on train tracks and each syllable of my name made up the train barreling toward her. The last "T", the caboose, came to a screeching halt inches from her frail body. She dropped her pen and looked up.

When God made her eyes, he evidently used dyes Yellow 5 and Blue 1 because they were the exact color of a lime Popsicle. After an awkward moment, she smiled, revealing she'd worn her retainer and her White Strips, and said, "Where's your machete?"

Machete? Oh, right. I'd written something in my letter about cutting his, now *her*, head off with a machete. It'd been a stress reliever at the time, even funny, but now it seemed a little over the top. "I left it in the car."

She laughed and her face creased in all the right places. I took this time to affirm I was here to give this person hell, not fall in love with them. I went over her bad qualities again in my head. Weasel reporter? Check. Big headed? Check. Money monger? Check. Nice rack? Check. Nice ass? Check . . . back later.

My thoughts were interrupted when she said, "I knew you'd show up here today. Actually, that was the whole reason for this book signing. It was bait. Thomas Prescott bait." She cocked her head to the side and asked, "Mind if I ask why you bit?"

I told her the truth, "I wanted to make sure you were ugly."

She laughed again, and I think my knees melted into my shins. "Then you must be disappointed."

Not the modest type, are we? I crafted my response carefully, making a point not to say extremely. "Extremely." Shit.

She grabbed a copy of *Eight in October*. Not the one in front of her, but the one she'd been writing in when I'd first approached. I found myself say, "Alexandria, is it?"

She handed me the book. "Call me Alex."

~

Back safely in the Range Rover, I opened my fourth copy of *Eight in October*. There was a map on the inside cover, underneath which Alex had scribbled:

1222 E. Amplewood Terrace. 8:30 Tonight. Bring wine.

Uh-oh.

Chapter 10

It was after three when I pulled into my drive. I hadn't eaten anything all day and I had a craving for a breakfast burrito. They say you crave things for a reason; red meat when you're low on iron, milk when your body is seeking calcium, and eggs when you're in need of protein. I had another craving but it wasn't as easily remedied as walking a couple blocks. It was in Philadelphia, even Seattle, not in Surry Woods.

The only thing on my mind on the walk to Little Benny's Big Burrito Stand, Little Benny's for short, was Alex's invitation to dinner. If I went, I had another opportunity to lash into her for writing the book. If I stayed home, I would just be waiting for something to happen which, sadly, was starting to look like the three-legged horse in the eighth race with Ricki Lake for a jockey.

When I first set out on my burrito pilgrimage, I'd been 90% in favor of not going to Alex's for dinner. Now I was down to about 70%. My goal was to somehow get down to fifty-fifty and go to the "old coin flip." I wonder how many big decisions have come at the hands of the old coin flip? I'm sure a couple wars were started because some idiot called heads. *Tails, we sign the treaty. Heads, we nuke 'em.*

Didn't people know you always call tails. Always.

When I'd completed the round trip, an elapsed time of twenty minutes, I found Lacy in the kitchen giving Baxter a bath in the sink. She heard me slide the glass door open and said, "How'd the book signing go? Did you give 'em hell?"

I set the Little Benny's bag on the kitchen table and said, "You mean, did I give *'er* hell."

Lacy stopped scrubbing the pug, who against the classic idiom, seemed to be enjoying the bath thoroughly. "Alex Tooms is a woman? No way. I wish I could have seen the look on your face. Oh, I would have given anything."

I took a burrito out of the sack, sat down at the small oak kitchen table, and said, "I'm still in shock."

Lacy sniffed. "Little Benny's?"

"Got yours right here."

Little Benny's took precedence over Baxter, and Lacy joined me at the table. After she'd taken a huge bite and sighed heavenly, she said, "Sooooo, drama at the bookstore. Spill it, bro."

I told her the story and she hung on every word. When I recounted Alex's dinner invitation for later that evening, Lacy started choking. I had to run and get her a glass of water. After she drank the glass and exhausted a coughing fit, she said, "You *have* to go."

That was all I needed to hear. Lacy's vote officially bumped it to fifty-fifty. Lacy went back to the kitchen sink—Baxter was in the dead pug's float—and I asked her if she had a dime. She yelled over her shoulder, "If I had a dime for every time someone asked me for a dime, I'd have a dime."

I guess that was a no, because no dimes came hurling my way. I walked to a wooden ledge separating the kitchen from the living room. Sitting on the ledge was an ivory colored ceramic vase, circa 1935—left over by the Farth's—that had become a refuge for Lacy's and my change.

I wasn't overly superstitious, but I did have a couple quirks and quacks that might fall into the category. After two minutes, I finally stumbled on a dime made the year I was born.

I flipped the coin and revealed—tails. See?

Lacy asked, "What's the verdict?"

I laughed at my own stupidity and said, "I'm not sure. I didn't assign heads or tails to either of the outcomes."

I primed the coin, assigning one outcome to heads and one to tails. Lacy interrupted my train of thought, "Wait. You can't assign the outcomes yourself. You need an unbiased third party to assign the outcomes. Like me, for instance."

"Why?"

"Because you're a retard and you always pick tails. So you're going to assign the outcome you want to tails, even if it's subconsciously."

She turned around, smiling, "Going was tails? It was, wasn't it?"

Oh.

Ohhhhhh.

I'd allocated *Going to Alex's for Dinner* to tails. This was not a good sign. "All right, you tell me what's what."

She thought for a second and said, "Flip for it."

I was confused. This was starting to be a common trend, "What?"

"Give me the dime." I handed her the dime and she said, "If it's heads then *Going to Alex's for Dinner* will be heads. If it's tails then *Going to Alex's for Dinner* will be tails."

This was like Abbot and Costello meets Benny and Joon. "So what's *Not Going to Alex's for Dinner*?"

"It's whatever *Going to Alex's for Dinner* isn't."

I was under the impression flipping a coin to make a decision was meant to simplify the decision, not complicate it. "Whatever."

She flipped the coin, then Braill-ed the top of the coin with her right index finger. "Heads. So *Going to Alex's for Dinner* is heads. Actually, if you wanted to be entirely unbiased, you would flip a coin to see which one of the outcomes you would flip a coin to see what heads and tails would be for the final flip."

I felt a migraine coming on and grabbed the coin out of Lacy's hand. "So let me get this straight, *Going to Alex's for Dinner* is heads and *Not Going to Alex's for Dinner* is tails."

"Right."

I flipped the coin and, for the first time in my life, I found myself praying for heads.

~

Tails. Best two out of three. Tails. Best three out of five. Tails. Best four out of seven. Tails. I'm telling you, it's always tails. To be honest, I was starting to get the heebie-jeebies, I couldn't remember the last time I'd had tails four times in a row. I kept flipping and things started to even out. And after about ten minutes, heads finally inched out tails in the best thirty-three out of sixty-five division.

~

After stopping by a liquor store, I turned the navigational system on, foolishly opting for the voice command option. The woman's voice came on and asked for my destination. The bitchy undertones of the woman's voice sounded vaguely familiar, but I still couldn't place the voice. The woman repeated the command and there was no mistaking it; Hillary Rodham Clinton was yelling at me from the dash.

I opened *Eight in October* to where the map should have been, but it'd either vanished or I'd brought the wrong copy of the book. I could have viewed this as a sign I wasn't fated to go to Alex's, but that would have been superstitious and I wasn't superstitious. Plus, my lucky socks would have canceled it out, had it been a sign.

I called Lacy and luckily Conner was at the house. Apparently, the two were about to head to a movie which, strangely enough, Lacy still enjoyed listening to. Conner found my signed copy of *Eight in October*, and I relayed the address to Hillary. Within seconds I was a blue dot blinking along I-95 headed to the red star more than twenty-five miles away.

I pulled a CD out of the glove compartment and slipped it in. I was bumbling along to Maroon 5 when I noticed a high-pitched background singer. In reality, it was Hillary bitching at me to merge onto Route 2 westbound. I turned the music down and followed Hillary's commands until I found myself in the town of East Madison.

Alex's house was on Amplewood Terrace. From my experience, there was only one house on a terrace and it was usually the biggest house on the block. I drove for a long par five and doglegged left for a short par three when the street suddenly ended at a huge wrought iron gate: 1222 Amplewood Terrace.

I didn't want to announce my presence at the gate box and was debating whether to jump the fence when the huge gate began to swing inward. Watching Alex's gate open was like watching a hundred-year-old paraplegic do the moonwalk through fresh concrete. The gate finally opened wide enough to squeak the Range Rover through. Or make that wide enough I *thought* I could squeak the Range Rover through. My passenger side mirror was now part of Miss Tooms' gate garden motif. Beats a garden gnome, I guess.

There was a gravel road leading up a hill, the house's slate roof shingles barely visible through the barrage of spruces and pines. As I drove, my nose detected a hint of lake or river, and I'd be willing to bet there was freshwater parked somewhere in Alex's backyard. Speaking of parking, there was a silver Jeep Wrangler parked next to a shed about twenty yards from the house and I headed the car in that direction.

I grabbed the bottle of wine and stepped out, my feet sinking into a bed of more than an inch of fallen pine needles. Walking around the car, I surveyed the wires dangling from where the passenger-side mirror once sat. In my frustration I may have kicked the front bumper which, in turn, fell off.

The house was that odd height where it could easily be comprised of either two stories or one story with high ceilings. It was made entirely of white cobble brick and the four pane windows sat back seven or eight inches. There was a series of rosebushes girdling the perimeter of the house, the bulbs readying themselves for the long winter slumber. The front door split the house evenly—two windows on each side—and was the only thing with paint attached. I lifted the bronze doorknocker and slammed it twice against the door.

I was pulling the doorknocker upward for a final thrusting when the door swung inward and I was left with the doorknocker and its hinged compatriot suspended from my fingertips.

Alex Tooms stood in the doorway holding the door with her right hand, her left hand appearing to be sewn into her hip pocket. She was wearing the same outfit as earlier, only she was now donning a derisive grin.

I offered her money for the brass fixture but she said she didn't have her credit card machine up and running.

She said, "I'm surprised you came. I wasn't expecting you."

Wasn't expecting me, my ass. She knew, as well as I did, the fancy soap was out. I ambled onto the recently lacquered wood floor, dividing my attention between both Alex and her home's delicate beauty.

We made our way to the kitchen, which I was surprised to see was fully loaded. Centering the kitchen was a black marble island with ten burners, four of which were occupied and simmering away.

I ran my hand over one of the cherry wood cabinet doors and said, "Nice place you got here." (This comment is only said when either the person saying it is uncomfortable, or they are impressed with the other person's digs. I was both so I wasn't sure where that put me.)

After turning one of the dials on burner one, three, five, seven, or nine, Alex said, "Can you make us some drinks?"

I wasn't sure if she was asking if I wanted to make drinks or if I were capable. She gave me instructions to the bar and put in her order for whatever I was having. I set the bottle of Cab on the countertop and exited the kitchen, finding myself in a spacious living room with a long oak bar at back. There were two paintings, one on both the east and west walls, respectively, and I knew immediately both were Winslow Homers. There was a small couch facing a mammoth flat screen television and the bar in the dim left corner was nearly invisible.

I meandered behind the high bar and fumbled through Alex's array of liquor bottles. I made two stiff gin and tonics and made my way back to the kitchen. Alex tossed two thick salmon filets on the grill splitting the island, inciting a cacophony of smells.

At the present moment I was leaning back against one of her marble counters, markedly uncomfortable both physically and conversationally, and hauled myself up with both hands. As I let my weight down on the counter a searing pain tore through my right butt cheek, and I heaved myself up and off the marble. The sound of my gasping began to fade and was soon barely audible beneath the rumbling laughter emitting from Miss Tooms.

I mustered the strength to look back over my shoulder and took in the sight. There were three corncob holders sticking out of my back right pants pocket. I pulled one out slowly. The blade was about an inch long and about a quarter of an inch thick, covered in a light red film, aka my fucking blood.

As I pulled the remaining two corncob holders out, the composed Alex said, "You can keep those as souvenirs. I don't think I want them touching my corn."

I smiled meekly, then walked—no, make that hobbled—out of the kitchen and directly across the hall to the sparse bathroom. It took me a couple seconds to get my pants unbuckled and my red boxer briefs peeled from the flesh, which I might add, were white when I bought them. If you are under the impression wounds of the butt don't bleed, let me be the first to tell you otherwise.

I cleaned up the wounds with toilet paper and warm water, then scavenged the bathroom cabinet for some Band-Aids. There weren't any Band-Aids but I did stumble on a box of maxi pads. Hmmm.

I took three pads from the box, unwrapped them, and smacked them down, securing the wings down tightly on the rosy flesh. Then I flushed the wrappers down the toilet, pulled my pants up, and then flushed twice more for good measure.

Let's take a minute and reflect on the night so far, shall we? I'd stripped my passenger side mirror, kicked off my front bumper, ripped off Alex's doorknocker, sat on a set of corncob holders, and now had three maxi pads stuck to my ass. Holy shit, maybe I should call it quits before I burned Alex's house down and put in a tampon.

Chapter 11

The 'Ol brothers, Alcoh and Tylen, were starting to get along and when Alex said dinner was on, and I didn't feel half bad. I followed her into the living room and saw the bar was set rather than the table. I thought about this for a moment and decided the bar was at the most desirable height for my present situation. The two of us sidled up to opposite sides of the bar, Alex playing bartender and me in the role of drunken patron or soon to be drunken patron, that is.

I took in the food; it looked amazing. There was a medley of grilled vegetables: mushrooms, baby tomatoes, green peppers, red peppers, and onions, surrounding a steaming filet of salmon. All were sitting on a bed of dirty rice, garnished with a sprig of parsley and two lemons. I wondered if Alex was trying to impress me or if she'd had an internship with Wolfgang Puck after college.

Alex had the bottle of wine open and breathing, and while she poured us both a glass I took the time to focus on the message I wanted to convey to this woman. I desperately wanted to scold her for writing the book. But could I blame her? It was a hell of a story and she was paid a substantial amount for the trade.

Alex pushed a full glass of scarlet Cabernet Sauvignon in front of me and said, "Let's clear the air. You first."

Here went nothing. I cleared my throat and said, "The man who killed those eight women is still out there."

Alex sat in stunned silence, obliviously popping a mushroom in her mouth, and garbled, "All right, let's hear it."

I replayed the events that transpired on that fateful day almost a year ago, Alex soaking up each detail like a thirsty sponge. She was a journalist at heart and I could see she was twitching to run and grab a pen and pad. I finished with a tirade of sorts, hitting a high with, "*Eight in October* is a death trophy to Tristen Grayer."

At my conclusion, Alex asked one of the few questions I hadn't seen on the night's docket, "Can I see the scars?"

I showed her the nickel sized scar on my left shoulder and said, "The other one isn't as easily accessible."

"I thought the second bullet shattered your femur?"

"It did. High femur." I raised my eyebrows. "High—inner—femur."

A pained expression blanketed her face and she covered her mouth, "Did it nick the old twig and berries?"

Did I hear her correctly? Did an acclaimed investigative journalist just use the phrase "Old twig and berries?"

I tried valiantly to hide a smile, and, as if reading my mind, Alex said, "Sorry, cock and balls."

I laughed and said, "It's your turn."

Alex shook her head, "Let's take a twenty." She tapped her shoulders with her fingertips twice, indicating a timeout. "For the next twenty minutes, this is a date."

"A date? Why not a prune? Or a raisin?"

She rolled her eyes at me, "Are you always like this?"

No, only when I'm in the presence of a beautiful woman, tipsy, and am wearing maxi pads. "Okay, it's a date. And, by the way, tapping your shoulders is the signal for a full timeout, not a twenty."

We argued over a couple referee calls (by the way, she was right about the timeout) until I ejected her from the conversation, which she thought was hilarious. The way to a woman's heart is through her funny bone and I was having inner strife about whether I wanted to tickle Alex's. I decided to tone it down a bit and said, "So, two cowboys are on the edge of a cliff when they hear the sound of war drums. One cowboy looks at the other and says, 'I don't like the sound of those war drums.' From below they hear someone shout, 'He's not our regular drummer!'"

When I pulled my hands away from my mouth (I'd cupped them to give an echoing effect), Alex was crumpled behind the bar. I was a third of the way into my salmon when Alex popped up wiping tears from her eyes, "That is the stupidest joke I've ever heard."

We ate and traded jokes—for the record, hers were much dirtier than mine—for the next twenty minutes. We moved on to sailing. Turns out, Alex was an avid sailor and offered to give me a lesson sometime. After we finished the meal and the bottle,

Alex disappeared into the kitchen, returning with a large slice of cheesecake. The two of us devoured the rich, creamy, almond swirled cheesecake, and I'd be fibbing if I said the orgasmic tremor at the end of my fork was the only one on my mind.

After we'd licked the plate clean, I looked at my watch. It was close to ten and I said, "Date's over, babe."

She threw me a look daring me to call her babe again then, after clearing her throat, said, "Now it's my turn. I believe you. I believe every word. I wish you would have told me all this ten months ago so I could have written the truth in my book. There, I'm done. Now back to the date. Where did you grow up?"

"No, no, no. Unacceptable. I went on a tirade, now it's your turn to tirade."

"I don't tirade. I get to the point. I believe you. Everything you said makes sense. Case closed. Did you have any pets growing up?"

"You can't play the high-and-mighty card. I threatened your life for crying out loud. This is your chance to get even."

Her emerald eyes penetrated mine as she said, "You were shot twice. You careened off a cliff into the Atlantic. You were in a coma for two weeks and a wheelchair for eight. Not to mention that at this very moment you're wearing maxi pads. Honey, I think we're even."

~

Alex carried the dishes into the kitchen and left me to sit in my own abashment. On her exit she'd said (this is a verbatim quote, mind you), "Well, Max, do you think you can make us some after-dinner drinks."

To which I'd piously replied, "I'll wing it." Guffaws all around.

I grabbed two Bud bottles from the bar fridge. Done. Alex reappeared from the kitchen, her right arm drooping under the weight of an enormous spotlight. She walked over to the bar and grabbed the beer with her free hand. I asked, "Looking for life on Mars?"

"Oh, this thing. This is for spotting wildlife."

"Like chimpanzees and elephants?"

She shot me an appraising glance. "Are you qualified to have an adult conversation?"

"I passed all the tests. They said my diploma was in the mail."

Alex shook her head as I followed her through a small stateroom and onto a small terrace overlooking a large lake feeding into thick woods. The reflection under the full moon made it hard to distinguish where the lake ended and the forest began. The tall pines afraid to move, lest they were only a reflection. There was a short gray brick wall surrounding the concrete terrace and I leaned against it for support. Alex nestled up to me and put her hand on my shoulder, "That's Lake Wesserunsett."

She flipped on the spotlight and began scanning the horizon back and forth. The spotlight appeared to be a smidgen less powerful than the moon, and I said, "Are you on call if one of the lighthouses ever breaks down?"

She laughed then yelled, "Look!"

Within its beam, the spotlight held an imposing moose at the edge of the forest. It shook its head, thrusting its horns around like the fearful beast it was and I said, "I think it's Rocky that likes the spotlight, not Bullwinkle."

She laughed and turned toward me, unintentionally blinding me with the one million watt bulb. When my sight came back, Alex had her hands around me in a rather intimate position. In hindsight she may have blinded me intentionally.

I could feel my breath reeling off her forehead and my stomach dropped like an elevator headed for BB2.

I slowly pushed her away and said, "I can't."

I glanced around for the ventriloquist hiding behind the terrace wall, but it turns out I actually said these words. In truth, I couldn't shake Caitlin from my mind's eye. I hadn't given her a chance, and I had fundamentally screwed her over. I owed her another shot. Scratch that, I owed us another shot. I'd loved her, possibly still loved her, and if it wasn't for my unrelenting stubborn streak we would still be together.

As for Alex, she threw me an inquisitive glance that might as well have asked me if I were gay out loud. When she opened her mouth, I expected her to ask if I were into ice skating as a young lad, but instead she said, "How did your parents die?"

She added, "You don't have to tell me if you don't want to. It's just something I stumbled on while I was doing research for the book."

Surprisingly, I kept my composure and said, "An airplane crash."

"Where?"

"Near the California-Oregon border."

"How old were you?"

"Twenty-six, it was my first year as a detective with the Seattle Police Department. I did the funeral thing then moved back in with my little sister, Lacy." I wisely skipped the part about the monumental inheritance.

"Then you up and moved to New York?"

"A couple years later, Lacy got a swimming scholarship to Temple and I decided to tag along. She was the only family I had left and I couldn't imagine not seeing her every day. Plus, I'd spent my entire life in Washington; I was ready for a change."

"Then you started with the Philadelphia Police Department?"

"Not exactly. I was more or less thrown off the force in Seattle and didn't think I could follow the protocols of another department."

She nodded.

I continued, "I had an old friend from college who was a Philly homicide detective and he would ask for my opinion on cases every so often. I broke a couple of his cases, and pretty soon the department had hired me on as a consultant. And then a year ago, the FBI came a knocking."

Everything I'd just recounted Alex knew verbatim, but I didn't feel like impeding the conversation. I saw an opening and swiftly asked, "Considering I thought you were a man until about eight hours ago, why don't you tell me a little about yourself?"

She shrieked, "You thought I was a guy?"

"Well the name doesn't leave much room for imagination."

"Yeah, well if I said I didn't do it on purpose, I'd be lying."

No shit? Why not just go by Façade Tooms, Hoax Tooms, or False Pretense Tooms. I asked, "So you started going by Alex instead of Alexandria?"

"Nope. Alex is my given name. My parents were convinced they were having a boy."

"So I guess you're lucky your name isn't Jack or Fred."

"Oh, I don't think they would have been that cruel. Although I think they're convinced they made me into a lesbian as it is."

I laughed. "Why would they ever think that?"

She ran her hands through her shoulder length, beaver brown hair. "Up until about a year ago my hair was always really short, like Demi Moore's."

"Demi Moore *Ghost*? Or Demi Moore *G. I. Jane*?"

She looked at me like I'd caught the short bus to her house and said, "I want to see that diploma."

~

Alex was indulging me with a little background information when I heard a rustling near the terrace wall. I grabbed the spotlight illuminating the wild beast, a bunny-wabbit. Maybe he was a friend of the guy who beat up Baxter and came to gloat. I also didn't rule out Bigwig, Fiver, Pipkin, Blueberry, or Hazel.

Alex started back up, "I was up to college. I got a scholarship to Boston College for cross-country and studied journalism."

Cross-country. That explained the figure. I remarked on this, "You look like a runner."

She smirked. "I opted against the traditional method of binge-and-purge for the less conventional binge-and-run." She looked at me and said, "You look like a runner too."

To a woman, this is an incredible compliment; to a man, it's an incredulous insult. "Thanks. I went on a lead-based diet."

"You mean bread?"

"No, I mean bullets."

She covered her mouth, "Oh, I forgot. But aren't you supposed to gain weight when you're in a wheelchair?"

I patted my stomach. "Good metabolism." There are no two words in the English language that anger a woman more when combined than *good* and *metabolism*.

Alex shook her head. "I hate people like you. If I don't go running tomorrow morning there will be a cheesecake shaped fat pocket in my ass."

I didn't believe that for a second. "How far of a run?"

She counted on her fingers. "Eight miles."

"How did you come up with eight?"

"One mile for each drink. Four miles for the cheesecake."

I wondered how many hours of sex that converted into. She studied my face and said, "Eight hours. One mile of running is equal to one hour of sex."

We both stood there for an unpolished Humpy Dumpty and if I said the thoughts running through my head were PG-13, I'd be lying. I heard a faint ringing in the background of the X-rated movie playing in my head, and the lead actress, Xela, said, "I think your cell phone is ringing."

The ringing was indeed coming from my pocket and I extracted my phone. I checked the caller ID; it was Lacy. If it'd been anyone else, I would have clicked on my voice mail. I flipped the phone open, "What's up?"

"I just called to tell you that you're the master. You got me *sooo* good."

Got her? Oh, my little practical joke. I'd strategically placed thirty fly traps throughout the house. If you aren't familiar with a fly trap, they unravel from the ceiling about three feet and are covered in a half tree sap, half Elmer's glue type concoction. I'd gotten three of them stuck to my face on the way out and I'd hung them. "Well thank you, Lacy Prescott. That means a lot coming from you, although it's easy when your prey is deaf, dumb, and blind."

"Just blind, you prick. Where did you get the parts, they feel so real."

"What parts? They're fly traps. I picked them up at the hardware store."

"No, the body parts in my bed. They feel so real."

As she said the words I knew my worst fears had been realized.

Tristen Grayer was back.

Chapter 12

My autonomous nervous system kicked in and my body couldn't decide whether to fight or flight. So I stood still, like a deer in headlights. No, wait, Alex was shining the friggin' spotlight in my eyes again.

She said, "Oops, sorry," and ran into the house.

I flipped my cell open and dialed Caitlin. She picked up on the third ring, "This better be good."

Caitlin should have asked, "Where?" The only reason I would be calling at 11:30 p.m. on a Monday night would be to report a murder or put in for a late night sex romp. "Where?" covered both bases. I cleared my throat and said, "My house." She was silent, the reality of the situation piercing her skin. When it hit marrow, she asked, "Are you there?"

"No, I'm thirty minutes out."

She didn't ask where I was. And if she had, I would have said the dentist. Lucky for me, this wasn't the time for questions or comedy routines.

Caitlin said flatly, "I can be there in twenty."

I flipped the phone closed and saw I had unconsciously made my way through Alex's house and was nearing her front door. Alex had absconded somewhere and I hoped she would understand my leaving without a proper so long, farewell, arrivederci, miss-me-miss-me-now-you-have-to-kiss-me.

I beelined it to the Range Rover, rammed the key in the ignition, threw the car in drive, slammed down the gas, then slammed on the brakes, nearly crippling Ms. Tooms in the process. Alex hit the hood with both hands and threw open the passenger door. Her chest was heaving as she said, "I'm coming with."

I would have thrown her out, but it would have wasted valuable time. And, to be perfectly honest, I didn't mind her presence. She apparently knew where I lived and directed me through a shortcut even Hillary wasn't wise to. (I would later go on to name the route "The Lewinsky.")

I kept my foot down on the gas and after two minutes I was rocketing up the ramp to I-95. Once safely on the highway, cruising at the breakneck speed of a hundred and ten miles an hour, I attempted to get my cell phone out of my pocket. It was a futile effort and I said, "Dial this number."

Alex pulled a cell phone from her pocket, sending something small and metallic onto her lap. She said, "Shoot."

I rattled off the number and she handed me the phone. After the first ring someone picked up on the other line and I said, "Where are you?"

Conner's voice shot through the phone, "I'm on my way to your house. What the hell is going on? Lacy wouldn't tell me shit."

I told him the situation and I could hear the pistons in his Camaro flex their muscles. It wasn't safe to talk on a cell at 120 miles an hour so I hung up and concentrated on the road. I handed the phone to Alex, who was fiddling with the small metallic object and, for what it's worth, didn't appear to be peeing her pants. At some point, I picked up one of Maine's finest, his twinkling lights cascading off the tunneling trees in my rear view.

The exit sign told me I had two miles until my stop. The three cop cars on my tail told me I would probably be on the next edition of *World's Greatest Police Chases*. Fifty seconds later, I exited and the three cops followed suit.

Oh no, someone must have broken into the Lighthouse Museum.

I covered the next three miles in record time, leading the parade of lights through a number of treacherous turns, slowing down when I hit my street. It was one thing to run over a hitchhiker on the freeway, it was another to run over your neighbor's curfew-breaking-pot-smoking teen. I found my inlet and skidded to a halt behind Caitlin's red Pathfinder. I bounded out of the car and immediately heard someone yell, "Down on your knees! Hands up!"

Someone else yelled, "Fuck off, I live here!"

Someone didn't like *Someone Else's* answer and the next thing *Someone Else* knew, they had their face buried in the leaves and their arms wrenched behind their back. *Someone Else* tried reasoning with them, but it was hard to get across the message there was a dead body in *Someone Else's* house with a mouthful of dirt, leaves, and grubs.

A woman's voice rang out, "If you don't get off that man this instant you'll be writing traffic tickets the rest of your life."

Oh, Caitlin. Sweet, sweet Caitlin.

I thanked my lucky stars and the cuffs flew off. Caitlin had on a pair of dark khakis and a light Bangor Police Department parka with the words "Medical Examiner" stenciled on the left breast pocket. Alex was at her side, and both brushed a couple leaves off my chest.

I asked, "Where's Lace?"

Caitlin cocked her head toward the house, "Conner called and said the two of them were in the back looking for Baxter."

I wasn't sure if I was supposed to introduce Alex and Caitlin, and to be perfectly honest, I didn't care if they ever met. I started a trot to the house and yelled over my shoulder, "How long have you been here?"

"I must have pulled up right before you. I was on my way up the stairs when Alex grabbed my shirt and said you were being arrested."

Alex? These two were on a first name basis? Did I miss something? I filed this information away somewhere in a folder marked *Relationships* in my cerebral cortex and said, "So you haven't seen the body?"

"Nope." Caitlin's mood did not convey there was actually a *body* to be seen.

The front door was open and the three of us filed through, heading for the stairs. Halfway there, I turned and started for the back deck. Corpses rarely, if ever, up and leave the scene of crime. Plus, I needed to see firsthand that Lacy was safe.

Caitlin and Alex followed me out to the beach where Lacy and Conner were visible under the moonlight thirty yards away, both shouting Baxter's name at the top of their lungs. Lacy heard us approach and raced in my direction. She was clad in a pair of yellow pajamas with snoring teddy bears. Let's just put it this way, if the blood soaking Lacy's pajamas had been hers, she'd be running about a quart and a half low.

Caitlin swallowed hard, it almost appearing as though she had an Adam's apple under the soft moonlight, and said, "I'm sorry, Thomas. I should have believed you."

~

Lacy didn't seem overly distraught about the possibility there was a dead body in her bed, but the idea that Baxter was missing was evident in the tears dribbling down her cheeks. This was probably one of the few situations in which it paid off to be blind.

I yelled to Conner thirty yards up the beachfront, "Have you been up there yet?"

He walked slowly up the beach toward our group. "Nope. Lacy was frantic when I got here, and I've been looking for that little shit since. She won't even let me wash the blood off her hands for Christ's sake."

I looked over my shoulder and saw Caitlin yelling into her cell phone. *That's it, load up the apology bus. Single file, please.*

Lacy wanted me to help with the pug search, and I told her I'd be more than willing once I took a gander at her room. I walked back into the house. Caitlin and Alex were nipping at my heels while Conner was evidently stuck with doggy duty for the time being. The three of us made our way through the house and up the beige carpet stairs. I was two steps from the top when I heard Alex's wispy voice state, "Walking upstairs, no sign of blood."

I turned around and saw Alex speaking into the small metallic object. I'd been too preoccupied earlier to heed I'd allowed the enemy into the castle. Not allowed even, escorted. I yanked the tape recorder from her hand, pressed Stop, and watched the tape cease spinning. "I can't let you up there, Alex. I don't know what I was thinking even letting you come here tonight."

I watched Alex until she was out of sight and put the tape recorder in my pocket. Caitlin and I continued up the stairway and into the hall. My heart was pounding in my throat and I blinked my dry eyes before taking the final steps into perdition.

I eased the door open, the door reverberating lightly off the oak trimming in the obscure blackness. I inhaled deeply, pulling every inch of the room in through my nostrils. My sister was a neat freak and the room usually reeked of Windex and ginger potpourri. Tonight it carried the acrid taste of blood, like biting on a penny. I flicked on the lights and my eyes converged on the bloody mess of limbs scattered on the once white down comforter.

Caitlin and I looked at each other in aversion. It was real.

I walked to the bed and saw, lying smack-dab in the middle of the carnage, our fugitive in question. Call off the search party. I plucked the seven pound scab from the carnage. Baxter awoke and did his best guard dog impression, three successive yelps.

Yeah, buddy. But where were you when this was happening?

I wrapped Baxter in an old T-shirt and walked into the hall where Alex was leaning backward on the top stair straining to hear. I handed the blood-caked-narcoleptic-guard pug to her and said, "Maybe you can help Lacy give this guy a bath."

Alex took the pug, wrinkled her nose, and asked, "Is it bad?"

"Yes."

She sensed this was the extent of her details and started down the steps holding Baxter like he was a canister of plutonium.

I walked back into the room and joined Caitlin next to the queen sized bed. I did a quick inventory of body parts and came up with twenty-one differentiated body segments. Then assembling the parts in my mind I came up with a compact, well-shaped woman, 5'6" to 5'8", between 120 and 130 lbs. The woman's head was facing down at the top left corner of the bed, her dirty blond hair matted down to her spongy red scalp. Caitlin and I met eyes and she asked, "You want me to?"

Yes. "No."

I slowly turned the woman's head over on the bed. It was similar to waiting for a carousel to come full circle with a sniper on it. The face was barely recognizable, painted red with blood. Her nose was smashed flat, her eye sockets pulpy black concaves, and her left cheek bone protruded her gaping mouth. I staggered two steps backwards and held myself up using Lacy's ragged dresser, the air being sucked from my lungs like I was attached to a vacuum.

Caitlin asked, "Who is she?"

It took me a couple seconds to fight back the salmon swimming upstream in my esophagus. Through clenched teeth, I said, "Jennifer Peppers. I was engaged to her a couple years ago."

I shook my head, my eyes falling on the wall opposite Lacy's bed. It took me a couple seconds to realize what I was looking at. Or, more accurately, what was looking at me.

Caitlin followed my gaze and gasped, "Holy shit. Are those her eyes?"

Chapter 13

I took two steps toward the lifeless, vacant eyeballs protruding from Lacy's wall.

I'm assuming the vast majority of you have never seen an eyeball when it isn't resting peacefully in the socket. The shape of the human eye is elliptical, with all the wiring hanging out the back. They look like tiny squids, to be frank. Through each eye, a nail had been pounded expertly through the pupil, plastering the optic nerve and his relatives outward like rays emitting the sun.

Jennifer had these magnificent hazel eyes; taking on a tawny lemon hue one day and a metallic bronze another. Now her eyes hung in a copper limbo against their bloody landscape.

I followed the stare of the inanimate eyes to the mangled limbs piled high on the bed. I stated, "He wants us to know Jennifer watched her own death, watched her own life be taken from her."

Caitlin said from somewhere, "Tristen Grayer with a twist."

I nodded. This was certainly a new development.

I walked around the room for the next ten minutes, taking three rolls of mental photographs. Jennifer's eyes had taken on a Mona Lisa quality, seeming to follow my every move within the small room. I'd seen my fair share of death as a homicide detective. Yet when it's someone you knew personally, emotionally, sexually even, it's different. I kept thinking it couldn't be real. Jennifer Peppers couldn't be dead. Tristen Grayer couldn't be back.

I laughed at my naiveté. Tristen Grayer wasn't back. He'd never left. He'd always been waiting in the shadows, lurking. Now, he'd struck at the heart of the castle, killing someone special from my past.

~

We made our way downstairs as two men dressed in white jackets with "Bangor Police Department" inscribed on their backs walked through the front door holding a collapsible gurney. A gurney? What did they think was up there? They needed a box. A big fucking box.

Caitlin directed them to Lacy's room, and the two of us walked out onto the front porch. The fresh air took on a cleansing property, and I suddenly wished for a torrential downpour. Unfortunately, it hadn't rained in about three weeks, and I surveyed my yellow lawn. There were six cop cars, three Bangor and three Penobscot County Sheriff parked in a semi-circle, their lights dancing on the grass up near the outskirts of the nearest oak where a band of onlookers had formed.

Through the kaleidoscope of lights, Alex appeared and walked up the drive. She wiped her hands on her pants and said, "Your sister just left with Conner. She wants you to call her and let her know where you'll be staying the night."

I hadn't thought of this little nugget. I sure as hell couldn't spend the night here. Come to think of it, I wasn't sure if I could spend another night under the roof. Too much death. One woman gets killed? Hey, let's get different drapes. Two women get killed? Hey, let's get a different state.

Apparently, Caitlin had already contemplated my sleeping quandary and said, "You're welcome to stay at my place. It's only a block from Lacy and I'm sure she'll want you nearby."

Case open and shut, right? Wrong.

Alex did not concur with Caitlin's analysis of my sleeping quarters and rebuked, "You know it's only me in that big house. You're welcome to crash in any of the guest bedrooms." She added, "You have to drop me off anyhow."

Caitlin didn't seem pleased with this information and pointed to a group of four cops, "Oh, sweetie, I'm sure one of those nice gentlemen would be kind enough to drop you off."

I told Alex I would drop her off but I needed to be near Lacy, and it would be best if I stayed at Caitlin's. Speaking of which, Caitlin would have to play coroner for the next couple hours, and I asked her for a house key. She removed her key chain from her pocket and was attempting to expunge her house key when she asked, "Don't you still have the key I gave you?"

Yes, it was in my glove compartment thirty feet away. "No."
Caitlin looked at me suspiciously. Alex looked at Caitlin suspiciously. I looked suspiciously at my feet.

~

Caitlin handed me the key and retreated into the house. Alex and I buckled into the Range Rover, and I navigated through the barrage of police cars. One of the police officers who'd tackled me threw me a salute and I saluted him back, only my hand was out the window and my thumb, pointer finger, ring finger, and pinky wouldn't stand up.

Once on the frontage road, my curiosity overcame me. I asked Alex, "How did Caitlin know your name?"

She raised her thin eyebrows slightly, "I interviewed her for the book. I interviewed everybody involved with the case. Well, almost everybody." She smirked. I dismissed this and said, "Caitlin never said anything about any interview. All she said was that she spent a week compiling her account of the events."

"Yeah, with me."

"When?"

"I'd say around the beginning of November."

"Where?"

"MCM."

What a coincidence, last November I'd been doing quite a bit of hanging out at Maine Coast Memorial hospital, albeit, I was in a coma. I was stunned and said, "Don't tell me you interviewed her in my room?"

"I had to." She looked like she wanted to stop there, but I think there was something in the small print of the X-chromosome contract. She added, "She wouldn't leave your side."

I thought about these last five words for the duration of the drive.

~

I pulled through Alex's open gate and parked on her doorstep, her rosebush to be exact. She said meekly, "Can I have my tape recorder back?"

I'd forgotten I'd confiscated her tape recorder and extracted it from my pocket. I checked to make sure it was still off and handed it through the window. "Sorry I had to take it, but from my standpoint you're the enemy."

I watched Alex recede into the house, then drove to where I'd parked earlier, picked my bumper from its leaf burial, and threw it in the trunk. Making my way down her drive, I noticed her gate had taken the liberty of closing. I pulled up to the sensor box and the gate stubbornly played dumb. I hit the green intercom button and said, "Alex, could you open your gate?"

Alex's voice broke the static, "Only if you promise to go sailing with me on Saturday."

I was being optimistic in hoping the case—case being Tristen Grayer—would be in custody or dead by this point and said, "It's a date."

The gate creaked alive and I took the minute and a half to pick my passenger side mirror from her garden. I threw the mirror over my shoulder into the hatch turned car-part cemetery and slipped through the gate. This was my first chance to be alone, and all the emotions I'd felt at the crime scene came flooding back. There's a dam built in my brain that separates all the good I've encountered in my life from the bad. Jennifer Pepper's death was a lot of water to take on by an already unstable barricade. A large chunk of dam chipped off that ride home.

I ran through the visual pictures of the crime scene. The last shot of Jennifer's eyes was nagging. In the past, Tristen had taken the women's eyes as souvenirs. Why the sudden change? Boredom? Maybe, but doubtful. Tristen Grayer was a serial killer, but he didn't fit the serial-killer mold. His killings were methodical and impulsive or, for lack of a better term, he killed with an organized spontaneity. Tristen Grayer was the ultimate paradox, a killing conundrum.

Tristen Grayer was scary as hell.

Chapter 14

I pulled up to Conner's nondescript apartment complex. Conner opened the bottom floor apartment door as I was approaching and said, "Caitlin just called. I guess I owe you an apology."

"You can take me out to dinner some time."

Conner followed me into the living room where Lacy was listening to SportsCenter. I sat down on the arm of the tan love seat and put my hand on her shoulder, "You all right, kiddo?"

She ran her hands over Baxter's small back. "I don't know. I wouldn't have been if you'd told me the truth. Thanks for keeping me in the dark. Really. I'm not being sarcastic. I can't believe it. That poor girl."

Not any poor girl. Jennifer Peppers had been Lacy's beloved art teacher at Temple. Lacy had been the one to introduce us. I'd hoped this information would have surfaced by this juncture. I brushed a couple strands of hair off Lacy's cheek and said, "It wasn't just any girl. It was JP."

Lacy gasped for air. "No. Not Jennifer. Oh my God. Jen."

Conner's voice shot in from the side of the room, "Who's JP?"

I relayed the deceased's relationship to both Lacy and myself and Conner said, "He's gunning for you, Thomas."

No, he was axing for me. Except I was still in one piece and I couldn't say that much for Jennifer. I didn't like where my thought process was headed and said, "I think you should get out of town for a while, Lace. Go visit some friends in Washington."

Conner and I met eyes. He seconded, "That's not a bad idea Lacy."

Through a fit of sniffing she said, "I'm not going anywhere. The gallery opening is less than two weeks away and I still have a million things to do. I'm not going to let MS, my blindness, or some chump dictate how I live."

I wouldn't exactly refer to a man who just hacked some girl to bits and, more probably than not, raped her senseless as a chump. I thought it was in Lacy's best interest to jump ship for a couple weeks but a large chunk of me was proud of her for standing her ground.

Conner motioned for the kitchen. He turned the faucet on and whispered, "Why don't you call up a couple of your students and see if they want to do some extra credit."

Why didn't I think of that? In January, I'd been offered a job teaching a course at one of the local universities (seeing as how I was convalescing in a wheelchair and wouldn't be chasing any criminals any time soon). There were five or six guys from my class who would die for any form of police work, even if it was as arbitrary as a stakeout.

Conner and I walked back into the living room and Lacy said, "Extra credit, huh? How about Caleb?"

Lacy's hearing had more than made up for her lack of eyesight. Conner asked, "Who's Caleb?

I decided to leave before the fireworks and kissed Lacy goodbye.

~

Caitlin only lived a short mile from Conner, and by the time I found a radio station not on a commercial break, I was turning onto her street.

Caitlin lived in a cookie cutter stucco house in a neighborhood that hadn't existed this time last year. The only thing distinguishing each house from the next was the systematic bump of the last two digits in the address. I think you had to petition the homeowners' association if you wanted to open a window. I crept down the brightly lit side street. 1238, 1240, 1242, 1244, ah, 1246.

I put the Range Rover in park and felt my cell phone vibrate in my hip pocket. I withdrew the phone and saw it was the good doctor. I flipped the phone open, "Yes, honey."

"Honey? Oh, okay. I just wanted to call and tell you that I'm home. They're taking the body to the Penobscot County Morgue. I tried to tell them this was connected to the *Eight in October* murders but they laughed it off."

"I don't think we need an autopsy to tell us the cause of death."

"I still can't believe this. I'm really sorry, Thomas."

"Yeah, I'm numb. I need to get some sleep and deal with this in the morning."

After a slight pause she said, "If you want to stay at Alex's, that's okay with me."

Thanks, but you forgot to sign my permission slip. I didn't like her checking up on me and said, "Are you sure? I guess I'll just crash at Alex's then. Although it seems all her guestrooms are under renovation and I'm gonna have to shack up with her."

"Doesn't she have any couches you could sleep on?" She only seemed slightly annoyed.

I ambled out of the car and started up Caitlin's drive. "She said all her couches were contaminated."

"Contaminated? With what?"

"Caterpillars."

"Caterpillars? I don't know how to tell you this Thomas, but I think she's just trying to get you into bed. Hey, can you hold on one sec? Someone's at my door."

Caitlin opened the door, put the phone up to her mouth, and said, "You're a dick."

I walked past her, noticing the pair of plaid boxers and extra-large Supersonics tee she was wearing were both once possessions of mine. I walked into her compact kitchen, grabbed a bowl from the synthetic oak cabinet, and snagged the box of Lucky Charms (my Lucky Charms) from atop the fridge.

From the corner of my eye I could see Caitlin smirking and no doubt getting all warm and fuzzy. Men hate when women come into their house and act like they own the place. Women, on the other hand, find the act a smidgen beneath a marriage proposal. I had the distinct impression Caitlin's ovaries were huddled together in her fallopian tube watching my every move like an episode of *Sex in the City*.

Damage control. I asked platonically, "Do you mind if I have a bowl of cereal?"

"Yes."

Damn, a trap. "Well, I'm having one anyway."

"Suit yourself." She'd been sitting on the back of a blue leather couch and fell back disappearing from view.

I ate two bowls of cereal and read the Sunday comics. I laughed out loud at Foxtrot and Zits, and both times Caitlin's head popped up like a periscope. I rinsed my bowl and put it in the dishwasher (I was a guest, remember) then walked into the downstairs bathroom. There was a small closet where Caitlin kept extra towels. I felt around the top shelf with my hand until my fingers found the edge of a Ziploc bag. The bag contained two disposable razors, a small can of shaving cream, a toothbrush, and a small tube of Aquafresh.

I stashed the kit and walked out of the bathroom. Caitlin patted the seat next to her, and I wasn't interested in the repercussions if I sat on the floor. She said I looked tense and asked if I wanted a massage. I don't think anyone in the history of the world has ever turned down a massage, and I wasn't going to be the first.

Chapter 15

Caitlin had fallen asleep on the couch while I was returning the favor and I'd taken the liberty of stealing her bed. I'm still confused as to how I woke up with my hand wrapped firmly around her waist. She must have snuck in bed at some point, and I guess old habits die hard, especially subconscious ones.

Caitlin squirmed, then turned and faced me. Our faces were inches from each other and I'm not sure who initiated it, but next thing I knew, Caitlin's tongue was tickling my small intestines.

It was a routine I knew well and one I enjoyed thoroughly. I slipped the Supersonics tee over Caitlin's head, exposing her perfect breasts. She reached for my boxer briefs and the reality of the situation hit me. I took a deep breath and said, "We can't. This would only complicate things for the both of us."

She nodded her head in agreement but I could tell she was bruised by my chastity. The both of us laid there basking in the awkward moment, similar to the dust particles dancing within the brilliant morning rays, when the phone rang. Caitlin plucked the phone off the bedside table and said, "Dr. Dodds."

I decided to make my getaway. I picked my clothes off the floor and snuck into the bathroom. I elected against a shower and washed my face with Caitlin's Clinique bar, then threw on my same duds from the night before.

Caitlin's stick of deodorant was sitting on the counter and I did a quick swipe under each arm. The perfume soap and baby powder deodorant created an overpowering feminine smell and I checked my pants to make sure my testicles hadn't slipped into my socks. Everything intact, I walked out of the bathroom, only to have the phone rammed to my chest by Caitlin.

She murmured, "Director Mangrove."

I covered the phone, "How does he know I'm here?"

"I told him." She sniffed, "Did you put my deodorant on?"

I pleaded the fifth and put the phone up to my ear, "Prescott."

"Sorry to hear about Jennifer. She was a nice girl."

"Yes, she was."

"And I guess I owe you an apology. You're going to be getting quite a few of those in the next couple days."

"I'll put a check next to your name."

"Good. The boys are on their way as we speak."

By *the boys* I assumed he meant my friends Gleason and Gregory. "Sorry Charles, I'm flying solo on this one."

"What's it going to take for you to help us out?"

I could have asked for three or four men to watch over Lacy, but the last thing I wanted was two FBI goons eating all my food and hitting on my sister. I had a thought and said, "For starters, you can come to my sister's gallery opening and buy a painting."

"That it?"

'That's it."

"That shouldn't be a problem."

Charles was an altogether good guy, and the two of us probably would have been friends if he wasn't in charge of the most corrupt group of guys this side of Leavenworth. I thought of something else and said, "Also, I want Conner Dodds on the task force, and I want him to have FBI status."

"That shouldn't be a problem."

The word, "Yes," wasn't in the FBI's vocabulary. "That shouldn't be a problem" was the closest you would ever get out of them. It left some wiggle room if they ever flaked, which they did frequently.

We did the *who*, *what*, *when*, and *where*, and I hung up.

I recounted the events to Caitlin. We were to meet the rest of the task force at the Federal Building in downtown Bangor at nine. She was on another planet and I said, "You okay?"

Her eyes darted around the room and came to rest around my left knee. She said, "I'll be all right. We good?"

I tilted her head, kissed her lightly on the lips, and left the room. I wasn't sure if I kissed her to satisfy my own anxieties or hers. It was my own version of "that shouldn't be a problem."

~

Caitlin showered and I ate Lucky Charms until the box was empty. I heard the newspaper thud against Caitlin's stoop and read the clock: 8:08 a.m.

A little late for the paper wasn't it?

Caitlin, like everyone else, had subscribed to the Waterville Tribune after the events of last year. The paper was now third in circulation only to the *Bangor Daily News* and the *Portland Press-Herald.*

I plopped down on the second of three porch steps, slipped the paper from its light blue plastic sheathing, and read the front-page headline. It was fortunate I was sitting down because my knees would have buckled had I not been. In 72-point font, plastered across the front page was the headline:

Maine Frame-Woman Found Maimed on Anniversary of Killings

Story by Alex Tooms

I started in on the article:

> *Jennifer Peppers' mangled corpse was discovered in the home of Thomas Prescott (Yes, the same Thomas Prescott from the infamous murders of exactly one year ago) at exactly 11:37 p.m. last night. The body was found in much the same fashion as the women from last October's massacre.*
>
> *The victim's, Jennifer Peppers' (Prescott's ex-fiancée), ragged mortal remains were dismantled and her eyes removed, prompting Bangor Chief Medical Examiner, Dr. Caitlin Dodds, to credit the MAINEiac, Tristen Grayer, with the slaying. The only recognizable difference between the Jennifer Peppers murder and the murders of a year ago was the fact the victim's eyes were present at the crime scene.*
>
> *Thomas Prescott was quoted as saying, "He wants us to know Jennifer watched her own death, watched her own life be taken from her."*
>
> *The big question is: If they're crediting Tristen Grayer with the murder, then just who was the John Doe from a year ago?*

How in the hell did Alex get wind of that kind of information? Lacy said Alex had been with her the entire time washing Baxter. Oh shit, the tape recorder. But how?

As I was pondering this, Caitlin emerged onto the porch dressed from head to toe in tan, an umbrella outfit covering homicide detective, medical examiner, and task force member.

She asked, "Did you call Conner?"

"I forgot." I stood, handed the paper to her, and said, "You better sit down."

I walked inside and called Conner. He thought I was kidding about the FBI status part, making me swear on my life. He said he'd be at the Federal Building at nine and I ran into the downstairs bathroom, did a quick brush and met Caitlin on the top step of her porch.

She was sitting cross-legged and looked up in horror, "We haven't even notified the parents and that bitch has the audacity to print the victim's name. And how the hell did she quote you on the eyes?" She looked at me skeptically.

"I didn't tell her anything, I swear." I crossed my heart.

I hadn't thought about Jennifer's parents. They lived in Jersey and Jennifer Peppers wasn't exactly the rarest of names. Still, it was unethical from a journalist's position to use names when they are yet to be disclosed. I made a mental note to give Ms. Tooms a truckload of shit the next time I saw her.

I filled in Caitlin about the tape recorder and she said, "But it was off when you put it in your pocket. I saw the tape stop spinning."

We put the article on the back burner and Caitlin asked, "Should we take separate cars?"

Of course we should take separate cars. I wouldn't not take separate cars if my brakes were out. I said mildly, "I think that might be best."

~

We retired to our respective cars and I checked the dash clock. It was almost 8:30 a.m. I pulled my cell phone out and made the dreaded call to Jennifer's father. I tried to keep it short and sweet, but it was closer to long and sour. I ended with the standard, "If there's anything you need, anything at all—," spiel and recused myself in order to, "Find, apprehend, and cut the balls off the man who did this to her."

Next, I dialed Caleb Barstow. After four or five rings, a groggy voice answered, "Someone better be dead."

"Someone is."

This grabbed his attention. "You serious, professor?"

"You get the *Waterville Tribune*?"

"Doesn't everybody?"

I told him to snag the paper, then heard him fumble out of bed and a door open. He came back on, "No fuckin' way. This happened at your crib?"

"Yep. I need your help with something."

"Name it."

"I want you to keep an eye on my sister for the next couple days. Watch her from afar. Stake her out basically. You might have to miss some classes."

"I don't go to class anyway."

I laughed and gave him stakeout instructions.

~

I entered downtown Bangor and pulled into the massive U.S. Federal Building parking lot. The closest FBI field office was located in Boston, which has jurisdiction over Maine, New Hampshire, Massachusetts, Vermont, and Rhode Island. In a case such as this, an adjunct task force office is stationed in the nearest US Federal Building for the duration of the investigation.

The Federal Building was a large red brick structure built when imaginative architecture was frowned upon. In the state of Maine, the building fell under the classification "skyscraper" because, at an outlandish height of twelve stories, it was the tallest building in the area and possibly the state.

I was on time for once, which meant I had twenty minutes to kill. I pulled *Eight in October* out of the utility compartment and flipped once again to the dedication page. I slowly read the eight women's names one by one. As I did this, the theory I'd been trying to tie together for the last year, ultimately came full circle. It was like getting hit with a frying pan, falling and hitting a light switch, which in turn spotlights the bacteria growing on the frying pan which is penicillin. Or something to that degree.

I was going over the finer points when Conner pulled up next to me in his jet-black Camaro. I was surprised to see he was clad in slacks and a black button down, sans tie. Stepping out of the car, I said, "You're gonna need to get a suit if you want to fit in with these fruitdicks."

He smiled. "I've got an appointment with a tailor at noon."

The two of us walked into the edifice and stopped at the front desk to retrieve our ID badges. We each took our respective badge and it appeared someone at the Bureau had a sense of humor.

I showed my picture to Conner and after a healthy knee slap he said, "Is that the mug shot from your BUI?"

It most certainly was the mug shot from my Boating Under the Influence arrest. Look out, Nick Nolte, you have some competition. I clipped the photo to my breast pocket and led Conner into one of the four elevator shafts. I pushed the button for the eighth floor, but the elevator didn't respond.

Conner wisely slipped his ID badge off his shirt, inserted it in the slot beneath the numerals, and the elevator creaked to life.

After scanning his card twice more, Conner and I entered a large conference room. The room was roughly the size of a third grade classroom, only instead of twenty desks there was one giant one, and instead of third graders there were FBI agents, aka kindergartners.

Caitlin Dodds, Wade Gleason, and Todd Gregory each had a coffee mug in hand, an attaché case on the table in front of them, and stood when Conner and I entered. Gleason was first to make his way around the large mahogany table and we did what he called "knuckles."

He said, "I guess I owe you dinner."

"How 'bout dinner and I never pay taxes again."

He chuckled, "I'll see what I can do." His eyes fell to my breast pocket and he roared back in laughter. Gleason wiped the badge clean of his saliva with the cuff of his shirt and said, "Hey, at least they got your good side."

Interesting, I was a detective at heart and either Gleason should be thanking the Academy or he was innocent of said crime. I looked at Gregory making his way around the table. Todd Gregory's sense of humor topped out with a good Ziggy, so he wasn't suspect. By default the guilty party was Charles Mangrove. I tucked this information in a file marked *Revenge-See Good Fun* and while I was there retrieved the file for Tristen Grayer marked *Revenge-See Pain and Suffering.*

Gleason moved on to Conner, and Gregory stepped into the batter's box. Gregory extended his hand and said, "Well, Prescott, I guess I owe you dinner as well."

Dinner with Todd Gregory sounded about as much fun as a vasectomy, but we were all being cordial here and I said, "Thanksgiving is right around the corner. Why don't you tell Momma Gregory to set an extra spot at the table?"

He flashed his annoyingly perfect smile and I wondered if I could knock all thirty-two of his teeth out with one punch. Caitlin came next. If the two of us were playing charades, the card would have read *Professional Gauche.* We shook hands and exchanged pleasantries and no one would have guessed the two of us woke up in the same bed.

In any other situation the five of us would have shot the shit for twenty minutes, each of us filling our respective colostomy bag to the brim, but today was all business. We'd let a killer go free and he was back doing what he did best; chopping and raping, and not in that particular order. From the eight eyes sitting on my chest and the ache in the pit of my stomach, I surmised I was father corn in this steamer. Caitlin played catalyst, "Your theory, Thomas?"

Oh, right. My theory. Here goes everything. I stood, coughed into my hand, and said, "Tristen Grayer . . ."

I coughed once more to add dramatic effect, then continued, ". . . is a twin."

Chapter 16

Blank expressions canvassed the faces of my peers. Gleason rocked back in his chair, steadfast, and did a rolling motion with his right hand, "Care to elaborate?"

I sat down and crossed my right leg over my left. "Do you guys remember Robert Elby? He was the neighboring farmer who stumbled on Ingrid Grayer's body."

They all nodded.

I continued, "Well, I tracked him down in late April and grilled him in depth about the Grayer family. He told me what he knew, and I went to the Aroostook County Records office to try to corroborate his story. Aroostook is so remote only about half the residents are in the record books, but I was fortunate enough to stumble on the Grayer family history. Penelope and Timothy Grayer were blessed with a daughter, Ingrid, of course, and identical twin boys, Tristen and Geoffrey."

None of the four blinked. Caitlin asked dryly, "Tristen had an identical twin? Why wasn't any of this researched at the time?"

"Because Elby initially told police Ingrid and Tristen lived in the farmhouse alone. No one had any reason to think otherwise. Why would we? I only went in search of the information months later because everything ended so neat and tidy."

Tristen Grayer had shown these people a torn photo Scotch-taped back together. I was in the midst of pulling off the tape.

Gleason asked, "So where was the brother Geoffrey in all this?"

"Dead. At least according to Elby. Apparently, the Grayer farmhouse went up in flames three years ago, whereby the parents and Geoffrey died in the fire. There was no investigation. Hell, there isn't even a record of any fire. No death certificates, nothing. It was during the winter and nobody noticed. Elby said when spring came he passed the Grayer farm and saw half the house had burned to the ground."

Caitlin said, "We knew about the fire. It was hard to decipher at first sight because of the condition of Ingrid's body, but while doing the autopsy I came across a large amount of scar tissue, presumably from a fire. Also, when Elby gave us the description of Tristen, he'd remarked how he was horribly disfigured from a fire he suffered years earlier."

I set her straight. "Elby mistook Tristen for Geoffrey."

Gregory looked flustered, and for the first time I couldn't blame him. He asked, "So where was Tristen in all this?"

"That's the question. My theory is that he flew the coop after he set the fire."

Conner said, "You think Tristen set the fire that nearly killed his entire family?"

"That's precisely what I think."

Gregory asked, "Why would he try to kill his whole family?"

"I would have to ask him that question but I'd assume it would have to be sexual. Everyone was probably doing everyone else. Mom, pop, sister, brothers."

He smirked, "And just what evidence do you have to back this assumption?"

"For starters, while I was at the records office I did a little background on the Grayer family and there appears to be quite a bit of incest. The parents, Penelope and Timothy, were once brother and sister. It goes all the way back to Johanis Elbert Grayer bopping his cousin in the late 1800s and trickles down."

Gregory threw me a skeptical look, "So the family fooled around. Tristen sets fire to the house and skips town. He's out of the picture. Geoffrey kills Ingrid and goes on a killing spree. So we got the name wrong. We still got the right guy."

I smashed my fists down hard on the table, sending a couple wayward drops of coffee spitting onto the table. "No, you fucking idiot, you didn't get the right guy because about ten hours ago I found a woman in thirty pieces in my sister's bed."

Todd turned into Zechariah before my eyes and I said, "Let me finish my theory. Three years pass and Tristen, for whatever reason prompts these psychopaths to return to the scene of a crime, feels obligated to go sightseeing. October first of last year, he makes his way back to the Grayer farmhouse and is shocked to learn his siblings somehow survived the blaze.

"He bursts in and finds his derelict, burnt-to-shit brother screwing his derelict, burnt-to-shit sister's brains out. Then, to top it off, Tristen discovers Ingrid is carrying Geoffrey's child. The fashion in which he killed Ingrid tells the story. Tristen enjoyed every second of it. He's never felt so alive. He's instantly addicted. He wisely holds off killing Geoffrey, knowing full well he has someone to take the rap for all the monstrosities he plans to commit in the coming days."

I could tell I was starting to turn the four of them and rode my momentum, "In the ensuing carnage, Tristen takes the eyes of each of his victims. I have this image I can't shake of Geoffrey Grayer tied to a chair with each of Tristen's victims eyes encircling him, as if to say, 'If you hadn't gone and fucked your sister, hadn't stuck your peepee in the family teepee, then we would all still be alive.'"

I walked to the dry erase board at the front of the room. "It didn't hit me until I read the dedication page of *Eight in October* about a half hour ago."

I grabbed a blue marker and wrote each of the eight women's names on the board: Ingrid Grayer, Bethany Eggers, Amber Osgood, Ginny Farth, Deana Farwell, Shelly Regginald, Amy Elles, and finally Sarah Yeirs.

I circled the first letter of each woman's last name, spelling out G-e-o-f-f-r-e-y. I turned around and stared at the four frozen faces. "Tristen wanted to cause Geoffrey more anguish with each killing. He wanted his brother to know he was responsible for these women's deaths. These women weren't Tristen's victims, *Geoffrey* was."

I wrote Jennifer Peppers' name on the board and circled the P. "I nearly killed him, I nearly ended his game."

Underneath the P, I added, r-e-s-c-o-t-t. "It appears Tristen has an insatiable appetite for death and I'm next on his list."

Chapter 17

We broke huddle at noon. Gleason and Gregory had an appointment with the crime scene. Caitlin had an appointment with the Penobscot County medical examiner. Conner had an appointment to get fitted for his Fecal Barometer Internship uniform. I had an appointment with Alex Tooms, a hammer, and her tape recorder. The task force was scheduled to reconvene at 3:00 p.m.

It appeared as though Alex's little article had created quite a stir and there was a barrage of news vans in the parking lot. It took me five minutes to get to my car and fifteen to get to the Pulitzer Prize runner-up's stately lake house. I pulled up to Alex's gate and eighty-three seconds later, I kid you not, I once again applied pressure on the gas pedal and pulled through.

Alex's Jeep was parked where it'd been earlier, and I mentally prepared myself for some ass-kicking. I had to rap on the door with my fist (seeing as how the pretentious scribe didn't have a door-knocker) which was pulled inward seconds later. Alex had her hair back in a ponytail and was clad in charcoal sweat pants and a huge Boston College hooded sweatshirt.

Uh-oh, of all the outlandish fetishes out there, mine was as simple as a woman in sweat bottoms and a hoodie. Beats a cankle fetish, I guess.

Alex smiled and said, "Don't be too hard on me."

I was optimistic her saying "hard on" was just a coincidence and said, "How could you be so reckless? Your little article has jeopardized our entire case, not to mention the fact you used Jennifer's name. What if someone from her family stumbled on the article? Did that ever enter your little bird brain?" I was going to add dummy-head, but I didn't want to play my ace too soon.

She didn't blink an eye. "I don't lie to my readers. People don't want to hear John Doe, they want to hear John Jacob Jingleheimer Schmidt. Plus, in defending myself, I figured you would have called the victim's family before this article even went to print. Correct me if I'm wrong, but this woman was at one point your bride-to-be?"

Damn, she was right. I should have contacted Jennifer's parents last night. I changed the subject, "That's beside the point. You weren't privy to that information. I want to see that tape recorder."

"Sure."

I followed Alex through a series of turns and finally into a large study-slash-library. The longest wall, serving as the front of the house, was covered in row after row of hardback novels. There was an espresso machine in the far left corner next to a pair of maroon love seats snuggled up to an old brass fireplace.

Alex went to a large cherry wood desk with a large fern at each corner and I heard a drawer roll out of bed. After fiddling for a couple seconds, she extracted the tape recorder and handed it to me, "There you go. Is this going to be Exhibit A at my trial?"

I rolled my eyes at her and stared down at the tape recorder. The sleek chrome contraption was equipped with more than twenty buttons and I asked Alex, "You steal this from James Bond?"

She plopped up on her desk as did I, sending a wave of fire through my gluteus maximus. Alex laughed and said, "How's your butt feel?"

Somewhere between a bee sting and a fraternity paddling. I kept this to myself. "Don't try to change the subject. You have a remote control for this thing or what?"

"Nope."

"So what did you do? It was off when I took it, and off when I gave it back."

She took the recorder. "You can program a time frame you want it to run. I programmed it to start recording one minute after I turned it off and run for ten minutes."

Alex showed me the simplicity of the operation and I asked, "Didn't you think I would hear it turn on?"

She clicked down the record button and the tape began rolling without the slightest sound. She hit *Stop* and said, "Never leave home without it."

I popped the tape out of the recorder and read in Alex's scrawl, "Oct. 1, 11:30 PM."

I put the tape in my pocket and asked, "Is every journalist as skilled in the art of deception as you?"

"No. But mine is in the pursuit of the truth." She grabbed my chin and turned it toward her. "Still, I'm sorry. You trusted me and I abused that trust. I won't use you for my story ever again." She kissed me on the cheek.

Well, there went another good grudge.

~

It was almost three, and it appeared as though I was going to be late to yet another meeting. I pulled up to the Federal Building at 3:15 to a buzzing parking lot, whereby, the news vans had mated and reproduced. It took me close to ten minutes and a hundred "No comments" before I found the revolving door.

There was a healthy chance my mangy Van Dyke would be paraded all over the eleven o' clock news. Maybe I should have shaved or at least worn underwear.

I opened the door to the conference room and before it was half open, Gregory's exasperating tongue spat, "You're late."

"No, I'm forty-five minutes early." I'd planned on being an hour late.

I sat down next to Conner, who was now clad in a navy blue suit and looking all the part of the asshole agent. Caitlin slid me a dossier across the table and said, "I met with the Penobscot County medical examiner, nothing out of the ordinary. The eyes on the wall were Jennifer's."

It's an ugly day when you can use the phrase "nothing out of the ordinary" in regards to a women who has been raped, beaten, dismembered, and turned into chicken feed. For some reason the fact the eyes were Jennifer's came as a relief. If they weren't hers then there was a fair chance they belonged to Tristen's next victim. Or as I'd started thinking in terms of Mrs. R.

I opened the folder and skimmed over Jennifer Pepper's autopsy report. I asked Gleason, "Anything from the crime scene jump out at you?"

Gleason shook his head, "Nope. We talked to your neighbors and no one said they saw anything conspicuous. Not that anyone can see your house in the first place, but no one reported seeing any odd vehicles or such. Zilch."

"Did you ask them about boats?"

Gregory scoffed, "Why would we do that?"

I leaned forward in my seat, "Because my house backs up to a huge body of water called the Atlantic Ocean. Do you find it infeasible for someone to dock their boat on the beach and drag a woman into my house? Do you find that fucking infeasible?"

He didn't respond and Caitlin said, "I don't think we're going to get any anywhere on this sitting on our asses."

Caitlin was right, the five of us weren't going to accomplish anything sitting around a giant coffee table playing *The View* when we should be playing *The Task Force*. I stood up and was out the door in a matter of seconds. There were a couple neighbors who I wanted to chat with personally. It's not that I didn't have faith in Gleason and Gregory's interviewing skills. It's that I didn't trust them.

~

There were two squad cars parked in my lawn and one of the occupants tried to stop me from entering. His partner notified him the house was well within my jurisdiction and he let me pass with minimal confrontation.

The house felt odd, like it was a set in a movie and the cast and crew were out to lunch. I went into the kitchen, grabbed a white garbage bag from beneath the sink and walked upstairs. I ducked under the crime scene tape cordoning off Lacy's room and straightened. The air flooding my nostrils smelled awful, like the Gingerbread Man's cremation. I wrinkled my nose, more at the sight of the blood soaked mattress than the stale odor.

The blood on the bed was lighter in some places than others and there was a distinct outline of where one.of Jennifer's hands had rested and another that looked remarkably like a set of shoulders.

I stuffed the garbage bag full of Lacy's clothes, a couple pairs of her shoes, and circled the room waiting for the Clue God to whap me on the head with a stick. I had no such luck and found myself situated in front of a long wall mirror hanging near Lacy's bed. I took an overview of myself in the mirror: my clothes looked like shit and I had five days' worth of stubble growing. I ran my hand through the coarse cinnamon follicles and decided it was in my best interest to shave.

I turned to check the profile of my budding beard (I was already having doubts about shedding it) and immediately saw my head had been blocking the reflection of Lacy's lighthouse painting. A great painting is like lasagna, it takes a couple days for all the flavor to soak in. I was admiring the painting when *whap*.

I turned from the mirror and walked toward the wall. Eight inches below Lacy's painting were the remnants of Jennifer's eyes' last resting place. Blood was caked to the wall in about a three-inch diameter, but the portion of wall where the eyes had touched the wall remained predominantly white. Within each of these havens was a small black hole, an artifact from where each nail had been driven, and the combined illusion was of a set of glaring eyes. It was creepy, super creepy to be honest, but I couldn't break away from the marvel.

I walked back around the room trying to place what brought about the *whap*, but nothing registered. I guess sometimes you just get whapped for staring at yourself in the mirror too long.

Chapter 18

I spent the next two hours canvassing the neighborhood talking to neighbors. Evidently, the G-Agents, or *Gents* as I like to call them, had been telling the truth. Not one person saw an iota of suspicious activity by land or by sea. The last people I talked to were the parents of the curfew-breaking-pot-smoking teen and when I asked where their son was, they said he was doing research for a paper at the library.

If I remembered my misfit adolescent days correctly, "doing research at the library" translated roughly into drinking a Colt 45 on a rooftop or trying to get the neighbor's daughter's clothes off. Again on a rooftop. The key word here was rooftop, and I knew the exact rooftop I would find our teen in question.

~

I walked up the beach about two hundred yards until I came to an inlet that was home to the Surry Breakwater Lighthouse. Leading up to the lighthouse was a stretch of granite boulders jutting three-quarters of a mile into the bay. Each boulder was easily five by five by five—we're talking feet here—and the walkway was stacked three high, five wide, and a par five long. There were about a thousand gulls lined up along the breakwater and each would fly a small circle when I passed, only to return to their perch.

The walk took about five minutes due to the large gaps between the rocks. Let's just say the lighthouse was not exactly wheelchair accessible. As for the lighthouse, it was built in late 1879 and appeared not to have been renovated since early 1880. From the back, the lighthouse resembled a small two-story which sadly should have been condemned sometime around the Reagan administration. All the windows were boarded up, the paint had long been washed from the exterior, and there were more nails poking out than poking in.

I could hear strained voices stretching from the lighthouse annex's quasi-shingled rooftop. I didn't want to induce a mad scramble and, after much debate, I settled on, "I'm coming up there. If you run, you die."

The voices fell silent. Using the guardrail, I catapulted myself onto the roof, ripping my pants on a nail that had long ago retired from active duty. Come to think of it, I don't think I could design a more perilous location for a teenage hangout.

There were four of them sitting Indian-style on skateboards with blank expressions on their jewelry studded faces. The two girls had all their clothes on and I wondered if I needed to have a quick chat with the boys and explain the objectives.

I walked to their little group sitting on the dining table expanse of flat roof, taking the liberty of stealing a beer from the case hidden behind the farthest boy.

The four of them sat in stunned horror as the hipster doofus cracked the beer and brought it to his lips. I stopped short and said, "There are a couple rules of etiquette when it comes to beer."

They all nodded, or it's possible they each rolled their eyes so violently their heads appeared to nod, and I continued, "There is an unwritten rule that you never drink someone else's beer unless they're drinking with you."

The group looked a shade puzzled and I asked, "This is your beer, right?" One of the girls nodded and I said, "That means all of you have to drink a beer so I can drink this beer. And I really want to drink this beer."

The four of them looked at one another and slowly one-by-one took a Keystone Light from the box and cracked it open. They tried valiantly to act thirty-five, but it's difficult when you can't stop giggling and are on the verge of peeing your pants. After they'd each taken a couple sips, I asked, "How old are you guys?"

A girl with pink and green hair spoke up, "Thirteen. We're seventh graders. Why, how old are you?"

"Eighteen. I'm a senior in high school."

A boy with about seven earrings said, "Liar, you can't be in high school, you're like fifty."

Ouch. If this had been my second beer rather than my first, I would have given the kid a wedgie. My neighbor looked like the only one not enjoying himself and I said, "Listen, I'm not going to say anything to your parents. I was doing the same thing when I was thirteen." Give or take five years.

He nodded and took a sip of beer. I pushed fast-forward, "I need your guys' help with something. Were you guys up here last night?"

My neighbor, the monkey off his back, said, "Yeah, we were up here."

I made them all stand and pointed to the coastline near my house. "I know it was dark, but does anyone remember seeing a boat?" A boat in these parts was a rarity. I'd seen two boats in all of ten months.

Three of them shook their heads, but I saw my neighbor was nodding. I prodded him and he motioned for me to follow him. He walked to the edge of the lighthouse roof and said, "I came up here to take a whiz." He showed me the flow urine would be likely to take with his hand and continued, "And I saw this boat floating way, way out there. I remember because it's the only time I've ever seen one of them small boats around here."

I asked him what it looked like. He thought it had two sails and was "medium sized."

I had each of them program my number into their cell phone and directed them to call me if they saw the boat again or anything else suspicious for that matter. I finished off my beer and, after an inner strife, thought better of smoking a doobie with them.

Once safely back on the granite, I ran through what I'd learned over the course of the last half hour. One, kids started drinking beer and smoking pot at thirteen. Two, I could no longer pass for a senior in high school. And three, there was a boat drifting close to shore on the night of Jennifer's murder.

All were equally interesting. All equally disturbing.

Chapter 19

I stopped at a liquor store on the way to Caitlin's apartment. I was in the midst of opening her front door when I thought better and rang the doorbell. Caitlin opened the door and threw me a look which I decoded as "Are you trying to piss me off?" Or something in that general vicinity.

I followed her into the living room and saw Conner and Lacy sprawled on the blue sofa. I hadn't seen Conner's Camaro and asked, "Where's your car?"

Lacy said, "I made him walk. It's a perfect fall evening."

Apparently, young women never get killed on perfect fall evenings. Conner butted in before I could threaten his life, "Your sister is quite persuasive."

Lacy had her hand clamped in a fist and said, "I held his dick hostage."

As much as I love to hear about my sister's sexual exploits, I retired into the kitchen. I put the case of Corona in the refrigerator and asked Caitlin if she needed any help with meal preparation. She threw me a look similar to the one at the front door and riding its coattails was the phone book. She said, "Here's your meal preparation."

I did a quick survey and it appeared Caitlin, Conner, and Lacy all wanted Chinese whereas Thomas Prescott wanted a pizza pie. Sometimes you have to take one for the team. I dialed a number and said loud enough for everyone to hear, "Is this China Dragon?"

"No, this is Domino's." Oops.

The doorbell rang twenty minutes later and I let Caitlin grab the door. She came back with two pizza boxes, my credit card receipt, and an expression of utmost annoyance. She said, "Chinese, huh? By the way, you just tipped the delivery boy seventy-four dollars."

Interesting play. I hadn't seen that coming.

If the three of them didn't like the pizza, they faked their aversion well. After we fought for crusts, we quickly cleaned up. It was common knowledge when the four of us drew together we would play a laggard game of Trivial Pursuit. We split up into what used to be Couple vs. Couple but was now labeled, politically correctly, Adults vs. Children. Caitlin begrudgingly sat next to me on the couch, choosing to ignore my hand patiently awaiting a high five. *What kind of team camaraderie is that?*

The four of us spent the next two hours drinking beers, getting questions predominately wrong, and basically reliving happier days. Caitlin forgot about her grudge, a combination of her competitive spirit and the beers, and we had a nicely choreographed end zone dance by the time we'd picked up half our pie pieces.

Lacy and Conner jumped out to an early lead then folded, leaving the door open for the team of Prescott/Dodds-Adults to claim victory. Conner was considerably razed about the loss and exited stage left to cool off. Lacy followed him out, and in the heat of the celebration I may have accidentally bumped lips with my partner. Okay, we made out. Heavily.

I assumed Conner and Lacy walked home because they didn't interrupt Caitlin and my heavy petting and weren't sitting on the front stoop when I went to check on them an hour later. I'm not sure if I was thirsty for Caitlin or for the touch of a woman, but either way, I was parched.

The next couple hours were a blur of skin, couch cushions, bed sheets and shower tile. Accompanied by a cacophony of pants, moans, and sighs. Lots of sighs.

~

I woke up to an amazing dream involving me and a woman. And as much as it pains me to admit it, the woman was not Caitlin Dodds. The dream had ended with one Miss Alex Tooms and I doing extremely naughty things. It took me a moment to register the correlation of the naughtiness in my dream and the naughtiness being performed by unnamed party at said moment. I have to admit,

I preferred this to the blaring of an alarm. Had I somehow given Caitlin the wrong impression by sleeping with her last night? If so, whoopsy daisy.

There was a clash of philosophies between Big Thomas and Little Thomas and after a long debate, Big Thomas prevailed as top Nietzsche. I wrestled LT from Caitlin's grip and rolled out of bed. She lifted the sheets from over her head and revealed her stark naked form, giving rise to an unscheduled October caucus. I found my boxer briefs and pulled them on before Paddington could get in his closing argument.

Caitlin gave me an arbitrary glance and said, "You seem to be in a hurry to get out of here."

Yes, one does not dillydally at the scene of a crime. I thought about those lucky black widow males, cleared my throat, and said, "You know how it goes, early bird catches the sadistic serial killer."

She furrowed her brow and said, "I see."

I see are two words that have never in the history of the world led to anything good when spoken from the mouth of a woman. Caitlin was suddenly Eve, covering all her fun parts with the bed sheet. I glanced around for a discarded apple core or a slithering snake but saw neither.

Caitlin languidly hunkered into the bathroom and I was left to ponder my position. Whatever emotion I felt, somewhere between guilt and entrapment, I knew it wasn't love. Caitlin and I would have to chat. I'd see if she had an opening sometime in February.

I heard the shower turn on and pulled on my ensemble (96 hours, for anyone counting). I knew Caitlin, and I knew she wasn't in the shower. She was sitting on the toilet with her face buried in her hands. I also knew the bathroom door wasn't locked. I could walk in, pull her to me, and erase all her troubles. I threw on my clothes and left before the notion crossed my mind.

Chapter 20

I was penciled in to meet the task force at nine, a meeting I—and at least one other person—knew I would be absent from. I wasn't a vigilante, but I preferred to march to the beat of my own drum or, less perfunctory, the plunk of my own cowbell.

As for Tristen, it was my move, and I had an inkling Mr. Grayer was the type of guy who needed a view of the board, needed to watch me move my bishop firsthand. I tried to brainstorm a place that would make me especially vulnerable to a tailing and decided on the Kittery outlets. The Kittery outlets are East Coast famous, more than a half mile littered with close to 300 retail outlets. I was squeaky clean, a silver lining to Caitlin's and my Lever 2000 enhanced copulation, but I did need some new duds.

I headed south on I-95 for Kittery, a small town just north of the Maine-New Hampshire border. During the hour drive my phone rang three times. The first call was from Jennifer's father notifying me Jennifer's funeral was set for the following Monday. I told him I'd be there. The second was from Conner warning me everyone was pissed at me for ditching the meeting. I told him I was in a car accident and would be there shortly. The third was from Todd Gregory informing me I had no such accident and to get there ASAP. I told him I was inside the Federal Building but my ID badge had somehow been programmed incorrectly, and I kept going to BB4.

~

I bought a pair of shoes and some running gear at the Asics outlet, two suits at the Armani Exchange, a couple costumes from

Kenneth Cole, and a bunch of sailing gear from Nautica. If I thought most of the stores were barren for customers, it was because they were all hanging out at the food court. All twelve of them.

The girl behind the Panda Express parapet looked of Asian origin, and for some reason I knew my orange chicken would taste better because of this. I washed it down with Dr. Pepper and traded glances with a group of girls a couple tables away. None of the other clientele caught my eye, which doesn't mean none of them were Tristen Grayer. It would be much easier if these serial killer types would wear their work clothes out. A blood-soaked cardigan usually drew my attention.

Chapter 21

Eaton College of Criminal Justice was located at the base of Eaton Mountain in the town of Skowhegan. To Mainers, Eaton was a mountain. To me, a native of Washington state, it was more of a hill with attached billboard. I think the elevation was something in the outlandish vicinity of 2,000 feet. *Uh-oh, better get the oxygen tanks out.*

The college was one of the best in the New England region for cop wannabes, budding detectives, and those with their eyes on the prize: the almighty Federal Dick. There weren't many cars in the student lot; the only bustling around campus were the leaves and the teachers going home for the day. I found my classroom and saw nearly every seat was occupied. Today's class session was the equivalent of a Hollywood premier.

I had a feeling my sister would be in attendance and picked her out sitting between Ashley Andrews and Caleb Barstow. Caleb Barstow was the spitting image of Keanu Reeves, only with blood pumping through his veins. Ashley Andrews was a Tuscan Princess who had formed a comrade-in-arms relationship with Lacy, being that there were only four other women in Criminal Justice 204.

The name of the course was "Investigative Techniques". Students learned the primary methods used in crime scene evaluation and search, the recording and collection of physical evidence, the basic techniques of crime scene management, photography, drawing and reporting, finger print and firearms identification, as well as serology and trace evidence. The course was two semesters. Each semester consisted of fifteen two-hour sessions, meeting once a week on Wednesdays. This was the fifth session of the second semester.

The student's faces went somber when I entered. I didn't wait for the questions, recounting my Tristen Grayer theory for the masses. We spent two hours dissecting the crime scene but made little to no headway. There just wasn't anything to go on. We could round up every woman in Maine with a last name beginning with the letter R, but I didn't have the National Guard programmed into my phone. To be brutally honest, I think there were only seventeen.

With an hour left, I retired to my office down the hall and ordered ten pizzas of different makes and sizes. I unlocked my desk and extracted an Eaton College of Criminal Justice inscribed check. This fell under classroom use, right?

Lacy was sitting on my desk when I returned. She turned as I approached, "Hey, prof."

I plopped down next to her, gently patted her thigh, and asked, "What did you get into today?"

"I ran some errands, or make that Caleb and I ran some errands." She pinched my leg.

I pinched her back. "I hope you know what you're doing, Lace."

"Just some innocent fun. Isn't his surveillance easier if I'm sitting shotgun in his car?"

I told her about my purchases at the outlet mall and she said, "Hmm, maybe I'll have Caleb surveillance me to the outlets tomorrow."

"Who's going to help you in the dressing room?" She raised her eyebrows and I couldn't help but laugh.

The pizzas came twenty minutes later and the students gave me a standing ovation. I grabbed two slices of supreme and retired to my desktop, Ashley Andrews plopping down next to me with a slice of cheese. If I were five years younger, I would have had no problem breaking the time-honored tradition of not screwing the brains out of one of your students.

Ashley had jet-black hair, dark olive skin, and looked like she commuted from Tuscany, which is where her parents still live to this day. Ashley picked a mushroom off my slice of pizza, placed it on a section of her cheese, and took a bite. She leaned forward to catch a gob of dripping cheese, exposing a small dolphin tattoo on her lower back as well as the infinitesimal beginnings of a purple thong.

Drool bucket, please.

Ashley sat back, "I think your sister has a thing for Caleb."

"I concur."

"Although she'll probably be disappointed with the size of his dick after being with Conner."

Conner's unit was the likes of an anaconda digesting a two-foot salami and I was wondering how Ashley had stumbled on the eighth wonder of the world. There was a rumor going around at the Bangor Police Department that when Conner took a leak he threw his wanger in the toilet and blew bubbles.

I asked, "Where'd you hear about Conner?"

"Your sister told me. She said it 'tickled her tonsils,' and not when she was doing what you'd think."

I decided to change the subject, "So how's your love life?"

She rubbed my leg, "Not as interesting as it could be."

~

Lacy said Ashley would drop her off at Conner's and I locked up the classroom. I was set to drive home, when I realized I had no idea where home was. My house would be sealed for another day or two, and Caitlin's place was out of the question. That left only one alternative—Alex's. I was only ten minutes from her house and, if I remembered correctly, her exact words had been "You know it's only me in that big house. You're welcome to any of the guest bedrooms."

I started toward her place. I mean, what's the worst that could happen? Then I thought about the best that could happen. I laughed to myself and smiled.

Chapter 22

As I pulled up to Alex's house, the gate swung inward. I had a notion to hop out and snip a couple wires, but I thought I'd already done enough damage to Alex's property. Her Jeep was parked in her usual spot and I parked in my usual spot.

I walked to the front door and a minute later the door swung inward. Alex had her hair pulled back and rimless glasses pushed down on her nose. She had on a white tank top, sans bra, and mesh BC gym shorts. I wasn't sure if Alex's nipples were hard because of me or because it was cold, but either way they were testing the limits of the cotton gin.

She folded her arms over her breasts and said, "Oh, it's you."

Not exactly the words a house-crashing guest longs for. She turned on her heel, leaving the door ajar, and I ran back to my car and grabbed the Asics and Nautica bags from the trunk. Alex was standing in the doorway when I returned, her torpedoes covered beneath an enormous Winnie the Pooh hooded sweatshirt. *What was it with women and that damn bear?*

I followed Alex to a large guest bedroom with adjoined bath. The shower was barren and didn't appear to have been used since its inception. I told her I needed to take a shower and she asked if I needed to borrow a razor. I had a feeling this was a loaded question; most women didn't care if you were clean shaven unless they planned on your cheeks touching either pair of their cheeks.

I told her I was okay in that department but could use some soap and shampoo. She retreated into the room directly across from mine and came back with the aforementioned necessities. I jumped in the shower, dried off, threw on a clean pair of boxer briefs and some light blue running slickers. I pulled a red, hooded sweatshirt from the Nautica bag and unfolded it. I wiggled my head through the hood opening and when I finally popped through, I had a new found respect for the rite of birth. Three or four inches of my wrists were exposed and when I took a deep breath the waist hiked up above my navel.

I walked into the living room where Alex was sitting on her leather couch flipping through the channels on her flat screen. She gave me a once over before erupting in laughter. I beat her to the punch, "I bought it at the Nautica outlet. It's an extra-large."

"Are you sure you didn't accidentally stumble into Nautica Kids?"

"There's a Nautica Kids?"

"Nautica is on the east side of the pavilions and Nautica Kids is on the west."

Well, since I hadn't even ventured to the east side, I guess we'd stumbled on the problem. "I wondered why the clerk asked if I were teaching my son to sail."

She grinned. "Here, switch me."

Before I could refuse she had the Pooh sweatshirt off and ready to trade. I pulled my head back into the womb and handed the sweatshirt to Alex. She pulled it on and it fit her immaculately. I pulled on the Pooh sweatshirt and I'd be lying if I said it wasn't the most comfortable garment I'd ever donned.

Alex retreated into the kitchen and I ran out to the car to snag my cell phone. I turned it on and saw I had five missed calls from the same number. The area code was 603. 603 meant Virginia. Virginia meant FBI. FBI meant Todd Gregory, Wade Gleason, or Charles Mangrove, none of whom I felt like being chastised by.

I dialed Lacy, made sure she was okay, then hung up when I heard Conner ask to speak to me in the foreground.

When I entered the living room, Alex was walking in with two beers and a plate of cheese and crackers. I grabbed a piece of salami, some cheddar, and a Triscuit before plopping down next to her. My cell phone chirped and I checked the number, again 603.

I switched the phone to vibrate and set it atop the glass coffee table. The phone stopped pulsating then started back up ten seconds later. Alex raised her eyebrows, "You gonna answer that?"

She picked up the phone and I asked, "Is it a 603 area code?"

"Yeah."

"Don't answer it."

She smirked. "Why, do you have a lady friend in New Hampshire you owe child support to?"

"No. Why?"

"603 is New Hampshire."

I resituated myself. "No, 603 is Virginia."

She shook her head. "My grandparents live in New Hampshire. It's 603, trust me."

The phone had stopped vibrating and I snatched it from Alex's open palm. I called the number back and it was answered on the first half ring, "Mr. Prescott?"

I didn't recognize the voice. "Who is this?"

"This is Kevin, your, um, neighbor."

Uh-oh.

I took a calming breath and asked, "Why do you have a New Hampshire area code?"

"That's, um, where my dad lives." His voice cracked. "You said to, um, call if I, uh, if I saw the boat."

Super uh-oh.

"When?"

"Half an hour ago. We were on our way out and saw it pull up to the lighthouse." I was already at the door. "Is the boat still there?"

"No, it just left."

Mega uh-oh.

~

I hung up as I reached the Range Rover. The only difference between this time and forty-eight hours earlier was that Alex was already buckled in the passenger seat.

As we approached the gate Alex rolled her window down to punch her exit code. I accelerated past the box and hit the gate going around forty, wearing it as a hood ornament for half a block.

Alex rolled up her window and said, "I hated that gate."

I looked at the dash: it was 10:37 p.m. The second woman was found at 11:11 p.m. on October 3rd.

We pulled up to my house at eleven on the nose. I drove through the yard, around the house, up the beach, and to the foot of the granite breakwater. There was a deep fog over the water, and the second half of the granite stretch was thoroughly obscured. I could make out two streams of light canvassing the shore and the lights turned out to be Kevin and his gang with flashlights. Alex and I made it to them as the foghorn erupted for the first time. The kids wanted to be part of the action and I had to do some yelling. To rub salt in the wound, Alex and I took their flashlights.

We made good time until we hit the fog. It was thick and the refraction from the flashlights made it difficult to see my contact lenses. Talk about eerie. You could hear the gulls squawk and waves crash against the side of the breakwater but could see neither. So there we were playing hopscotch across the large gaps, gulls whining, waves crashing, foghorn blaring, Thomas Prescott screaming obscenities.

The two of us made it to the back of the lighthouse as the foghorn blared for a fifteenth time. There was a small dock at the southern edge of the lighthouse and I noticed the mooring lines billowing in the current. I etched this on the dry-erase board in my brain and pulled myself up the seven feet to the lighthouse's concrete foundation. The door to the lighthouse had long ago been torn from the hinges and the concrete steps were soaked to the bone with seawater. I shined the flashlight up the spiral staircase, illuminating three and about half a fourth stair. No blood so far.

As I took the first stair, I took in a deep breath of the acrid lighthouse air. The walls were caked with lime and sodium nitrate deposits, somewhat reminiscent of my bathroom in college. Alex and I made the first turn and continued our ascent up the spiral stairway. The foghorn erupted, shaking the structure to near collapse.

We took the last turn and an intense white light filled the room. The concrete was slippery wet and I fell to my knees, my flashlight reverberating off the stone floor. When I lifted my head I saw my hand was lying in a thicket of black hair. I ripped my hand from the tangles, sending the attached skull, brain, and what was left of the victim's face cascading across the small chamber. Alex had fallen just behind me and was rolling amid the carnage, her arms and jeans caked in blood.

I hauled her up and pulled her to a corner, shielding her from the gore. After a good minute, Alex's heavy breathing stabilized. I felt the light make its pass behind me and wheeled around, beholding the scene. There were more than fifteen pieces of body within a ten foot diameter of blood soaked concrete. Alex's flashlight was lying in the middle of the carnage, holding within its beam the unmistakable tattoo of a dolphin.

Chapter 23

Ashley Andrews was dead, her body destroyed. I closed my eyes and felt the anger burn in my chest. It felt like every red blood cell in my body had stopped in their tracks and went into a dead sprint for my heart. I couldn't help thinking Ashley was dead because she was in my class, because she was connected to me. In a sense, I killed her.

Luckily, I couldn't afford the luxury of despair and I struggled for my cell phone, dialing Caitlin. She didn't answer and I left a detailed message as instructed. Seconds later my cell phone vibrated and I flipped it open. Caitlin blurted, "I'm on my way."

The light was making its way full circle and Alex hit a large red switch as the horn began its bellow. The light went out, the bellow waned, the motor died. Alex plucked her flashlight from the carnage and brought it to bear on the lens languidly coming to a halt. In the dim light reflecting off the lens I witnessed Alex's delicate features form into complete aghast. She shouted, "Holy shit!"

Caitlin was still on the phone and yelled, "What?"

Ashley's eyes were affixed to the revolving lighthouse lens like two fried eggs. The flesh around the eyes bubbled, cracked, and hissed.

It took a second for the abomination to register with Alex. The flashlight in her hand crashed to the ground, engulfing us in gross darkness. I clawed my way to her and led her down the lighthouse stairs. We emerged from the lighthouse and both took in a long awaited heave of the innocent ocean air.

I pulled myself under the railing and slid down the concrete foundation. Alex was in lemming mode and followed me down to the small wooden lighthouse dock. I bent down at the edge of the small, ten-foot wide dock and pulled the anchor chords from the water. Both ropes had clean edges, their fugitive better halves sailing away into the night.

I sat down on the edge of the dock and absentmindedly draped my legs over the edge. Alex plopped down next to me, sinking her feet into the deathly blue chasm. I caught a wave between my palms and splashed the water onto my face, an attempt to somehow wash the image that had been painted on the lids of my eyes: Ashley's watchful eyes affixed to their man-made equivalent.

I could feel Alex shake her head next to me. She asked, "Who is—*was*—she?"

"Ashley Andrews, she was one of my students."

"I'm sorry."

"Me too."

Those were the only words muttered.

~

Ten minutes later, sirens began to wail in the distance and steadily became more audible. The fog had lifted a bit and if I squinted I could almost make out Alex next to me.

Alex said, "Time to play tour guide."

I nodded and whipped my legs from the current, kicking my new running shoes into the ocean. Alex was about to do the same and I said, "Don't bother. You can't go back in."

She nodded and shoved her heel back into her shoe. "What do you want me to do? Caitlin will kill you if she sees me."

Alex was right. Caitlin would frown on Alex's presence both professionally and personally. I looked around, "Why don't you go to the west end. There's a small landing just to the front of lighthouse. In a couple minutes we'll be inside and you can make a go of it."

Alex hesitated, came close, gently kissed me on the cheek, then disappeared from view.

A half minute later, three bouncing balls of light matured into full-fledged streams of illuminated fog. I turned into the light, shielding my eyes, and heard Wade Gleason's distinct drawl, "Nice sweatshirt. I hope Pooh has an alibi?"

And I thought I looked foolish because I was barefoot and my pants were rolled above my knees. I pulled the sweatshirt out from the bottom and said, "His hand was stuck in the honey jar. Plus, I don't think he can hold an ax." I twiddled my thumbs in the spotlight. "No opposable thumbs."

The lights fell off me and crawled up the lighthouse foundation, then continued up the eastern wall. Out of the corner of my eye, I saw Alex's figure duck into the shadows, a movement the other three apparently missed. I pulled myself up to the foundation and the four of us congregated at the edge of the entrance.

Caitlin asked, "Are you positive it's Ashley?"

No, I wasn't positive. Plenty of women had black hair and dolphin tattoos weren't exactly rare. But, I didn't know any other women that fit the description who had a relationship with yours truly or, more corporeal, who Tristen Grayer would benefit from killing, raping, and puréeing.

"Yep, it's her."

"Sorry."

Both Gregory and Gleason nodded their sympathies. The three of them followed me up the lighthouse stairs with a settled excitement. A homicide detective walking up the stairs to a crime scene is similar to a little kid walking downstairs on Christmas, only the presents aren't wrapped. I'd snooped, I knew the present, and I was feeling more of a settled unsettlement.

We came forth from the spiral staircase and three flashlights closed in on the defilement. It was more horrific than at first glance. A terse minute passed, each of us soaking up the scene. Caitlin broke the silence, "What's this?"

She was standing near the lighthouse lens pointing at two condensation pockets on the glass. I couldn't believe it. Ashley's eyes were gone.

~

I walked to where Caitlin was standing. Condensation had built up behind the glass where the eyes had been. Other than that, there was no evidence that twenty minutes ago Ashley's eyes had been scrambled to the lens sunny-side up. I looked for some sort of explanation. Could the eyes have fallen off? Even if they had, there was nowhere for them to go. Maybe the motor had started and the rotating lens had taken the eyes outside with it. No, Alex and I would have seen the light go on, and the lens would have had to come to a stop in the exact same position.

I gaped at the three people staring at me and I wouldn't doubt if they thought I had Parkinson's. I flexed my temples to make my head cease shaking and said, "Her eyes. Ashley's eyes were stuck to that lens like two fried eggs."

Gleason didn't look like he bought it, "If that's the case it looks like someone came and picked them clean with a spatula."

His words echoed in the lighthouse chamber. "Picked them clean with a spatula." I'd said it myself, *He wasn't back, he'd never left. He'd always been waiting in the shadows, lurking.*

The shadow I'd seen was not that of Alex, but of Tristen Grayer.

I took the spiral staircase like a fire pole and had it not been for the railing across from the door I would have been doing a frightful rendition of YMCA on the ocean stage. I flung myself under the railing and hit the granite, seven feet below, midstride. How long had it been since I'd seen the figure? Three minutes? Five minutes?

The fog had lifted, but it was still pitch dark. It was impossible to see where each granite boulder ended and the next began. They hadn't constructed a lighthouse here for shits and giggles. I didn't see any lights bobbling and weaving in the blackness. If Tristen was making the pilgrimage, he was doing it without the aid of a flashlight.

I pulled my cell phone from my pocket. Should I call Alex? No, Alex could very well be dead. I tried Conner, but he didn't answer. I could only think of one other person and dialed.

The other end picked up on the first ring. I was about forty feet from the lighthouse and navigating the stones with the phone to my ear was not a simple task. I could hear him breathing on the line and said, "Kevin? Are you there?"

He finally sputtered out, "Uh, yeah. What's going on? We heard all the sirens and saw the two police cars drive up. Is someone dead?"

"Where are you?"

"At the memorial stone. Is someone dead?"

The memorial stone was maybe an eighth of the way up the breakwater. I told him the truth, "Yes, someone is dead. The killer is coming your way right now. Start walking to shore. Go now."

He didn't respond, and I think he might have shit his pants.

Kevin came on, "I think I shit my pants." There you go.

I could hear him walking and asked, "Do you see the car I pulled up in?"

"Yes."

"The code on the side is 2321. Repeat that back to me."

"2321."

"Right. There's a spare key in the ashtray." It wasn't like I was throwing these kids into a shark feeding frenzy. They'd be safer in the Range Rover than where they were now. It was more like throwing plankton in the path of a humpback. "When you get in, lock the doors. Then I want you to drive to the edge of the water and turn the car lights on." I gave him instructions.

He repeated, "2321. Spare in ashtray. Drive to water. When I see a figure, shine the brights on him."

"Perfect."

~

I was making decent time and I estimated I was three-quarters of the way to shore when the Range Rover's lights flipped on, illuminating the better part of the homestretch. About a hundred feet up the breakwater, stopped like a deer in headlights, was Tristen Grayer. He was clad in all black and had a tan ski mask pulled down over his face. I took a step forward and a hand clasp around my arm. It was Alex.

Our eyes met and we both took off. I felt my right foot pound into the memorial stone as Tristen took the final granite boulder. Then a strange thing occurred, the lights from the Range Rover began to move. The SUV reversed up the beach, stopped, spit sand, then zoomed toward the deft figure. Kevin was going to run Tristen Grayer over with the Range Rover. Priceless.

The Range Rover just missed clipping him before smashing into the cliff wall. Tristen ran toward the car, jumped on the hood, and catapulted himself over the cliff and into the woods.

A minute later, Alex and I reached the Range Rover. I wrenched open the passenger side door, emitting a cloud of smoke. The kids were somewhere between a state of shock, hysterics, and pot. The girl in the passenger seat looked at me and giggled hysterically, "Look, guys, it's Weenie the Pooh."

Chapter 24

I woke up on Alex's couch. The night had ended dismally. None of the kids lost any more brain cells in the car crash than they had hot-boxing the Range Rover with their joint. They fled to their respective houses while Alex and I drove the frontage road for close to three hours before calling it quits. I couldn't put Tristen's time table together. It didn't fit with my logic. Not that I'm logical.

I mean, if he left in the boat, how had he returned and, moreover, why had he returned? I needed some Lucky Charms. I didn't find any Lucky Charms, grabbed a peach Yoplait instead, and looked at the clock over the oven, 7:45 a.m. I wondered if Alex subscribed to the *Waterville Tribune*. Of course she did.

I took the yogurt and walked to the front door. There were three other papers, but no *Tribune*. I tossed the three papers onto Alex's stoop and surveyed the damage to the Range Rover. One headlight was smashed beyond belief and the other one was in decent condition, only it was not attached to the car, per se. I added the headlight to the trunk-slash-car part sarcophagus and slid into the driver's seat.

I found a Dunkin' Donuts in downtown Waterville and walked inside. The slots for the *Bangor Daily News* and the *Portland Press-Herald* were both full, however the slot for the *Waterville Tribune* was vacant. I ordered a large coffee and two glazed donuts then asked the clerk if he had a Tribune hidden back there anywhere. I gave him a ten dollar bill and he handed me a disheveled *Waterville Tribune.*

Walking out of Dunkin's, I shuffled through about ten different sections until I found the front page. I spit a mouthful of coffee, splattering the paper. The coffee streaked headline read:

Heartbreak at Surry Breakwater
Story by Alex Tooms

I read the article and ripped the paper into about ten pieces before tossing it into the gusting wind. A couple of people threw me dirty looks; littering was more than taboo in Maine, it was barbaric. Speaking of barbaric, I was going to scalp Alex Tooms. How could she do this? Both literally and figuratively. Most papers went to press at ten or eleven at night. Alex and I hadn't even reached her house until close to two, plus she would still have had to write the article. Alex hadn't mentioned the eye's disappearing, not to mention the chase. All this was missing in the article. It wasn't like Alex to withhold information from her reader. Why had she held back?

I was stumped. I was still going to kill her, but I was stumped.

~

I rolled into the Federal Building parking lot at 8:30 a.m. There wasn't much for hoopla which would not be the case in an hour. Every other media outlet in the state was getting their Tristen Grayer report over coffee and donuts, much like I had.

I pushed the conference doors open and all conversation stopped mid-syllable. Caitlin, Todd, Wade, and Conner each had a copy of the Tribune sprawled out on the large mahogany. Why was it that every time I was in this room I felt like my fly was down? I checked—no fly. Buttons. I was checking my wallet for my Kenneth Cole receipt when Todd interrupted my scavenger hunt. He flapped the paper open in case I'd somehow neglected to notice the table looked like the floor of a hamster cage.

Todd spat, "Would you like to tell us how Alex Tooms wrote this story?"

"No." I wanted to find my Kenneth Cole receipt.

I had all my receipts on the table now. The Kenneth Cole receipt had to be in there somewhere. It was yellow, definitely yellow.

Caitlin thought she'd take a stab at it. "Did you tell Alex Tooms about Ashley Andrews?"

"Yes." What a relief. I put the yellow Kenneth Cole receipt in my back pocket and looked up.

Caitlin looked confused, "Yes, you told Alex about Ashley Andrews? Or yes, you found the stupid fricking receipt you're looking for?"

Good question. "Uh, the second one."

I gathered my receipts, poured myself a cup of coffee from the carafe, and pulled up a chair across from the four of them. I made eye contact with Conner and said, "And where exactly were you last night?"

"I got there right after you left. You drove right past me."

I didn't remember driving past his Camaro, but I had other fish to fry. I didn't like that Glease had yet to speak. He was leaning back in his swivel chair with what looked to be fermenting annoyance. Not a good sign. I put the shenanigans behind the bar with the good scotch, and said, "Remember when Todd asked what we would accomplish by asking my neighbors if they'd seen a boat and I'd said, *because my house backs up to a huge body of water called the Atlantic Ocean. Do you find it infeasible for someone to dock their boat on the beach and drag a woman into my house? Do you find that fucking infeasible?*"

They all nodded. Except Todd. Todd did not nod.

I kept my rhythm, "Well, it turns out there was a boat floating near the shore the night of Jennifer's murder. My source called me last night at 10:30 to notify me the same boat was docked at the Surry Breakwater Lighthouse. I'd been at Alex Tooms' house at the time, chastising her for the callous article she'd written when the call came in. Alex overheard the conversation and the next thing I knew she pulled out a sawed-off shotgun and said she was coming with me to the lighthouse. Who was I to dispute her? I mean, she had a sawed-off shotgun."

Caitlin, Conner, and Wade rolled their eyes. Todd's parents hadn't opted for the eye-roll software upgrade, and he remained motionless.

I recounted the rest of the story in relative accuracy. I didn't have to give false testimony about how Alex had written the story because I didn't have the slightest fancy. I also had no idea how Tristen Grayer left in a boat and managed to swipe Ashley's eyes.

Wade brought his chair back to its full upright position and rested his elbows on the table. He said, "Well, you hadn't been lying about the eyes. I talked with forensics earlier; they found traces of eye tissue on the lighthouse lens. Also, Ashley's prints were on file and checked out. It's her. We contacted her parents in Tuscany after the match was verified. They want to have the funeral here."

When you're accepted into the criminology department, you are fingerprinted and entered into a national database. I'd expected them to run her prints, and the absoluteness of her death put a huge knot in my throat. There was a big difference between being 99% sure of something and 100% certain. Hearing the words "It's her" sent that 1% up in smoke. Now I was pissed. I think best when I'm pissed. I said, "Here's how I see it. We have two dead so far. Tristen's hitting on the hot dates, killing these women on the exact date and time we found them last year."

Wade said coolly, "He's changed his pattern. No R in Andrews. He's not spelling out P-R-E-S-C-O-T-T. What do you think he's up to now?"

"He's obviously going after women in my life. It doesn't matter the name. And he's striking on the same hot dates as a year ago."

Gleason remarked, "We have the *who* and the *when*. That's two of the three W's. *Where* is the only mystery."

Conner added an insightful tidbit, "If we protect the *who*, we don't need to know the *where*."

Wade nodded to himself and walked to a dry-erase board at the far end of the room. He erased my irrelevant dribble from Monday and picked up a red marker. "Thomas, we need a list of every woman you've come into contact with in the last five years."

~

I spent the next hour thinking of every female whose life was in danger. I thought this was a bit overkill. That was, until Tristen Grayer killed a woman not on this list. Then it would be six-feet-under-kill.

Half an hour passed and her name still wasn't on the board. I sure as hell wasn't going to say it and she didn't seem too keen to offer it. Conner finally said, "Caitlin."

Caitlin and I locked eyes and I felt like the disciple Peter. I didn't hear a rooster crow and thought I might have been in the clear when Conner snapped his fingers and said, "Alex. Put Alex Tooms on the list."

Caitlin threw him a look that would have withered a man twice his size. I held back a grin. Better to be Peter than Judas.

~

Alex's name was the last addition to the list. When it was all said and done, I'd come up with twenty-seven different women who I thought might be on Tristen Grayer's hit list. Or make that twenty-seven names my colleagues on the task force felt might be on Tristen Grayer's hit list.

I skimmed the list; Tristen Grayer wasn't going after August the flight attendant or Margery the bookstore owner. Ashley's murder ached more than Jennifer's. Tristen had to up the ante each time. Each kill would be more critical than the last.

I looked at the list and put myself in his shoes. Who would I kill next? Who was in jeopardy? I came up with six names.

Chapter 25

The next thing on my to-do list was to talk to Lacy. She was most likely the last person to interact with Ashley Andrews before she was killed. I dialed Lacy's cell and she picked up on the first ring, "Hey."

She sounded grim and I countered, "Sucks."

"I can't believe she's dead. First Jennifer, now Ashley. What's going on?"

I ignored her question. "Did Ashley say anything to you in the car?"

"Nothing important. Just sex talk."

"Was she getting any?"

"She was always getting some. She was a slut. A cool slut, but a slut nonetheless."

"Where was she headed after she dropped you off?"

"She wouldn't say, but she had an I'm-about-to-do-some-kinky-ass-shit look on her face."

A thought struck me. What if Ashley had been fooling around with Tristen? I changed the subject, "So what do you have planned today?"

"Caleb's coming to pick me up in about ten minutes to take me to the gallery. I have a meeting with a lady from the MS Society and a caterer. Oh, and I need you to take care of Baxter until we can move back home. Conner almost killed him last night when he found him asleep on some suit he'd just bought." She paused for a half second, then asked, "When are we moving home?"

Good question. I told her to give the pug to Caleb, hung up, and dialed Mr. Barstow. He didn't try and hide his despair over the phone, audibly broken over Ashley's death. I told him I needed three more guys to help out with surveillance. He said he'd make some calls and to meet him at a bar a couple blocks from campus in a couple hours.

It was almost noon and I was starving. If I were going to yell at Alex I might as well do it over a burger and fries. I dialed her number and she picked up. She knew I knew about the article. And I knew she knew that I knew. I think we both found it easier to act like we didn't know.

~

Alex pulled into the Burger King parking lot two car lengths ahead of me. I parked next to her and the two of us ghosted to the burger joint entrance. I was nice enough to let her hold the door open for me seeing as I was a selective genius and a selective gentleman.

I was in an artery clogging mood and ordered a double Whopper, large fries, and a vanilla milkshake. Alex's eyes darted to the salad menu and she bit her lip as she said, "I'll have the same."

I visualized her calculating the math in her head. I think the caloric intake equated to back-to-back marathons.

We found a booth and each ate a fry awaiting the other person to speak. I was the only one with any ammo and said, "Write anything good lately?"

She swallowed a fry. "Yeah, I wrote a book. Maybe you've heard of it, *Eight in October*? Number one on the *New York Times* Best Sellers list as of today."

I was going to ask her when I could expect my royalty check but settled on, "I was thinking more along the lines of journalism."

Alex took a huge bite of her burger and I might be mistaken, but I think I heard her jaw dislocate. She grappled the bite down and said, "An article of mine ran in the *Waterville Tribune* a couple days ago."

"I was thinking more like today."

She looked up into her brain and it was my turn to take a bite. I lifted the burger with both hands, brought it to my lips, and was left with only the top and bottom buns eclipsed between my fingers. Alex cackled as I attempted to piece my burger back together. I was halfway through an enthralling game of burger Jenga when Alex answered my question, "Nope, I didn't write anything that ran in today's paper."

I stood up, tossed the wayward burger in the trash, and coincidentally spotted Exhibit B in the receptacle. I snagged the discarded copy of the *Waterville Tribune*, sat back down, and flipped the paper open. I pointed to her story and said, "You didn't write this?"

"Nope."

"Hmm. But it says your name right here. You sure you didn't type this story?"

She had both cheeks full of burger but somehow managed, "I told it to someone over the phone and they typed it."

"Big deal. You're not getting off on semantics." Yes, she would.

"Yes I will." See.

"When?"

"While I was in hiding at the lighthouse."

Made sense, that's why all the second half details were lacking. That's also why she hadn't noticed Tristen's loitering. She'd been gabbing on the phone. I checked my watch. It was a little after one. I was to meet Caleb and his recruits at 1:30 p.m. I grabbed my fries and shake and said, "You're working for Tristen Grayer. Your stories are paying homage to his evil. Promise me I won't see your name on another story in the Waterville Tribune."

She promised.

I turned to leave and said, "I can't believe your boss lets you get away with this shit. He's going to get his ass sued."

Over my shoulder I heard, "She."

I turned.

"*She's* going to get her ass sued."

~

When I arrived at the bar, I wasn't surprised to see Caleb sitting at a table with three of my other students; Blake, Tim, and Tim. To save a couple trees here: Blake is black, Tim 1 is tall, Tim 2 is fat.

They had a couple pitchers on the table and lying between them was Baxter. They handed me a frosty glass and we toasted Ashley. None of us cried, but funny enough we all developed the same allergy to beer. The five of us took down the pitchers fast and I dropped the ball on them. They were all thrilled to be selected and doubly to help take down their friend's killer. The six women from the list I felt were in harm's way were Caitlin; Lacy; the three other female students in my class: Kim Welding, Ali Marker, and Holly Gibbs; and Alex Tooms. Caitlin would have more than enough protection with the three Agenteers, Caleb seemed like he was doing a fine job with my sister. I put my other students on their classmates. And I took Alex.

I'd picked up three pairs of long-range walkie-talkies on the way to the bar and divvied them out at my car. I told the Thomask Force, as they'd aptly named themselves, the channel we'd be sticking with and to pack like they were going on a three-day camping trip. I also told them they could count on an FBI goon showing up on each of their marks' tails in the next twenty-four hours. They all drove off with grins on their faces, and I don't think it was attributed to the booze.

~

By 6:30 p.m. that night I'd dropped by a mini-mart and picked up enough food to last me and Baxter the next seventy-two hours, bought three books on CD, ordered new carpet for Lacy's room, and was now stationed outside Alex Tooms' gateless drive.

I picked up my walkie-talkie, turned it to channel nine, and said, "Everyone on their mark?"

I received three, "Checks," and one, "Get set. Go."

This was going to be a long night. I ran through some stakeout protocol and airway decorum, then ended with, "You can catch a couple winks tomorrow during the day, but I don't even want you guys blinking tonight."

I looked for Baxter but it appeared he'd had an episode and was snoring up a storm in the back hatch. I tore the cellophane packaging from one of the books on CD and slipped the first disk in the drive. A voice shouted, "Welcome to *Prey* by Michael Crichton."

How fitting. I was listening to a book entitled *Prey* while I was trying to protect Tristen Grayer's prey. Does irony come any thicker? After the first disk played through I looked at Baxter, who at some point had appeared in the passenger seat, and asked him, "Do you understand any of this shit? Explain a nanoparticle to me."

He couldn't and I started Disk One over. I was listening to the first disk a third time when the walkie-talkie crackled, "Hey, would you guys rather have a dick on your forehead or balls on your palms?"

Balls on my palms.

Definitely.

Chapter 26

Whack. Whack. Whack. I casually opened my eyes to daylight peeking in from every angle. *Whack. Whack. Whack.* What's with all the whacking? I brought my seat up and read the clock, 7:30 a.m.

Whack. Whack. Whack.

I calmed my heart beat down under 200 and rolled down the window. "You scared the crap out of me."

Alex was wearing short maroon Boston College running shorts and my red Nautica sweatshirt. She said, "Let's go."

I told her one minute and rolled up the window. I picked up the walkie-talkie and said, "Rise and shine, maggots."

All parties were accounted for. I guess I'd been the only one to take a nap. I called Lacy to make sure she was okay, and she said Conner had just left and she was going out to breakfast with Caleb. So the good news was that nothing had happened last night. The bad news was that the Range Rover smelled like dog doo.

It took me a minute to locate Baxter. I eventually found him in the pocket behind the driver seat, looking the part of a Joey in his mother's pouch. I hopped out of the car, opened the back door, and lifted him from the pocket. Baxter hadn't gone out of his of way to hide his push and I pulled the pouch open. It looked like someone emptied a bag of Reece's Pieces in there on a hot summer day.

I turned around and tossed Baxter on the grass near where Alex was stretching. Baxter landed with a thud and rolled to within a foot of her. So it's cats that land on their feet, not narcoleptic pugs.

Alex looked up at me in horror and said, "You killed him."

If only I was so lucky. "He's probably not dead. Sometimes it takes a couple throws until he wakes up."

I changed into my second pair of Asics and plopped down next to Alex. Baxter was alive and trying to wiggle his way underneath Alex's leg and into the warmth of her running shorts. Looked like Baxter and I had more in common than our nanoparticle knowledge after all.

~

The two of us walked and jogged for the better part of an hour. And I had to credit Baxter: he only fell asleep a few times and only once with his head in a gopher hole.

We were about a quarter mile from her house when Alex started picking up the pace and said, "Race you to the door. Loser buys dinner."

I let her get a sizable lead then turned on the afterburners. Alex called it an asskicking, I called it a photo finish. Either way, I would be footing the bill for dinner.

I showered, put on my black tweed pants with a lavender dress shirt, and sat down to a plate of sausage and eggs. I could get used to this. I took a swig of orange juice and a thought came to me. "You never asked why I was sitting in my car outside your house."

"Oh, I just figured you were staking my house out in case Tristen Grayer decided to try to kill me."

I cleared my throat and tried to speak but nothing came out. Had I walked to Alex's door during my little siesta and confided this all to her?

She asked, "Are you going to follow me around all day?"

"Why? Are you going to try to give me the slip?"

"No. In fact, I made you an itinerary while you were in the shower."

How thoughtful. She slid a piece of paper to me and I unfolded it. Alex's day schedule was rudimentary and PG. Her night register, on the other hand, was lurid and NC-17. Remember she is a professional writer. Here are just a couple flag words I encountered in her "overnight" allotment: wheelbarrow, coitus, engorgement, pollinate, zenith, flora and fauna, carnal appetite, and habeas corpus.

~

I followed Alex's Jeep to the Waterville Tribune building in downtown Waterville. It was a small, white, clapboard building, huddled between a ninety-nine-cent store and a Hallmark shop. Alex walked to my car and asked if she could borrow Baxter. Well, don't put a gun to my head.

She waved Baxter's paw at me and disappeared into the building. I had no intention of sitting there for the next eight hours and drove off. When I was on the highway I dialed Caitlin and said, "We need to talk."

We met at a coffee shop in walking distance of the Federal Building. I was sitting in a black wiry chair at a black wiry table in the back of a counterfeit French coffee parlor when Caitlin pulled up a seat across from me. Caitlin sat down, a beacon of poise and abatement. She was wearing a black skirt and a tan sweater, looking the part of off-duty librarian. Was I supposed to read into this? Was she trying to tell me something? Did I have an overdue book?

Everyone knows breakups are done like Band-Aids, but I wasn't sure what this was. This was more of a *You've just been one-night-standed* and I wasn't sure how to proceed.

Caitlin and I sipped our drinks in silence. Halfway through my drink, I noticed Caitlin had developed a previously nonexistent allergy to Caramel Macchiatos. I don't like making women cry. I swear, I don't.

I set my coffee down and said, "I'm sorry Caitlin. I don't know what I was thinking . . . We never should have . . . I mean . . . You know what I mean."

For some reason she didn't look like she knew what I meant. She nodded and found a tissue in her handbag. After a couple dabs she said, "Thomas, I love you, but if you don't love me then you have to be true to yourself. It would be selfish of me to think otherwise. So, if you don't love me, tell me so I can get on with my life."

I told her and she left.

Chapter 27

After my breakfast, breakup, breakdown, I broke neck to the breakwater. I did a hasty walk-through, took some mental snapshots, and left as quickly as I came. Next stop, Lacy's gallery. I decided to keep the news of Caitlin's and my demise to myself. For all I knew, Lacy wasn't wise to the fact there was anything to demise.

I opened the door to the gallery to Lacy's bugle, "Conner says you and Caitlin are back together. That's great."

So much for Plan A.

I went to Plan B: deny, deny, deny. I denied and Lacy didn't bite, "You're the worst liar. Don't tell me you hooked up with her, then broke it off. Again."

Plan C: blame, blame, blame. I blamed and Lacy shook her head, "Yeah, I'm supposed to believe Caitlin forced you to sleep with her."

Not in so many words, but at one point I did have a gun trained on me. I kept this to myself and told her what really happened while she gave me the grand tour. I gave her a bear hug when I left and told her I wanted her at arm's length from Caleb at all times. She winked at me and said, "That shouldn't be a problem."

I was walking outside in the parking lot when I saw Conner getting out of his Camaro. He walked over and I asked, "What's up?"

"Lacy said she needed to talk."

Uh-oh. Could this be the first brother-sister dump of a brother-sister in the history of the world? Now I understood why Lacy had said "Arm's length from Caleb at all times. Shouldn't be a problem."

I gave him ten minutes until he was doing the Dodd's Eye Dab. I quickly changed the subject, "So what's your game plan for tonight?"

"Agents are driving up from the Boston field office as we speak. We should be able to post a man on all twenty-seven women."

"I thought they were coming in yesterday."

"We decided against staking out last night, seeing as it wasn't a hot date and all."

Conner fit right in with these FBI bozos. I had my doubts about last night but at least I'd been prepared. Granted, I'd slept for close to seven hours, but that was beside the point. I said, "So that's it. Protect the masses. Don't let him get close enough to strike."

He paused too long and I kicked him in the shin. "Tell me."

He rubbed his shin and said, "We're using Caitlin as bait."

"You're what?"

"We figured if we have her staking out a house by herself, she'll appear vulnerable."

I laughed. "So you're staking out Caitlin doing stakeout."

He nodded.

The reason these idiots never solved a case is because they never respected their opposition. They appraised Tristen Grayer as being incompetent when he most likely had an IQ higher than their little task force combined.

I patted Conner on the back and said, "Good luck with that." Caitlin couldn't be safer if she was on a desert island, in a bubble, with a chastity belt on.

~

I pulled up to the *Waterville Tribune* building at 4:00 p.m. on the dot. Two more hours to kill. I put the second disk of the *Prey* book in, and after thirty minutes I had two of three migraine symptoms and had called information twice.

I pulled the key from the ignition and decided while I was at the *Waterville Tribune* building I might as well pop into the Editor in Chief's office and put the scare of death into her. I opened the door and walked into a bustling newsroom. No front desk. No secretary. Just twenty people behind laptops trying to meet deadlines.

I tapped a young man of about twenty-five on the shoulder and asked him where the boss's office was. He gave me a once over and said, "You're Thomas Prescott."

No use trying to get anything by this guy. I said in my best cockney accent, "Nopers. But if you see him, tell him General Van Furgle is looking for him."

For some reason he looked confused, and I moved on to the next guy in his row who directed me to a large office in the back right corner. I weaved my way through the maze of desks and didn't happen by Alex nor did I see an unoccupied desk with a pug shaped paperweight. Alex's Jeep was parked where she'd left it earlier. She was probably in the break room, or in the print area, or maybe she'd caught the red eye to Belize with Baxter. Lucky dog.

I came to an office that reminded me of my ex-captain's in my Seattle PD days. It occurred to me how similar a newsroom and a police department were, most noticeably the number of criminals present. I surmised the office was that of Alex's she-boss seeing as *Queen Bee* was stenciled where *Editor in Chief* had been scraped off.

I rapped on the glass—the white shutters on the inside swayed—and a hollow female voice yelled, "Come in."

I did a quick inventory of what I wanted to express to this woman. I wanted to make sure no more of Tristen Grayer's heroics showed up in the paper. The papers were our allies, not his. This yellow journalism, this sensationalism needed to be stopped. Although to be honest, every scrap of print thus far had been unexaggerated and accurate. But lucky for me, we weren't being honest, we were rationalizing. Big difference.

I pulled the door open, took two steps inside the modest office, and took an overview of the woman behind the desk. She was quite attractive and I felt like I knew her from somewhere. She motioned to the chair in front of her desk and said, "Have a seat."

I sat down, crossed my left leg over my right, and said, "So, you're Queen Bee."

Alex smiled. "I bought the paper."

I returned her smile. "Of course you did."

Chapter 28

When Alex walked out of the *Waterville Tribune* building the sun was crashing into the western mountains.

I followed Alex home, put the car in park, and then called Lacy. She said that she and Conner were quote "Doneskee." The Prescott-Dodds era had come to a bitter end. She and Caleb were on their way to pick her stuff up from Conner's and take it to his house. I told her to be careful and hung up.

Gleason called and he went over the same information Conner had filled me in on. He said he heard I had a couple students working for me and asked which women I was staking out. I gave him the names and we both wished each other luck. We were on different teams, but we still played in the same conference. He asked if I wanted to talk to Todd, and we both had a hearty chuckle.

I called Caitlin, not expecting an answer, and left a message on her voice mail to be circumspect of the FBI's game plan. At 7:30 a black sedan with tinted windows pulled up two car lengths behind me. Yippee, my FBI goon had arrived.

After I'd let him stand outside his car for close to a minute I opened my door and stepped out. Professional courtesy and all that. My Fed was a young buck somewhere in the vicinity of twenty-five. He had charcoal black hair cut short, almost orange eyes, and, apart from the thin scar running down the right side of his face, he would've made a good Colin Farrell stunt double.

We shook hands and he said, "Gary Strinteer, two 'e's."

"Thomas Prescott, two 't's."

How chummy.

Gary smiled and I asked, "How was the drive?"

He shook his head, "Twenty-seven black Caprices in a row and it wasn't even for a funeral. You'd have thought Mangrove himself had gone to Bureaugatory."

I liked this kid, he didn't seem all that keen on his peers. We had a lot in common and traded a couple FBI jokes, neither of us noticing Alex's Jeep until she nearly ran us over. Gary gave a quick salute and we both moved briskly to our respective vehicles. Out of my peripheral I thought I detected a slight kink in Gary's gait. Nothing obvious, just a heaviness in his step.

~

I'd never heard of the restaurant Alex spoke of, and it ended up being located in old Portland, or Old Port. Alex parked in the Freddy's Fresh Fish lot, which served two other similarly themed shanties. I parked on the side of the road closest to the restaurant, and Gary the Fed did a U-turn, parking on the far side.

Alex stepped from the Jeep, dressed in blue jeans and a lime green tank top. She didn't look my way and I juggled with the possibility she was actually meeting someone. Where was my gun?

A minute passed. I knew I would go in eventually, the debate was whether it would be before or after Alex ordered the appetizer. I double buckled, popped the hood, the trunk, and the gas latch. By the time I unbuckled and closed all three, Alex would have her credit card out, right?

I rolled all the windows down, turned the wipers on, and locked the doors. Just bought myself another thirty seconds. I was opening the moon roof when a car passed and drove into the restaurant lot, parking alongside Alex's Jeep. The door to the Passat opened and Caleb stepped out. He walked around to the passenger side and helped a beautiful young lady, rumored to have 0/0 vision, out of the passenger seat. I'm not big on conspiracy theory, but something here was amiss.

By the time I unbuckled, turned the wipers off, rolled the windows up, unlocked the doors (then locked the doors), closed the gas latch and the trunk, Caleb and Lacy were through the weather-plagued doors.

I put my cell phone in my pocket, grabbed the extra walkie-talkie from the backseat, and walked across the street to the black sedan. The darkly tinted window rolled down and I said, "I'm going in there for a while." I handed him the extra walkie-talkie, "If anything happens I'll be on channel nine."

He nodded.

I walked across the street, took a deep breath, and approached the maître d'. I inquired, "Is there a party of three awaiting a Thomas Prescott?"

She checked a list and said, "Follow me."

We didn't have to go far. Alex, Caleb, and Lacy were sitting at the closest booth, all three huddled against the window. Alex was prying the wooden shades open with her hands and I asked, "What are we looking at?"

The three of them turned in unison. Alex smiled and said, "Oh, just some idiot who left the hood up on his Range Rover."

I knew I forgot something. I stared at Lacy and the smirk on her face told all. I asked, "Was this your stupid idea?"

"Just trying to get you laid, bro."

We all gave a nice uncomfortable laugh. That's what we Prescotts do best. We don't feel comfortable unless everyone else's faces are flushed and they're having heart palpitations. I said, "Not that I don't appreciate it, Lace, but next time can I have a little advance notice? If you had sent me a memo, I could've asked Tristen if we could do this whole stakeout/murder thing next week."

I couldn't get that upset. Lacy was at arm's length from Caleb, and I didn't mind Alex arm's length from me. We put the stakeout on the backburner, and the four of us dined as if the world was in the hands of the PBS executives. I cut Caleb and myself off after one beer, the girls more than making up for our lack of alcohol intake.

Alex and Lacy were into their second bottle of Chianti when Caleb pulled the shutters apart and said, "A guy just walked across the street, shut your hood, and got into a black sedan."

"Oh, that's Gary. He's Alex's FBI tail."

Caleb appeared dazed. He looked at Lacy, "Didn't Conner say the Feds could only get twenty men so they weren't going to put a man on the women Thomas had covered?"

She nodded. "Yeah, Conner said that he told some guy named Gleason that you had your students working for you and Gleason was pulling the tails off those women."

That would explain why a black sedan hadn't followed Caleb's car into the parking lot. So that's why Gleason had called; he wanted to confirm the women I had covered. But still, he wouldn't be so callous as to yank a man off Alex or Lacy and put them on Margery the bookstore owner. Then again, he was a Fed at heart.

This was easy, I would simply call Gleason and have him run Gary's name. I'm sure it was a simple miscommunication. Problem was I forgot Gary's last name. I pulled the walkie-talkie from my hip and said, "Hey Gary, you there?"

There was static, then, "Where am I gonna go?"

"Right. What did you say your last name was?"

"Strinteer, two 'e's. Why?"

"Just curious." I clicked the radio off and said to myself, "Gary Strinteer, two 'e's."

I pulled out my cell phone and Caleb grabbed my arm, "Wait a minute. I need a pen."

Alex pulled a pen from her purse and handed it to him. He scribbled something on a napkin, then peered up, his mouth gaping, "You might want to look at this."

He slid the napkin in front of me and I stared at it in horror. Caleb had crossed off the letters:

G-A-R-Y S-T-R-I-N-T-E-E-R and written T-R-I-S-T-E-N G-R-A-Y-E-R.

Gary Strinteer *was* Tristen Grayer.

Caleb flipped the shutters open, but oddly enough the black sedan was gone.

Chapter 29

I couldn't believe it. I'd shaken hands with Tristen Grayer. I'd shaken hands with the devil. How insolent was this guy? He was goading. "Here, take a good look because you'll never be this close to me again, Thomas Prescott. Let me shake the hand of the poor sap whose life I'm ruining, who can't even come within a stone's throw of a clue."

The both of us knew the next time we crossed paths, only one of us would be coming out alive.

I started to notice the *unnoticables* about my friend Gary Strinteer. He had a thin scar running down the length of his right temple to his lower jaw. I looked at my right thumb and recollected the large amount of skin they'd scraped from beneath the nail. Also, Gary had an awkward gait, and running the clip back in my head, he appeared to drag his left leg. Funny, I'd shot a man in the left patella a year ago. One does not forget the sound of a bullet blistering a kneecap.

I shook off my anger at Tristen and channeled it to my friends at the Federal Bureau of Investigation. Here was a prime example of the FBI's parsimonious disposition. Had they informed me they were pulling their agents, I might have found Gary Strinteer a wee bit suspicious and maybe, just maybe, put together that his name was an anagram of Tristen Grayer. Truthfully, I had my doubts I would have pieced it together if he'd said his name was Gristen Trayer, but I wanted to be pissed at my friend Todd Gregory. Wait, it'd been Gleason who'd pried the information out of me. Damn it, Glease.

Caleb asked, "What should we do?"

We could jump in the car and canvass the neighborhood, but the chances were slim we'd pull up next to Mr. Grayer at a stoplight.

I could call Wade Gleason, tell him what happened, and see how he wanted to play it. Or I could try to get Tristen on the walkie-talkie. I wasn't in the mood to swap info with the Feds and I had a feeling Tristen wanted to talk.

~

The three of us packed into the Range Rover. Lacy sidled up with Alex in the backseat and Caleb jumped in shotgun. Lacy asked, "Where's Baxter?"

"He's around." I hope.

We looked for the pug, but he was, in fact, un-around. I pulled the walkie-talkie up and everyone fell silent. I pushed the button to talk and said, "Tristen, stealing a blind girl's pug is unethical even by serial killer standards."

A voice broke in, "I didn't steal him. I went to close your hood, and when I got back he was asleep on my dash. Listen, that was really a nice piece of detective work you did back there."

"Don't mention it." I didn't know what else to say.

"Not you. The kid, Caleb. If it wasn't for him, you probably would've invited me back to Alex's for after-dinner drinks. Tell me, Thomas, are you going to fuck her tonight? I would. And you can be assured I will."

I looked into the backseat at Alex, her lip was quivering. I yelled into the mouthpiece, "What you do to these girls will be nothing compared with what I do to you. Just keep that thought in the back of your head."

Lacy ripped the walkie-talkie from my hand. "Listen, you ass-wipe, you so much as touch that dog I'll see to it you choke to death on your own dick."

Tristen gave a shrill laugh. "Lacy Prescott. I was hoping your brother would be nice enough to introduce the two of us. Well, in due time. Listen, I'd love to chat, but I have a date with a beautiful young lady."

The walkie-talkie went dead.

~

Lacy was crying and Alex was trying to console her. Or vice versa. It was hard to tell. The walkie-talkie crackled, "Professor, was that who I think it was?"

I went to speak, then thought better of it. Caleb saw I didn't want to communicate on our present channel and said into his walkie-talkie, "Everyone go to the channel of UM's back-up goalie."

University of Maine hockey had a cult following. Caleb looked at me and said, "Channel forty-one."

I turned to forty-one. "Everybody here?"

Everyone was there. "To answer your question—yes, that was exactly who you thought it was. First things first, I want everyone to go and touch their mark. Don't check back until you have their shirt in your hand."

A tense minute and a half passed, but all the women were accounted for. The ten of us were spread out in about a twenty-five mile radius and smack-dab in the middle was the town of Waterville. I looked over my shoulder at Alex and asked, "You haven't gone to print yet, have you?"

Alex gave a puzzled look, then smiled.

We arrived at the *Waterville Tribune* building at almost 11:00 p.m. On any other night the paper would have gone to print around eight but Alex had postponed it for some reason or another. Imagine that.

When a witness goes to the police station to give testimony for a composite sketch they use a computer program called Sketch-a-Villain 6.0 which can shrink ears, enlarge noses, tint skin, and make zillions of tiny adjustments until the witness is content with the image. Lacy and I would have to go old school. One shot at glory.

Alex rummaged up some pencils, a set of pastels, and a sheet of gloss paper. It took thirty minutes for Lacy to complete the sketch. After she was finished, she handed the piece of paper over. Lacy's and my efforts had produced a near spitting image of the face I'd seen less than an hour earlier. I found myself staring into the sunset orange eyes of Tristen Grayer. My demon.

Chapter 30

We pulled into Alex's drive to three cars parked in the middle of her yard. The three girls from my class gave me hugs and asked why I hadn't involved them in the case. Anyhow, Kim is trim, Ali is a lot of woman, and Holly is mole-y. I promised them from that point on they would each have a stake in their own survival.

The clan—Kim, Ali, Holly, Lacy, Caleb, Blake, Tall Tim, and Fat Tim—followed Alex into her house as I whipped out my cell phone and dialed Gleason.

The phone was answered on the first and half ring, "Gregory, Special Agent in Charge."

Piss. "Where's Wade?"

"Getting some coffee? What can I do for you, Mr. Prescott?"

Hold your breath until you die for starters. "I shook his hand."

"Whose hand?"

"His hand. *Tristen Grayer's.*"

I could hear him straighten up in the car seat. "When?"

I recounted the events for him. Now while the facts weren't completely sober, they would have passed a breathalyzer. A thought occurred to me that hadn't yet, and I said, "He was in a black Caprice with FBI plates, so you might want to check to see if all the men in your platoon are accounted for. I'd be willing to bet you come up one PFC short."

If one of his goons was gone, it was safe to assume the woman the goon had been staking out was also gone.

Todd started cranking up his drawbridge, "Our men have been checking in every half hour."

You know how I'd been having the kids say "check" to check in? I'd filched this wizardry from the Feds. I asked Todd, "Are you asking for their social security number every time they check in?

That's how my bank ensures that it's me on the phone and not a serial killer impersonating me."

"I'll call you back." Fill the moat. Get the gators.

The phone rang a minute later. It was Gleason. Not a good sign. If all the men in Todd's army had been accounted for, Todd would have called. I skipped over the fundamentals, "Which woman was your man staking out?"

"Samantha Jackson."

Samantha Jackson was one of ten black girls in the entire state of Maine. She was a waitress at a small diner in Camden. Gleason said, "We're sending our closest man right now."

"Don't. He might be thinking along those lines and be waiting for a man to abandon his post."

"Good point. How do you want to play this?"

I must be hearing things. Did the FBI just ask for my input?

I said, "He knows everything we do. He knew we had twenty-seven women as possible victims, he knew Caleb was working for me. Hell, he probably knows what kind of toilet paper you wipe your ass with and where Todd keeps his strap-on. Listen, I know where Sam lives. I'll be there in five minutes."

I jumped in my car and skidded out of Alex's drive. This didn't fit the mold. Samantha was a waitress who'd waited on me ten, maybe fifteen times. Conner had come up with her name simply because he'd eaten with me at her restaurant on a couple occasions.

I knew Tristen, or at least I knew how his mind worked. Each kill had to be bigger, better, and bloodier than the last. He couldn't move down the ranks from Ashley Andrews to Samantha Jackson. Maybe this, my driving to her house this instant, had been his ploy. I called Caleb and told him to be on the lookout.

~

I exited US 1 northbound and entered the town of Camden. I'd driven Samantha home once when she'd gotten food poisoning from her shift meal. I'd taken her home, then gone back for the meat loaf which, coincidentally, had been the very meal to make her ill. Go figure.

I pulled up to Samantha's, a small row house, sitting in the epicenter of a class-six earthquake of a yard. I jumped out, pushed a hotwheel and a scooter out of my way, and knocked on the thin door. I watched the hand on my Tag tick full circle. A pessimistic streak in me had the thought, "It's hard to answer the door when your feet and ankles are in different rooms."

I walked around to the back of the house and peered through a sliding glass door. I put pressure on the door and it slid easily. There was a small kitchen and I flipped the light. There weren't many places to hide a bedroom in the small house and I walked out of the kitchen and into a cramped hallway. The hallway was devoid of light and I failed to see the baseball bat being swung at my midsection. The bat was a Nerf one and I ripped it easily from the grip of the small black woman attached to it.

Samantha Jackson was sporting plaid boxers, a bright yellow T-shirt, and an expression of menacing doom. She was in a state of panic, and it took me two or three minutes to calm her down. I'd been fully prepared to find a woman-turned-3-D puzzle. And as elated as I was that Samantha was alive, it threw me for a loop.

I'd just completed a thorough walk-through of all two rooms, when there was a knock at the door which I opened to Conner, Caitlin, Gleason, and Gregory. I told them everything seemed to be in order and asked Gregory if all the other agents had checked in.

He nodded.

I had my doubts about Todd's system here. I inquired, "And might I ask what rigorous data your men are disclosing to ascertain their identities?" I think the size of Todd's dick would have been a good verifier.

He threw me his holier-than-thou glance. "Mother's maiden name and blood type."

"O-Really."

"Yes, 'Oh, really,' you condescending prick."

"I thought you wanted my blood type and mother's maiden name: O-Really."

If Todd Gregory could have looked hotter under the collar, a Brad Pitt blow-up doll would be involved. So I'm AB positive, and my mother's maiden name is Reid. But I was pissed at these shitheads for withholding information from me. I waited with Samantha until her mother picked her up and threw in the towel. As I pulled the door to my Range Rover open a hand clasped my forearm. It was Caitlin.

She looked me in the eyes and said, "What do you think?"

I'd lied to Caitlin one time too many. No more lies. "Tristen said he had a date with a beautiful young lady. So I imagine he's killing her right now and we'll find her when he wants us to."

Chapter 31

I woke up with my head on Alex's kitchen table. It was still dark outside and my cell phone told me the sun would be rising any moment. Four hours of sleep is plenty when there's a psychotic killer popping his head into every dream. I went for a long run on the trail running along the lake making up Alex's backyard. About half the lake was surrounded by dirt and prairie, and I spent this time dreading Tristen's next move. The other half of the lake was girdled by spruces, and I spent this time dreading ticks and Lyme disease.

My cell phone chirped as I walked through Alex's front door, and I shied away from the voices resonating the kitchen. Gleason's drawl shot through the phone, "Well, the good news is that all the women are accounted for."

"That is good news, Wade. What's the bad news?"

"It's a double dose actually. Our agent never showed up. We put an APB out on the car, but I'm not very optimistic."

Ditto. "What's the second round of bad juju?"

"Charles wants Todd and I on the next flight back to Quantico."

I said my scripted line, "I thought you said you had bad news?" Hardy-har-har.

I added, "So throwing in the towel, are you?"

"Not completely. The next hot date isn't for five days. We'll pick the brains of a couple guys at the Bureau before heading back. We'll need to get a composite from you and run it through our mainframe. There's a slim chance this Grayer fellow is in our system or an even slimmer chance it's someone else altogether."

Don't count on it. I asked, "Have you seen today's paper?"

"Which paper?"

If I'd been talking to Gregory I would have said, *The North Dakota Free Press.*

"Uh, the *Waterville Tribune*."

I heard Gleason rustling with the paper. He came back on, "Holy shit, how did you pull this off?"

"I've got a contact at the paper."

"Tooms?"

"Yep. She bought the paper."

He seemed to give this some thought. "This picture is pretty creepy. I think they may have gotten the wrong color on the kid's eyes. They're orange."

"Nope, that's them. They say if you look deep into Satan's eyes you can see hell."

"You think they're contacts?"

"Doubt it. He's not going to put on a dress and dance for us."

"You mean for you."

"Exactly."

"Unbelievable you got this in today's paper. It might throw him off when he sees it."

Tristen Grayer knew his picture would be in this morning's paper. He knew my next move before I did. "Let's hope. Hey, tell Gregory to fuck a duck for me."

He said he would. I made him write it down and repeat it back to me.

I walked into the kitchen. All eight of Alex's guests were crammed into the kitchen eating cereal. They all stopped when I entered, and I assumed they wanted to know where I'd gone last night, who was on the phone, and if another woman was dead.

I grabbed a glass of orange juice and said, "Here's the deal, all the women are accounted for. But the agent whose car Tristen stole is MIA, missing in action, which subsequently means he's probably DIA, decomposing in the Atlantic." I briefed them on the phone call with Gleason and that the Feds were going home for a long weekend.

Caleb raised his hand and I called on him, "Yes, Caleb."

"What do you want us to do? Should we stay on stakeout for one more night or what?"

"At least for another day. I don't have the slightest clue what Tristen is up to. Why don't the eight of you stick together at least through the weekend?"

Sixteen eyes congregated on Alex, aka House Mom. She shrugged. "You're all welcome to stay here for as long as you like. I hate being in this big house all alone."

Kim Welding shook her head, "Don't you want us to appear vulnerable. I mean we want him to come after one of us, right?"

No, I didn't want to use three of my students, my sister, and Alex as bait. I'd already lost two worms, and I didn't even know I had my line in the water. "We'll play that card when we need to."

This repartee seemed to satisfy her. My sister was the only sourpuss of the group and I asked, "You all right, Lace?"

She did a dramatic frown, "I miss Baxter."

I wasn't too worried about him. I'd tried to kill him on several different occasions and come up short. Baxter was a survivor. If anyone could escape the reaches of Tristen Grayer it was the narcolepugtic.

Alex steered me out of the room. "Let's go grab a paper. I want to see how the picture came out."

"I can't believe you don't get your own paper delivered to your house."

"I like to separate work from play."

I was curious which category I fell under. She added, "We'll pick up a paper on the way."

Huh. "On the way?"

She smiled. "We have a sailing date, remember?"

~

It was close to ten when Alex and I had a cooler packed and were buckled in the Range Rover. I pulled through the gateless drive and Alex said, "Are you sure you want to go sailing?"

I'd been asking myself the same question. Tristen's picture had landed on the doorstep of close to fifteen thousand homes this morning. By now, there'd probably been twenty or thirty calls to the police about the photo. Two-thirds of them would be crackpots, and the other third would be people who mistook the weird-kid-who-lived-down-the-hall for Tristen Grayer. None of these would pan out. Tristen Grayer was too smart, too methodical, and too damn spontaneous.

Tristen didn't leave clues at the scene, and if he did they were meant to be found. He was in total control. So that was my rationale in going sailing. "Yes."

We passed a Dunkin' Donuts and Alex ran in. She came out with two coffees and two papers. Alex tossed one on my lap, my eyes immediately training on Tristen Grayer's vivid tangerine oculus. It was like staring into the face of a lion.

That's what he was. He wasn't a demon, he was a lion. Tristen was the ghost in the darkness. Slinking off at night from his remote lair and picking off the group till it no longer existed.

I looked up at Alex and she said, "He looks like a lion."

~

We hit the kite shop in Portland, and by noon we were parked in the Bayside Harbor loading lot. Alex hauled the cooler out of the trunk and I picked up the kite. In hindsight, I think Alex may have expected me to relieve her of cooler duty which is confusing because she'd picked the cooler up of her own accord.

She hoisted the cooler up with a grunt and said, "You really know the way to a woman's heart."

Each time Alex set down the cooler she gave me a look as to say, "You've got to be kidding me." When she set it down for the fifth and final time, about twenty feet from the boat, I said, "Here let me get that for you. That looks a little heavy for such a pretty lady." I didn't want to blow my chances for a little skinny-dipping completely.

I knelt down to pick up the cooler, but Alex slapped my hand away. She ambled off grunting obscenities as I scanned the premises for Kellon. There were only a couple little guys milling around the pier, none of which was Kellon. I walked up the small wooden walkway to the dock manager hut and opened the door. Kellon's dad was on the phone, and from his silence and the disgruntled look on his face I suspected he was on hold. Kellon's dad fell somewhere in between the terms Big and Obese. He was balding and sunburned to boot, making his head appear vaguely similar to a hairy Italian in a red tank top. I waved the kite near his peripheral and said, "Is Kellon here?"

He shook his head and stared at the phone jack on the wall as if it were the man's face who'd put him on hold. I wonder if I were getting more attention than Kellon would if he was on the ground having a seizure. I said, "If you see him, tell him Captain Dipshit has something for him."

I turned and stepped through the open door.

From behind me the beast murmured, "If I see her. Kellon is a girl."

Chapter 32

I did a U-turn in the door frame, "What do you mean Kellon is a girl?"

Kellon's dad didn't answer me, so I pulled the phone base from the wall and threw it over his head.

He didn't look pleased and screamed, "What in the hell?"

I prodded, "Kellon is a girl? Are you sure?"

He was silent for a second. Thinking. Can you believe that? Two plus two is four, oil and vinegar don't mix, and your offspring either has a penis or a vagina.

Finally, he said, "Yeah, Kellon's a girl."

Highly doubtful. He probably flipped a coin at the custody hearing. I asked, "Where is she?"

He glared at me. "You owe me a fucking phone."

"I'm gonna owe you a hefty dental bill if you don't tell me where Kellon is." I think he thought I was serious because I'd pulled him over the desk by his shirt collar.

He stammered, "She's with her mother this weekend."

Thank God. "Are you positive?"

"Of course."

I let go of his Bayside Harbor tee and said, "Thank you. The next time you see her, tell her Captain Dipshit has something for her."

I took sixty bucks from my pocket and left it on the desk. "Forty is for the phone and twenty is for Kellon for docking my boat last weekend." I gave him a look that I hope conveyed, *Try me, motherfucker. I've got a lot of steam bottled up and beating the piss out of a deadbeat dad might just be the remedy I've been looking for.*

Walking out of the hut, I had a strong premonition Kellon would not only see the twenty bucks, she might even get a hug out of the old man.

~

As I made my way to the *Backstern*, I surveyed Alex untying the boat and imagined she'd been similar to Kellon as a child. Penis envy was big at four and five. It was at about the age of ten that girls thanked the Lord they didn't have to walk around with a Twinkie in their undies.

I thought about how scared I'd been when I'd heard her dad utter the words "You mean her. Kellon is a girl." They echoed through my head, a refrain slightly audible behind Tristen's chorus: *Listen I'd love to chat, but I have a date with a beautiful young lady.*

I was grateful Kellon was at her mother's this weekend. Kellon once told me that her mom lived in Kittwery. How in the hell had the mother not gotten custody of the child? I'd seen the mother once during the summer and while she wasn't Princess Di, she didn't seem like Queen-crack-head either.

Alex threw the mooring lines onto the boat and said, "Off we go. Why do you still have the kite?"

"She wasn't around."

I saw the word "she" hit her eardrum and blow up like a shotgun shell. Alex's eyes widened like there were two invisible fingers holding them open. I beat her to the punch, "Yeah, Kellon's a little girl not a little boy. I freaked too, but she's at her mom's this weekend."

Her eyes said, "Whew," and she hopped aboard the boat.

We disembarked and I retired to the captain's chair with Mick and Lob. The three of us studied the ease with which Alex walked about the boat as only one could who'd grown up on the water. She immediately caught us a breeze, a breeze I hadn't felt until my brain told my body there must be one if we were moving. I'd say ten knots south by southeast.

I sank my hand into the cooler and handed a beer to Alex. She swigged in silence and did a couple minor adjustments on something called a jib. I inquired as to when the poop deck came into play and was rewarded with an eye roll so violent you'd have thought Alex counted her lashes. When we had eclipsed the harbor she finally sat down and said, "Perfect day for sailing."

It was perfect. There wasn't a cloud in the sky or a chop in the water. We sipped our beers and chatted, and every so often she would get up to correct the sails or jimmy this or jimmy that, all the while spatting all sorts of sailing jargon. In hindsight, I should have forgone Hieroglyphics in high school and opted for Sailish.

We traded war stories from the high seas, hers having mostly to do with inclement weather, mine, inclement brain activity. She thought I made up the part about the *Maine Catch*, and I told her I could prove it. But I couldn't prove it and melted into my boating-under-the-influence parable, my personal favorite.

She smacked her leg and said, "What'd you do while the kid sailed the boat back?"

What a stupid question. "I drank."

She put her beer out and the two of us toasted the high seas. We ate some sandwiches we'd picked up from a deli near the kite store, and Alex cut the sails which I learned does not involve scissors. So that's where I went wrong. With me it was like *Amelia Bedelia Goes Sailing*.

I went to check my cell phone, and the next thing I heard was a splash. I glanced up and saw the majority—nope, make that all—of Alex's clothes lying on the boat deck.

Gulp.

I walked to the edge of the boat and peered down. Alex was treading water and I could see the tops of her buoys. She waved for me to come in and I think I saw one of her nipples.

I love sailing.

Chapter 33

I did a spot check. The only boat close enough to see us would have needed binoculars and appeared to be heading in the opposite direction. I unbuttoned my shirt. Slowly. Pulled my shorts down. Again slowly. That one nipple had awakened Paddington Bare and I didn't want my paddle out when I jumped in the water. I turned so my butt was facing Alex and pulled my boxer briefs off. Technically, I could have faced front, but my mother always told me not to point. If the pirate critters onboard needed someone to walk the plank, I was their man.

I heard Alex whistle and decided my best option was to jump off the opposite side of the boat and swim around. Selective genius, what did I tell you? I dove into the water and swam around the boat until Alex came into view. The two of us swam about thirty or so yards from the boat, coming to rest roughly a wave from each other. She spit a stream of water in my direction and said, "I didn't see any scarring from the maxi pad flaps."

I smiled and said, "Can we talk about sharks instead?"

She laughed then submerged her head under water. I was under the erroneous impression she was going to play shark and I was to play harpoon. She popped up and said, "I can't believe you dove in naked."

"I didn't want you to feel awkward skinny-dipping alone."

Alex pulled two straps up and secured them over her shoulders. The treacherous devil had a swimsuit on. She said, "That's for making me carry the cooler you asshole."

I stopped treading water and let gravity do its thing. It was cold, really cold. And, come to think of it, I not only no longer had a stiff paddle, I couldn't locate my paddle at all. An old Seinfeld episode breached the surface of my brain. *Elaine: It shrinks? Jerry: Like a frightened turtle.*

I kicked my legs together and felt my head break the surface. I blinked the water from my eyes and assume I blinked some onto Alex seeing as she was only inches from me. Neither of us said a word, both of us bobbing up and down with the current. A wave slightly bigger than all his relatives carried Alex's small body the last six inches to mine. I felt her warm body touch mine, then her legs wrap around my back. Whatever was left of the turtle poked its head out, but I'd be surprised if Alex felt a stir.

Alex wrapped her hands around my head and I wrapped one arm around her small waist. Alex leaned over my shoulder and nibbled my earlobe then she proceeded to burst my eardrum with a bloodcurdling scream. Her legs and arms came undone and I peered over my shoulder.

"Leave dah screwing to dah whales."

I looked up and saw seven men standing on the bridge of a ship wearing coveralls and toothy grins. I spit a mouthful of water, "You guys have the best timing. First, when I'm lost at sea. And then when I'm saving this woman from drowning."

They all let out a roar and one of them said, "Yehah. I saved dah girl from drownin just lahst nawght." They all bellowed and slowly retreated to the cabin.

The lone man winked and said, "You come on down to dah bah and buy dah boys a cuppleha beahs, they'll keep to demselves about dah size of yer hook der."

The boat roared to life and I scanned the water for Alex. Her head popped up ten yards to my left. She whispered, "Who were they?"

"Those were my friends I was telling you about."

She squinted and I could see she was trying to read the name of the boat off the side. She said, "Catch." Her eyes widened, "So you were telling the truth."

I nodded.

The *Maine Catch* was now close to three football fields away and Alex had steadily trod closer to me. We looked at each other clumsily. I decided to take one for the gipper and did a half breast-stroke, half running man thing, until I was arms distance from her.

She gaped at me and I thought I might have a boog dangling. I wiped my nose, but the expression on her face remained immutable. Maybe she'd seen my turtle and wanted to know where the rest of him went.

I asked, "What?"

"Baxter's on the boat."

I shot a glance over my shoulder at the lime green lettering bobbing in the current. I laughed, "It's *Backstern*. Like back and stern. It's a pun on my sister's pug, Baxt—"

She nodded. "Yeah, I know—Baxter—is on the boat."

I turned and saw Baxter asleep in the captain's chair. If Baxter was on the boat, then Tristen Grayer had been on the boat.

Oh dear God.

~

How could I be so stupid? And I was supposed to be a detective? Maybe it wasn't Baxter. Maybe someone else's pug from the harbor had slipped into the boat. Nope, the pug in question was asleep at the helm. Definitely Baxter.

This did not guarantee that a woman of the deceased variety was stuffed somewhere in the boat, but it didn't bode well. I put my head down and swam hard to the *Backstern*, then clambered up the schooner's water ladder. It's peculiar how you don't really care that your pecker could fit inside a beer bottle when there is, in all likelihood, a dead woman stashed somewhere on your boat. I slipped on my shorts and edged my way to the top of the cabin stairs.

There were six small stairs leading to a narrow galley. My heart was crashing against my ribs, and it felt like each beat might be its last. I took five or six calming breaths before sauntering down the steep steps. The air was stale and musty, and since I'd never been down in the galley before, I couldn't tell you if this was bizarre. I found a small light and it flickered twice before illuminating the six foot by eight foot cabin. There were no body parts strewn about and my heart beat slowed down to the two hundreds.

Had Baxter somehow found his way to the boat? I mean, I was always hearing these fantastic stories of dogs finding their way home. But Baxter hadn't been awake longer than sixteen or seventeen continuous minutes. His life was a series of comedy shorts. How in the hell would he ever navigate to the Bayside Harbor and slot 23B?

I sat to ponder the impasse and heard a hollow thud echo from the cushion below. I stood and surveyed the long green cushion. It appeared to lift for storage. I had the ephemeral thought not to lift the cushion. I didn't know if I could stomach any more death. I edged my fingers under the padding and delicately pried up the cushion.

Kellon was not at her mother's.

Chapter 34

Kellon's body was in shambles. Her face looked like it had been dropped from a ten story building and her short hair clumped together in the places where the skull was still intact.

I dropped the lid and ran up the galley stairs, dragging myself to the edge of the boat. I was choking on my own breath, my own life. A coursing dry heave caused every infinite muscle strand in my body to pulsate, and it felt like my spine was going to snap in thirds. After a stream of near epileptic fits, I crumbled to the boat deck. Why? Why was Kellon dead? How could I let this happen? Didn't I say that each kill would be bigger, bloodier, and closer than the last? Hadn't I known this would happen?

I looked up and saw Alex staring at me in studded silence. I read her thoughts: "What horror could possibly cause a grown man to behave in such a way?"

Well, that was me holding back, babe. What I really wanted to do was jump overboard and dry heave at the bottom of the Atlantic, suck in one lung full of water and turn off the lights. Forever. Kellon and I would go fly a kite.

Alex had tears in her eyes and she couldn't stop shaking her head. She said, "Tell me it isn't her. Lie to me. Tell me it isn't. Tell me there's isn't a little girl down there slaughtered."

I wish someone else had found her and I could be the one lied to. Alex was an investigative journalist, she needed to know the truth, good, bad, or ugly. I nodded, "It's her."

She turned her back and went to fiddle with one of the sails. Her charade ended as soon as it began. Alex tucked her head in her hands and glued them together with an unrelenting stream of tears. I urged myself up and walked to her. As I enveloped Alex in my arms, she buried her face in my chest. She'd never laid an eye on Kellon, never seen her big brown eyes, never heard her lisp, yet Alex was broken.

She looked up, her Popsicle green eyes melting in the heat, and I said, "Kellon is dead, there's nothing we can do about that now. I need you to be strong, I need you to get us back to shore as quickly as possible."

She wiped her eyes and nodded.

~

I found my cell phone and punched Caitlin's number. She picked up on the second ring and I said, "Bad news. I found her on my boat five minutes ago."

The line went dead for ten seconds and I checked to see if I still had a connection. Caitlin finally shot back, "Who is she?"

"I'll tell you when you get here."

"Where are you?"

I covered the phone and asked Alex, "What's our ETA?"

She looked out to sea, puffed her cheeks, and said, "Forty minutes. Fifty, tops."

I told Caitlin and she replied, "I'd better call Gleason before their flight leaves."

"When you get to the harbor, don't say anything to anyone. I don't want a circus awaiting our arrival."

I hung up and put the phone in my pocket, then faced toward the galley stairs. I took the six steps to Hades, took a deep breath, and lifted the bench. The stench of death washed over me like a wave from the Atlantic. The dampness of the boat expedited the breakdown process and the body smelled twelve hours worse than it looked. What I'd really come down here for was to see about Kellon's eyes. I needed to know if her big, brown, puppy dog eyes were resting peacefully in their sockets.

I used the blunt end of a screwdriver to gently push Kellon's head to the side. Her skull was soft and I had to apply more pressure than I wanted to, but the skull finally lulled to the left. Kellon's eye sockets were vacant. I wasn't surprised. Come to think of it, I would have been surprised if her eyes had been present. I checked every nook and cranny in the small cabin and didn't stumble on Kellon's chocolate fudge brownies.

There was a small window, with the shade slid shut, like the kind on an airplane, and I approached it. I slowly slid the shade open, but no dice, snake eyes that is. Maybe Tristen had reverted back to his earlier pattern of taking the eyes as souvenirs.

I spent another twenty minutes fussing over the scene before retreating into the sunlight. We were closing in on land and I guessed we had less than ten minutes before we entered the Bayside Harbor. I surveyed Alex. She seemed in total control, the antithesis of the person I'd seen thirty minutes prior.

I scanned the deck for my shirt, but couldn't locate it anywhere. I tried to think back to what I'd been wearing. A tan polo, right? I'd thrown it haphazardly when I'd undressed. Alex's nipple had sort of short-circuited my hard drive. On my third canvass of the boat, I spotted the sleeve of the tan polo at the very back of the boat. Sorry, starboard. I rescued the shirt from its brush with death and slipped it over my head. There were two fishing poles rigged to the back of the schooner that had come with the boat (I'd yet to touch either one), and I couldn't help noticing both had their lines out.

I slipped one of the poles from its mooring and hoisted it up. The pole was heavier than I was used to, and the fishing line was thicker than the kind I used with my dad on the Puget Sound. I slowly began reeling in the line. After a good thirty seconds I saw a ripple where the line fed into the Atlantic. I reeled in the last twenty yards and saw I'd caught a tiny fish. On closer observation, it appeared to be a baby octopus or squid.

I held the pole with my left hand and grabbed my catch with my right. It was one of Kellon's eyes.

Chapter 35

The hook had been pushed through the pupil and into the meat of the eye. I wasn't sure if I should pull the eye off the hook or if I should throw the eye, along with the line and pole, into the watery waste. I broke the hook off the line and walked the eye over to the cooler. There were three beers left and I slipped them out, setting the eye atop the ice. Two of the beers fell over on their side, Alex striding over to pick them up. She handed me one of the beers, her gaze passing over the cooler.

She popped the top of her beer and asked sedately, "Where were they?"

"The son of a bitch baited the two fishing poles at the back of the boat and tossed them out to sea." Speaking of "them," I should probably go reel in the other one.

Alex nodded solemnly like this was practical, even routine, and said, "What's the deal with the eyes?"

"I've been racking my brain and I don't have the slightest clue."

This seemed to appease her and she went back to work on the sails. The next five minutes were spent reeling in the second line. If anyone was watching me they would have thought I was having a grand old time, doing some fishing, swigging on a beer, living the good life. Nope, buddy, I'm reeling in the eye of a seven-year-old girl I just found in my galley.

Salúd.

I had the ripple within about ten yards when a five-foot sailfish decided to have Kellon's eye for lunch. I heard a barrage of whistling and screaming, and noticed two passing boats on their way out to sea. There were about ten people leaning over their respective railings screaming the likes of, "Give 'em hell," and, "Kick his ass."

I leaned back, heard the distinct snap of fishing line breaking, and toppled backward landing on my ass. There was a collective, "Ahhhhh," from my spectators and one gentlemen yelled, "Can't win 'em all!"

I tossed the pole in the ocean absentmindedly and readied myself for the onslaught of Feds, forensics, and father. Kellon's that was.

~

As we neared Bayside Harbor, I had to rub my eyes once. I thought I'd seen Kellon's small frame amongst the larger bodies, but it was, in actuality, Todd Gregory. He was standing next to Caitlin, only she was a head taller than him. I closed one eye and squashed him between my thumb and forefinger. *Squish, squish, squish.*

Do I deal with death efficiently or what?

We entered the marina and I made out Kellon's deadbeat dad amid the burgeoning throng. I wanted to despise the man, but couldn't muster the strength. He'd just lost a daughter, and I would be the one to tell him. Hey, if the world didn't suck, we'd all fall off.

They'd cordoned off a slip for the boat and Alex eased us in. I threw the mooring lines to Gleason and he fastened the ropes to the dock. Gleason uprighted and said, "Nice boat."

"Thanks. Want to buy it? I'll give you the Fed discount."

He threw a half smile he does sometimes but said nothing. There were about ten people that looked ready to storm the boat the second we departed the premises. Alex had Baxter in her arms and Gleason helped her over the small gap between the boat and the dock. As she passed Caitlin, they traded looks like each had suspicions the other let go a silent stinker.

Caitlin grabbed my shirtsleeve but I ignored her and continued on to Kellon's father. I strode toward him and he gave me the once over. He cleared his throat and said, "People talking like there's a dead feller on your boat."

I guided him to his office and informed him about his daughter. He didn't believe me at first and called his wife. I only heard his side of the conversation, but it was evident Kellon was not supposed to be with her mother this weekend. He broke down and I told him how sorry I was, then left before I lost it. I found my cell phone and dialed Lacy. Her excitement at Baxter being alive and Kellon being dead, averaged out to mildly upset.

Speaking of Baxter, Alex was standing forlornly at the top of the pier with the squirming pug. I walked over to her and she asked, "How bad was it?"

I assumed she was referring to my interlude with Kellon's father. "On a scale from one to a ten? Five hundred, forty-eight thousand, six hundred, and forty-two."

I found my keys in my front pocket and handed them to her. "Take my car. I'll be here for a while and catch a ride with Caitlin."

She nodded. At her taking my car or my riding with Caitlin, I wasn't sure, she didn't specify. I wasn't certain what the right parting words were in this situation, but from the expression on Alex's face, "I saw your nipple" were not them.

Chapter 36

The Range Rover disappeared in a cloud of dust and I turned my attention to the schooner. There was only one person on the deck of the *Backstern*, which by default put nine people in the already cramped cabin. Caitlin and Conner emerged as I ambled onto the deck.

Caitlin said earnestly, "Horrific. Who was she?"

"Kellon Atkins. She was my pal."

A voice from behind Conner spat, "Why didn't you mention her name when we were making our list of possible victims?"

Gregory had slipped up the stairs without my notice. I faced him and said, "Hey, Frodo Baggins, I didn't see you down there. If you must know, I didn't mention her because I like little girl jigsaw puzzles. It's kind of a hobby of mine."

He glared at me. "How is it you're always the one who stumbles on these girls' bodies?"

I looked at Caitlin, then Conner, and finally back to Gregory. I was speechless. When my capacity to speak came back, I said, "I hope you're not suggesting what I think you are."

Gleason came up the stairs and Gregory said to him, "I was just telling Thomas about our little theory."

Someone smashed their fist into the bridge of Gregory's nose and he fell to the ground. I looked at Conner and said, "I can't believe you hit him."

He smirked, "You hit him."

Did I?

Blood was dripping from Gregory's nose and he screamed, "You broke my nose, you son of a bitch! I'm gonna sue your ass, Prescott."

I offered my solution, "How 'bout I just give you this boat and we call it even." Gleason helped Todd to his feet and I leaned into him, "If you ever so much as mention me in that context again, it will be your neck next time. Capiche?"

Caitlin edged herself between the two of us and said, "Tell us what happened." I recounted the events in 70% truth. I left out the part about Alex and my skinny-dipping—make that just my skinny-dipping—alleging that Baxter appeared from below deck while we'd been sailing. And I left out the part about the sailfish. They followed me over to the cooler in the far back corner and I showed them Kellon's eye.

Conner asked, "Where's the other one?"

"I have no idea." I lied.

~

Conner dropped me off at Alex's around nine. We hadn't had much for small talk the duration of the ride. I think my screwing over his sister, both literally and figuratively, and Lacy dumping him had negatively impacted our relationship.

I opened the door to his Camaro and he asked, "Are you going to be at the meeting tomorrow?"

"Probably not. I think I need to find a lawyer before I'm in the same room with the Toddler."

He nodded and said, "Well, if you want the run down, give me a call."

I nodded, slammed the car door, and watched as he peeled from the drive. I found the eight young bucks nestled in the living room. They were each wearing a different, yet similar expression. Let's see here: Kim was flashing despair, Holly was donning anguish, Ali was clad in gloom, Tall Tim was sporting melancholy, Fat Tim was up to his ears in dreary, Blake was modeling woe, Caleb was showing affliction, and Lacy was displaying morose. Speaking of Ms. Morose, she was sitting on the ground between Caleb's legs, Baxter prancing over hers like he was in the steeplechase.

Caleb shook his head, "I can't believe this shit. What do we do now, professor?"

"The next hot date isn't for another five days. I want you guys to stay alert, but it appears Tristen is only striking on the hot dates."

Kim Welding asked, "Can we do anything to help?"

"Right now, I'm not sure there's anything we can do."

I retreated into the kitchen. Alex was slurping up the last bites of the Froot Loop primordial soup and I asked, "Mind if I have a bowl?"

She slurped down the last bite of her cereal. "Yes."

"Well, I'm having one anyway."

"Suit yourself." Wow, Déjà vu. I grabbed a bowl, a spoon, and the milk, and joined her at the small table.

I picked up the box of Froot Loops. Empty. I couldn't help but notice Alex now had a heaping bowl of cereal. She smiled and said, "There's more in the cabinet."

I walked to the cabinet and opened it. Cha-ching. House Mom had evidently gone grocery shopping. There were seven different boxes of cereal, including an unopened box of Lucky Charms. I poured the cereal and asked Alex, "What are the odds I find an article about this in the *Waterville Tribune* tomorrow?"

She picked a green Froot Loop from her bowl and held it up.

Chapter 37

Today was October 7th, which meant today was Jennifer Pepper's funeral in New York. The service started at 1:30 p.m. which meant I was running late. Is it possible to be running early? If so, I'd never experienced the phenomenon. Lacy was snuggled up with Caleb and Baxter on the floor under a down comforter and I shook her lightly. I said, "Up and at 'em. We have to be dressed and on the road in half an hour."

Lacy said groggily, "All my stuff is at Caleb's." Lacy was roughly the same size as Alex, give or take a cup size. "I'll see if Alex has something black you can wear. But you need to hop in the shower."

I led her to the shower in the guest bedroom and walked across the hall to Alex's room. I knocked on the door and Alex yelled, "Come in!"

Alex was fastening the top button of a turquoise blouse, and said, "Well, now he comes knocking." She looked at her watch, "We're going to have to make this fast though, I need to be somewhere at nine." She unfastened the top button on her blouse and started in on the second.

She appeared serious and I said, "I'll have to take a rain check."

She pouted dramatically and I rebuked, "Sorry, I have a funeral that takes precedence over whoopee." Her mouth straightened. The word "funeral" is in the same boat as black plague, gingivitis, dungeons & dragons, and genital warts. They all seem to drain the romance from a situation.

I said, "Lacy's stuff is at Caleb's and we're running a little behind schedule. Do you have anything Lacy can borrow?"

She nodded and went to her closet. She came back with a decent length black skirt and a black blouse. I asked, "Where is it you have to be at 9:00?"

"I have a meeting with my publisher to see about a sequel to *Eight in October.*"

Grand, another book I would have to buy five friggin' times. "What are you going to call it, *Encore in October*?"

She cocked her head sideways and grinned.

~

Lacy and I settled into the car at nine-ish. We stopped at a Dunkin' Donuts on the way out of town and I picked up two large coffees, five donuts, and one *Waterville Press.*

Waterville Press? What ever happened to *Waterville Tribune*?

Under the new title was a letter from the editor:

The *Waterville Tribune* has undergone a name change. The *Waterville Press* promises to deliver the same caliber of undiluted coverage you've come to expect from the *Waterville Tribune.*

—Editor in Chief, Alex Tooms

That sneaky, conniving wench.

Under this was the headline: *Hero Catches Eye of Local Girl.*

My hands were trembling, and I was forced to read the article on my lap. Thankfully, Alex didn't describe the particulars of Kellon's mutilated corpse, and I recalled that she'd never ventured down to the galley.

I was rolling up the paper when I noticed after the *Press* in *Waterville Press* were four tiny letters, c-o-t-t. Unbelievable, Alex had renamed the paper the *Waterville Press-cott.*

I was contemplating doing Tristen Grayer a favor and killing Alex Tooms myself.

~

Jennifer's funeral was a nice service, and we made our journey full circle by 10:00 p.m. later that evening, both of us deciding to crash at Caleb's. I didn't trust myself around Alex. Although, whether it was my sleeping with her or killing her was a bit fuzzy.

I still couldn't believe what she'd done, but I guess when you own a paper you have a lot of leeway. Alex truly was the Queen Bee. With one hell of a stinger. I called Conner at 11:00 and he gave me the rundown on the meeting that afternoon. The new task force was stumped. I wasn't and had never been a suspect. The eye was in fact Kellon's. And Todd's nose now slightly bent to the left.

I wasn't sure if I was glad or disappointed they were stumped. God knows I was stumped. We needed a break other than Todd's delicate little nose.

~

Caleb, Lacy, and I ordered Chinese and played a couple games of gin rummy. Lacy and Caleb beat me twice before retiring to the living room to watch a movie. Yours truly, on the other hand, went for a night jog and scrutinized each crime scene in my head. At mile five it hit me: the eyes. It came down to the eyes. I wasn't sure in what context or why, but I was sure the eyes meant something. Perhaps Tristen would be nice enough to detail it for me the next time we bumped into each other. Speaking of which, that was the exact reason I was jogging at 12:30 a.m. on a Sunday night.

Nothing out of the ordinary happened on my run, and I was drinking water straight from Caleb's faucet a little after 1:00. Caleb and Lacy had retired to the bedroom to watch a little Discovery Channel or, more likely, to play a little Discovery Channel. I thought about the word "channel" and I ran out to my car and grabbed the walkie-talkie.

I flipped the channel back to nine and said, "I know you can hear me, you piece of shit. I was going to bring you down and let the justice system punish you, but now I've decided to kill you. I'm going to strangle you with your own guts. Sweet dreams."

Chapter 38

I slept next to the walkie-talkie, half expecting it to crackle sometime throughout the night, but either Tristen hadn't heard my message or he didn't want to play my game. More likely, the latter. This was his game. And we would play by his rules.

Lacy made breakfast for the three of us and I asked what her plans were for the day. She turned from the skillet and said, "I was going to finish a couple last minute things at the gallery, but Ashley's funeral is at noon, after which I plan on getting extremely wasted. I recommend you do the same."

I'd totally spaced Ashley's funeral. Back-to-back Christmas parties are fun. Back-to-back funerals, not so much. Well, if there was a silver lining it was that I hadn't spilled anything on my suit at Jennifer's wake.

~

Caleb, Lacy, and I walked up the path, through the Franklin Cemetery gates, and found a crowd of close to a hundred gathered around where Ashley was to be buried. I could make out the majority of the students in my class, in addition to Ashley's family.

It wasn't difficult to spot her mother, her resemblance to Ashley was uncanny. As the three of us joined the back of the group, the priest began his spiel, and I was glad I wouldn't have to fumble through the oddities of funeral banter with any of my students.

The priest gave an angelic ceremony, and I felt Lacy squeeze my hand in its finality. I forgot a handkerchief and was forced to wipe my eyes with the cuff of my jacket. I don't cry when I'm sad, I cry when I'm angry. Angry tears don't dribble off your cheek. They're absorbed, as if you can't part with that anger, you need that anger to go on, to live. I was so angry. Angry with Tristen Grayer for Ashley's death. Angry with Ashley for letting herself become Tristen's prey. But predominantly, I was angry with myself for letting her death happen. Ashley had been killed in the storming of my castle. She was a chambermaid within my walls and I hadn't been able to protect her.

Ashley's mother was walking up to the podium to render the eulogy, and I was losing it exponentially. I could almost hear the dam splintering in my brain. I slid my hand from Lacy's, retreated a couple steps backward through the grass, and walked away from the procession. I made it about a hundred or so yards over a small hill before the dam burst. A high school friend lost to a car accident, my parents' funeral, every snapshot I'd taken as a homicide detective, the eight women's mutilated corpses from a year ago, Jennifer, Ashley, Kellon; each of these memories poured from my tear ducts and played over my eyes before trickling to the ground.

I found a stick on the ground and broke it in half until it would no longer break. I'd only heard a neck break once, but it sounded almost identical to that of a twig snapping in half. Anyway, with your eyes closed, you get the idea. So after breaking Tristen Grayer's neck six or seven times, I felt remarkably pacified.

I walked the grounds for about ten minutes. There were a couple old people visiting their friends at the big buffet line in the sky but apart from them I didn't encounter anyone else. I made my way back to the procession and noticed the group was forming a line in which to put a rose, or other tokens of expression atop the casket. I noticed at the midpoint of the line, in a black pantsuit, was Alex Tooms.

What was she doing here? Did she know Ashley? Of course she didn't. Was she here just to see me?

I fell in at the back of the line and mentally traded Alex for Ashley. This was her time. I concentrated on how much I'd enjoyed the short time I'd known her, how much she'd made me laugh, and how much she'd tempted me to break the time-honored code. I thought back to a night at a bar about a month ago when she'd said she'd do "Anything for an A. *Anything*."

I reached into my pocket and removed a small piece of paper about an inch wide and six inches long. It was the piece of paper I gave kids at the end of the semester with their final grade. I'd written a short passage on it and circled her grade, 89.1%, an "A" in my book.

I put the folded sheet in with all the flowers, gave my condolences to Ashley's parents, and walked to where Caleb, Lacy, and most of my class were huddled. I scanned the grounds for Alex, but didn't come across the jade-eyed jaded journalist. The conversation turned to which bar we should take the festivities to. Caleb made an executive decision, The Pale Norseman Pub, and the scrum slowly started to move toward the cemetery gates.

As we neared the entrance, I spied Alex in my peripherals. How could this woman be so selfish? First with the articles, then coming here? I knew goldfish who were less self-serving. She sidestepped me as I eclipsed the gate and said, "You haven't returned any of my calls."

I ignored her question and said, "What are you doing here? I thought you only wrote the Tristen Grayer High Praise column. I didn't know you did obituaries too."

She looked like I punched her in the stomach. I cut her off before she could reply, "Don't call me anymore."

I thought I saw a tear form in her eye, but turned before I could be sure.

Chapter 39

Here's the million dollar question. Make that plural, million dollar *questions*; Who threw me down a flight of stairs? Why was I in the fetal position in a bathtub? And finally, and most consequential, why was I naked?

I pushed myself up and sent a blinding pain searing through my skull. It felt like my temples were playing Pong with my brain. I peeked over the rim of the bathtub basin and saw my pants atop a pile of puke drenched clothing. All right, so I'd found my clothes. Now where was I? Caleb's? One of my buddies from the *Maine Catch*?

I stood up shakily, and surveyed the bathtub and shower, again shakily. I had a strange sense of déjà vu, but since I'd never woken up naked, in a bathtub, in the fetal position before, I didn't know when, or where, to attribute the feeling.

There was a pink loofa hung around the shower spigot, and I crossed off the crew of the *Maine Catch*. I didn't cross off Caleb; my sister had a pink loofa and may have relocated it. I picked up a bottle of liquid body soap and turned it over in my hand. A haunting memory filled the infinitesimal area of my brain functioning at the moment; *I was squeaky clean, a silver lining to Caitlin's and my Lever 2000 enhanced copulation.*

Blimey.

I was at Caitlin's.

How in the hell did I end up here? I could have slept on the beach, on a park bench, or in a jail cell, anywhere but with the woman I'd just screwed under then screwed over.

My first priority was Tylenol. I couldn't defuse this time bomb until I defused this hangover. I stepped out of the tub and walked to Caitlin's medicine cabinet, extracting a bottle of Tylenol. After pouring the last of the capsules down my throat, somewhere between one and eleven, I tossed the bottle in the small wastebasket next to the toilet.

Back up, *beep, beep, beep*. Clear the etch-a-sketch, *shake, shake, shake.* We have a new million dollar question: What is worse than waking up naked in your ex's bathtub with a blinding hangover and your new suit caked in throw up?

The answer of course is: *Finding the packaging box from a home pregnancy kit sitting atop your ex's bathroom trashcan.*

I picked up the tiny blue trashcan and rifled through the contents for the actual pregnancy test. I tried to get mentally prepared. Blue is good, Red is bad; - is good, + is bad; Da is good, Da-da is bad.

Luckily, the pregnancy test was MIA. I'm not sure what I would have done if I'd stumbled on it and it'd been positive. It isn't that fatherhood scared me, because it didn't. Marrying Caitlin, on the other hand, scared the little green dog turds out of me. Don't get me wrong, I'm a stand-up guy. If one of my regiment somehow infiltrated Fort Dodds, then I would stand by her. I mean, there was a 90% chance I would stand by her, and only a 10% chance I'd send her a check once a month. No, it was more like a 70% chance Caitlin and I would get married, and only a 30% chance I would change my name and move to the depths of the Amazon.

The more I think about it, dime, we need a dime over here.

~

I put the trash back how I'd found it, placed the empty Tylenol bottle back in the cabinet, and picked my puke-drenched suit off the bathroom floor. I opened the door to the bathroom and peeked out. No sign of Caitlin. Caitlin's dresser was positioned against the far wall, and after a minute I found a pair of my boxers, a shirt of mine, and an old pair of sweat pants.

I looked at the clock, saw it was almost 10:00 a.m, and dialed Lacy on my cell. I started with, "Mind telling me what happened last night?"

She laughed, "You said you were walking down to have a beer with your *Maine Catch* pals and disappeared."

This jarred a vague recollection of taking a boilermaker with six bearded men, although this may have just been a recessed memory from Lumberjack Camp. After a bit of cajoling, I was able to persuade Lacy to call Caitlin and fish out her present location.

Lacy called back a minute later and said, "Caitlin said, quote, 'I'm pulling up to my house right this second to check on your bastard of a brother.'"

I hung up on her and went to the bedroom window, corroborating Lacy's statement. Caitlin was opening the door of her Pathfinder as we spoke. I grabbed my damp suit and ran out of Caitlin's bedroom and into the hall. Her key went into the lock as I skipped past the front door and slipped behind one of the large drapes in her living room. My only chance was if she went directly to her bedroom to check on me as I suspected she would. The door opened and Caitlin yelled at the top of her lungs, "Thomas! Are you alive, you jerk?"

I let ten seconds pass, then slipped out Caitlin's front door for the last time. After two blocks I stopped running, retrieving my ringing cell from my pant pocket. Let's just say I wasn't shocked when I saw Caitlin's number on the caller ID. I clicked my voice mail on and saw I had four other missed calls: two from Caitlin, two from Alex. Two from a woman who was a coin flip away from wearing my last name the rest of her life, and two from a woman who pissed me off and turned me on more than *Chicago* had.

~

It was a two mile jog from Caitlin's cookie-cutter to the High Tide Tavern, and when I opened the door to my car, I was feeling like a champ. Well, a champ who had been dethroned the night before, but a champ nevertheless.

Back on the road, I whipped out my cell phone and dialed Caleb. I told him to get the gang together and meet me at my house by 6:00 p.m. I wasn't taking any chances. The next two nights would be spent behind the castle walls, and nobody, not Tristen Grayer, the Grim Reaper, or fucking William Wallace himself, would be able to storm the gates.

Chapter 40

Caleb and the gang showed up at 6:00, each with their respective overnight and sleeping bags. Noticeably missing was Kim Welding and I asked Caleb about her absence.

He said, "She has a midterm tomorrow. She said she was going to study in the library until like 9:00 and then shoot over. I told her we'd call her every hour."

If it'd been a day later and this had been the case, I would have called her teacher and had him postpone her midterm. But since the hot date was still more than thirty-six hours away, I let it slide. Holly and Ali started preparing dinner at 8:30. Fat Tim, Tall Tim, and Blake retired to the living room to watch the Mariner's playoff with Lacy. And Caleb and I busied ourselves putting the finishing touches on Lacy's new room.

In the last forty-eight hours the room had been recarpeted and painted to Lacy's specifications which I regret to inform you were yellow, yellow, and more yellow. Actually the carpet was closer to Taupe, but the refraction off the Bright Canary walls gave it a yellow cast. The room smelled of fresh paint, but the walls were dry to the touch.

Caleb and I spent the next twenty minutes hanging Lacy's many paintings, picture frames, posters, and wall mirror, identically to how she'd left it when her lights had gone out. The police had removed Lacy's bed as evidence, and the Big Bird walls seemed miles from one another. Seeing as I was yet to sleep a night in my bedroom, Caleb assisted me in moving the queen-sized bed into Lacy's room.

In the final stages of dressing the bed, I asked Caleb, "When's the last time you talked to Kim?"

"Forty minutes ago."

"What's her ETA?"

"9:00, no later than 10:00. She has a midterm in Forensic Psych tomorrow. The teacher, Jameson, is a crackpot. Hundred multiple and, like, ten short essay."

The two of us congregated in the door frame and Caleb said, "You'd never suspect a woman was murdered in this room. Where again were Jennifer's eyes?"

I showed him.

He walked over and brushed his hand over the textured groves as a blind man might brush the cover of a new book. He said, "And they were facing out, not against the wall?"

"Right. A nail was driven through each pupil."

He turned around with his back against the wall and slid down. He looked like he was doing a wall sit in gym class. I looked at my watch and started counting. He went for thirty-seven seconds. Good, but not great. Caleb continued to stare off in the distance as if Lacy's wall was a mere hurdle.

Finally, he cocked his head up at me and stated, "The victim's eyes see."

"What do you mean?"

He said the words slowly, "Jennifer's eyes saw where the next victim would be killed."

To say I was confused would be an understatement. I was befuddled. What in the hell was Caleb talking about, *Jennifer's eyes saw where the next victim would be killed?*

He instructed me to sit how he'd been and I indulged him. As I slid down the wall, my bad quad screamed, but held. Caleb asked, "Now tell me what you see?"

I glanced around the room and Caleb said, "No, keep your head straight. Imagine your eyes are the eyes on the wall. What do you see?"

I followed his instructions and stared straight ahead. "I see the bed. I can see myself in the mirror."

"What else do you see in the mirror?" He prodded.

"Nothing. It's just me and Lacy's painting." The words hit my ear before they'd hit the air, like they'd come from someone else's mouth. I repeated, "Lacy's lighthouse painting."

I pushed off the wall, "Holy shit. Jennifer's eyes saw where the next victim would be killed. Jennifer's eyes saw Ashley would be killed at a lighthouse."

Caleb nodded. I detected in his eyes he knew more but wanted to let me reach my own conclusions. I thought about Ashley, the lighthouse, and her eyes.

"Ashley's eyes were affixed to the lighthouse lens. They were watching over the water, watching the incoming boats. Ashley's eyes saw the next victim would be killed on a boat."

Caleb chimed in, "The eyes see where the next victim will be killed, but in relation to you. It's Tristen versus you, remember that. Jennifer was killed in your house. Ashley in your lighthouse. Kellon in your boat."

I recollected my encore visit to Lacy's room when I'd been looking at myself in the mirror and the clue god had whapped me on the head. But it'd never clicked.

Caleb broke my muse, "Now we need to think about what Kellon's eyes were seeing."

I didn't get an opportunity to give Kellon's eyes any conviction. Holly ran through the door holding a walkie-talkie, the ensuing stampede on the stairway flexing Lacy's walls like rumbling speaker boxes.

Holly panted, "This just went off. It was him. It was Tristen."

I grabbed the walkie-talkie from her. It was silent. I pushed the talk button, "Hey, coward boy. What's your excuse? Your mommy make you breast-feed until you were sixteen? Or maybe daddy made you jack him off, that it? Your sister wanted to screw your brother over you? Am I getting warmer?" I tried a couple more taunts about his family's incest but he didn't bite.

Everyone was in the room now, steadying themselves for the second leg of the biathlon. Speed then accuracy.

I caught Holly's eyes and asked, "Did he say anything?"

She nodded. "Yeah, he said, 'Two-twenty.' That's it. I heard it three times, I'm sure of it, 'Two-twenty.'"

What in the hell did two-twenty mean?

Lacy offered, "Maybe he's going to kill the next woman at 2:20 a.m. tonight, or 2:20 p.m. tomorrow afternoon."

I shook my head, "No, the fourth woman wasn't found until

5:30 p.m. last year." Plus that wouldn't help us. Tristen was trying to even the playing field. He was killing me, pun intended, and wanted a little competition. This was charity.

I looked at Caleb. He shrugged, "Got me."

Two-twenty. Maybe they were initials. Tristen had spelled out Geoffrey's name and he'd rearranged his name to spell Gary Strinteer. He obviously wasn't averse to wordplay. I didn't know any woman with the initials BU and hit a dead end. Somewhere I knew there was a file marked "two-twenty," a file I'd opened in the last couple days.

I walked out of the door and found myself staring at the door to the guest bedroom. *Whap.*

That was it. I'd skipped over the fourth murder in *Eight in October*. I'd earmarked the page so I could come back to it later. I'd earmarked page 220.

~

I ran out of Lacy's room, vaulted down the stairs, and raced out to my car. I grabbed *Eight in October* off the backseat and slid into the front. I flipped on the reading light and found the earmarked page 220. I had an inkling why Tristen Grayer had me reading this particular passage and skipped to the final sentence on the page:

> *Task force member, Dr. Caitlin Dodds, said after the complete autopsy, "Ginny Farth had been dead for a substantial period of time before we found her. Time of death would be close to 10:00 p.m. on the evening of Oct. 9th.*

That was it. We'd marked the hot dates the women had been found. How could I have been so asinine? This was a death ritual: same time, same day, same MO. Tristen Grayer wasn't concerned with when the women were found; the hot dates were when the women were killed.

Chapter 41

I ran back to the house and said to the awaiting assembly, "Two-twenty was page 220 of *Eight in October*. The fourth woman was found on October 11th at roughly 5:00 p.m., but her time of death was approximately 10:00 p.m. on the evening of October 9th."

We all looked at the clock, it was nine-fifteen. Holly said, "Oh my God."

"We still have forty-five minutes. Tristen wouldn't have called if the woman was dead." I hit mute for a terse commercial break. We still needed to know where tonight's murder site was. Where did Kellon's eyes see?

I assumed Caleb had briefed them on his eye theory and said, "The last victim's eyes were baited on a hook and slung out to sea, so think about that in terms of Tristen in relation to me."

I looked at Caleb and could see from the look on his face that he knew where. He said modestly, "The cliff you fell off. Where you drowned in the Atlantic."

I nodded, "The east bluffs."

I looked around, everyone was waiting for the play. "Caleb, you ride with me. Fat Tim and Holly, follow behind us. I want the rest of you to stay here."

They all nodded.

Holly yelled from behind me, "I just tried Kim's cell. She's not answering."

~

The east bluffs run for about twenty-five miles northeast on US 1. US 1 curves along the entire Atlantic coast of the eastern United States, but in Maine its treachery is unrivaled. This had greatly to do with the limited number of streetlights in the state. I think the Federal Government allocated Maine something like a thousand streetlights and they used them all up in a four-block radius of Bangor.

It was curvy and black, not ideal conditions to be zooming along at eighty-five. I nearly missed the exit for the Roque Bluffs, screeching across two lanes at the last second. Caleb closed his cell phone and said, "Kim's still not answering her phone. I have a bad feeling about this."

Really? Because I was strangely optimistic. We were driving through pitch-black going close to ninety. Kim Welding was MIA and would probably be DOA. And Tristen Grayer was watching me run around like a dog chasing my tail. It all looked rather upbeat if you asked me.

We made our way through Columbia Falls and into a narrow inlet running to the Roque Bluffs. A few lane reflectors had fallen off at a sharp right turn and the Range Rover hung on the guardrail before fish-tailing back onto the road. I looked in my rearview mirror just in time to see Fat Tim finish crossing himself in Holly's white Accord passenger seat. I guess Holly had a bit of trouble with that turn as well.

I slowed down a bit, seventy-five, and took the majority of the turns on four wheels. I hadn't seen a streetlight in ten miles and nearly ran headlong into the Roque Bluffs sign. I pulled the Range Rover over on the side of the road, the white Accord parking directly behind me.

Caleb pulled out his phone for the fifth time and shook his head, "No luck."

I was going to say, "It's difficult to answer a phone when the hand your cell phone is in and your head are fifteen feet apart," but decided on, "She probably turned it off so she could study without interruption."

He threw me a skeptical look as the two of us hopped out of the car and walked to Holly's Honda. I instructed them to call Caitlin if they didn't hear from us in the next ten minutes. And by no means to leave the vehicle.

Caleb and I walked across the street, resting for a moment, straddling the guardrail. I could smell the ocean, taste the ocean, and hear the ocean, but I could not for the life of me, see the ocean. And I hoped I didn't touch the ocean. The last time I touched the ocean in this spot, I'd stopped breathing for fifteen minutes. Which a doctor once told me isn't healthy.

I didn't turn on the flashlight. Half the reason being I didn't want to alert Tristen to our presence; the other half, I'd forgotten the flashlight on the kitchen table. From the guardrail to the bluff face was less than thirty feet in some places and as much as seventy in others. From the cliffs to the water was about a twenty foot splash if the tide was in and about a forty foot smack if the tide was out. The rocks jutted out on both sides and converged without touching, resembling something of a horseshoe. I had my apparent brush with death halfway down the left side of the horseshoe and that's where Caleb and I were headed.

We reached the rocks at the edge of the bluffs and stared down. I knew there was water down there but I still couldn't see it. Caleb sidled up next to me and whispered, "How far down is it?"

"About twenty feet. We have to get down there. I can sense Tristen's presence. He's down there. I'm sure of it."

"So what do you want to do? He'll hear us climbing down and that could take five minutes."

More like half an hour. Plus, the prospect of the two of us climbing down the rock ravine without falling into the lagoon was about as likely as Michael Jackson landing a day care license. I enlightened him, "We have to jump."

"Hell no."

I guess we both knew where Caleb stood on the jumping issue. I patted him on the back, "So you're in. Good. We go on three."

Caleb came to terms with the issue quickly, "What if he has a gun?"

"He won't."

"How do you know?"

"Because he'll have an ax." Duh.

~

I set the walkie-talkie on the rocks and said, "One." *I hope this is the same lagoon I fell in and not a rock museum.* "Two." *It's almost 10:00, the tide should be in by now. Right?* "Three." *I can't believe he jumped.*

Caleb went right, I went left. I didn't see the water until I was inside it. My feet didn't hit bottom, and I kicked hard, neutralizing my body in the freezing water. My head broke the surface and I shook my eyes open. My eyes had started to adjust and there was a touch of hibernating light nestled just above the waterline.

I could barely make out the shadow of a figure about fifty feet up a rock strip against the horizon. I caught an incoming break and rode the small wave the fifteen feet to the rocky shore. The figure was unmistakable now. This cove was a hot spot for fishermen setting up illegal lobster cages, and since the figure was clad in a yellow slicker I didn't discount the possibility.

Caleb was pulling himself from the surf a foot to my left, his eyes trained on the ghost in the darkness. We hushed across the loose rock, closing the gap to a mere twenty feet. The figure was moving diligently, bent at the waist, looming over what appeared to be a lobster cage. I didn't like the odds of your average Joe being out here on this exact date and time, but better safe than sorry.

I yelled, "Excuse me sir, can I speak with you for a moment?"

He didn't turn and I saw him stuff something in the cage. Who puts things in a lobster cage? Aren't you supposed to take lobsters out of them?

Caleb yelled, "Sir, would you please turn around? A lot of people have been getting sick from the lobsters in this area. We really need a minute of your time."

Good thinking, but no.

We were within ten feet of the man when I noticed him place something else in the trap, then secure and latch the top.

I yelled, "There's a gun trained on you this very second. I'll give you until the count of three to turn around and state your business or I'm gonna start shooting. One. Two. Three. Four. Five. If I get to six you're a dead man. Six. Seven. Eight. Don't let me get to nine. Nine. Ten. Eleven." Shit, I was a terrible bluffer.

I looked at Caleb and he shrugged.

Splash. Splash.

I whipped my head around. The figure was gone. The cage was gone. And my suspicion was they were censurable for the succession of splashes. I ran forward and gazed out on the water but couldn't distinguish a humpback tail from a fugitive sneer.

Caleb dove in and began scanning the ocean ten yards out. I watched as he swam back and trudged from the surf. He looked me squarely and said, "That was him, wasn't it?"

I hadn't dismissed the possibility of a neurotic, self-conscious lobster-trapper, but all fingers were pointing toward Tristen Grayer. I let his question slip and asked, "Did you see the cage?"

He nodded.

Neither of us came out and said, "Kim," but we both thought it loud enough to scare off two osprey resting on a rock nearby. I walked over to the edge of the surf and found the beginnings of a thick yellow rope. Caleb and I pulled the cage, which was roughly the size of a small aquarium, from the surf. Before it was completely void of ocean, it was evident the cage did not house lobsters. The cage lolled to its side, a finger poking out one hole, a bone splintering through another.

I unlatched the top and saw sitting, atop the pile of limbs, a soiled copy of *Introduction to Forensic Psychology.*

Chapter 42

Caleb was glaring over my shoulder and saw the book. I helplessly watched as his patellas turned to jelly and he crumpled to the rock bed. This would have been the time I took out my cell phone and called in the cavalry to search the shores for Tristen Grayer. That would have been a realistic possibility if either Caleb or I had been smart enough to remove our cell phones before plunging into the Atlantic. I'd had the sense to leave the walkie-talkie on the edge of the cliff. Why hadn't I thought to take out my cell?

Caleb yanked on my ocean-saturated pant leg and told me to be quiet. I asked, "What? Do you hear sirens already?"

It'd only been about five minutes since I'd chatted with Tim and Holly at their car window, the police couldn't be on their way. Unless the FBI had stumbled on the same information we had. But the chances of that were about as slim as the remains in the lobster cage not being Kim Welding.

Caleb said, "Listen closely. I think I can hear your walkie-talkie."

I blocked out the sound of the swirling Atlantic, the whining osprey, and the eroding rock only to hear the distant sound of rumbling laughter. Caleb looked into my eyes and said, "He's laughing at us." Then added, "But how?"

There was absolutely no way Tristen Grayer could have made his way to land and to a walkie-talkie. It was a half mile swim to any point feasible to exit the ocean. Plus, I could see for at least a quarter mile and there wasn't a boat in the general vicinity. I was mystified. I was also mystified as how to proceed. Caleb and I were cut off from the world. There was no way either of us could climb the rock wall. We would have to sit and wait for the world to find us.

~

Twenty minutes passed before we heard the first siren. The whirlwind of lights gave the image of a sun rising from the west. Another five minutes passed when a large spotlight shone down from where it had been erected at the bluff's edge. A large silhouette shouted, "How in the piss did you get down there?"

It was Gleason. I was in an odd mood and replied, "Pencil to can opener—full pike."

After a quick conversation with someone, his shadow disappeared. Seconds later, there was a large splash. Gleason's head popped out of the water and Caleb and I helped him from the water. He brushed his hands over his bald pate like he had a long flowing mane and said, "Damn, that water's cold."

Gleason peered upward and yelled, "Come on, Todd! It's nothing."

I yelled, "Not yet."

Gregory's annoying voice echoed into the cavernous ravine, "Why?"

I cleared my throat and screamed, "It's adult swim! I'll blow the whistle when you can come in." The manner in which I had decided to channel my anger could be construed as childish and counterproductive.

Gleason, Caleb, and I made the short ten steps to the lobster cage, and Gleason peered at the contents, a steadfast aura about him. I heard noises behind us and turned to see Caitlin and Gregory, clad in bright yellow harnesses, shimmying their way down the bluff. Gregory had a spotlight similar to the one at the top of the bluffs clutched in his palm and set it high on an arbitrary rock, illuminating the small inlet.

Caitlin reached the epicenter and asked, "Who is she?"

"Kim Welding."

I didn't have to tell her Kim was one of my students. In another life, Caitlin had frequently popped in on my class sessions. Gregory made a final adjustment to the spotlight and joined the party. He had a butterfly strip over the bridge of his nose which, as much as it pains me to say, looked about as perfectly symmetrical as before. Shucks.

I ran through the story for them, letting Caleb take over when I reached the point of his consequential discovery, and took back the reigns at my *Eight in October* revelation. I could almost see Gleason mentally slap himself on the forehead. He stamped his foot, "How could we be so stupid? The hot dates are when the women were killed, not when they were found. What were we thinking? Good catch, Thomas."

I was going to tell him that I never would have thought differently had Tristen not communicated via walkie-talkie, but I liked them thinking I stumbled on the marvel while sitting on the pot. Todd Gregory did not show his adulation as outwardly as Gleason, and if another one of my students hadn't just been killed, I think he may have shot me.

Chapter 43

I rolled off the couch and strapped on my running shoes. I'd walked through the door last night at close to 3:00 a.m. Caleb and I had been the first two removed from the scene and I had the pleasure of wearing the harness fitted for Gregory's size 26 inch waist. My balls still felt like they were vacationing in my stomach. It hadn't hit me until I'd been halfway home that I hadn't given the slightest conviction to Kim's eyes. I assumed they were somewhere in the melee of body parts. But what was their significance? They needed to see the site where the next woman was to be murdered.

I clipped the walkie-talkie to the top of my running pants and started out the front door. I started up the beach feeling rigid. Body, mind, and soul. It was like Kim's murder hadn't happened. I needed to limber up mentally and physically so the world could come crashing down. How many women were dead? Let's count, shall we? Jennifer Peppers, Ashley Andrews, Kellon Atkins, and now, Kim Welding. Four in all.

What I couldn't understand was how Tristen had moved down the ranks from Kellon to Kim Welding. Was Kim simply a filler in his massacre? Did he kill her out of simple convenience? The only thing I knew for certain was that Tristen wouldn't stop until eight were dead.

I also knew somewhere on Tristen's list, whether it was fifth, sixth, seventh, or eighth, was Lacy's name. Probably written in blood on a wall somewhere. No, Lacy would not be taken from me. In fact, no other woman would be taken. I would die before I let that happen.

I ran hard for more than an hour before the tears came. I consoled myself with the confidence that Tristen Grayer and I were now on a level playing field. He'd gone out of his way to make the odds fair and I would make him regret his charity. There were two hot dates left and the only possible victims I could think of were Caitlin, Alex, Lacy, and possibly myself. I also knew the exact date and time Tristen would strike. He would not stray from the rules, he would never cheat at his own game. The one thing I needed was the site of the next murder. I needed Kim Welding's eyes.

~

After my run, I walked through the door and immediately dialed Gleason. He picked up on the third ring and I said, "Kim's eyes. We need to find them."

"One step ahead of you. I talked with Caitlin about twenty minutes ago. She just got all the parts sorted out at the morgue."

"And?"

"No eyes."

Shit. "Could they have fallen through the openings in the cage?"

"Theoretically, yes. But my gut tells me Tristen placed the eyes somewhere in the general vicinity of the Rogue Bluffs. Caitlin has twenty of her men helping us canvass the area later this afternoon. She even got three volunteers from the canine unit."

"If we don't find those eyes and Tristen thinks we have, we're up a shit tree without a paddle."

"It's 'up shit creek without a paddle.'"

"Whatever. We're fucked."

He said the team was meeting at the Roque Bluffs at 9:00 a.m., and I told him I'd see him there. Part of me thought Tristen had taken Kim's eyes and that they'd show up in my life somewhere unexpected in the next twenty-four hours.

Another part of me thought he'd placed her eyes strategically at the scene and they'd either gone out with the tide or were sitting in the belly of an osprey.

~

I ate three bowls of Lucky Charms for good luck and jumped in the Range Rover. As I pulled up to Caleb's apartment, he and my sister were getting into his Passat. I honked and yelled, "Change of plans! Get in."

The two of them hopped in the back and I said, "Lace, I assume you need a ride to the gallery."

"Don't you know it? I have 5,000 things to do before Friday. Did I say Friday? What day is today?"

"Wednesday."

She looked the opposite of calm. "There's no way I can get all the stuff done I need to in two days. No way, no how."

I dropped Lacy off at the gallery and had a quick chat with the security guard that I didn't want her out of his sight. He nodded and I slipped him a fifty.

We passed a Dunkin' Donuts on the way out of town and Caleb darted in. He came out with a bag of donuts, two tall coffees, a newspaper, and a subdued expression. Opening the passenger door, he said, "You're not going to believe this." He tossed the paper on my lap and he was right. I didn't.

The front page headline of the newspaper, today entitled the *Waterville Daily*, read:

No Bluff! Student Found in Lobster Cage

How in the hell did Alex get wind of the story? For once, I don't personally escort her to the crime scene and she's still able to stab me in the back. It wasn't like there had been a small army at the scene. It'd been me, Caleb, Caitlin, Gregory, Gleason, and two of Caitlin's men at the Bangor PD. Conner hadn't even been there.

I opened the driver side door, walked around the SUV, and said, "Slide over, you're driving."

Caleb reversed the car and I sank into the article:

Don't ask for this "Catch of the Day" unless you like 'em young, pretty, and blonde. At approximately 10:00 p.m. last night, a young woman's body was found dismembered and stuffed inside a lobster cage at the base of the Roque Bluffs. (Yes, the same bluffs where the last three victims of the Eight in October string were found.) The victim, Kim Welding, was a student at nearby Eaton College of Criminology, which subsequently lost another alum, Ashley Andrews, in a related incident almost a week ago. Both young women were students under Thomas Prescott. This must be a hard pill to swallow for the convalescing FBI consultant. We're all starting to wonder, is any woman in Prescott's inner circle safe? It appears not.

That was all there was. The article should have been in the editorial section for crying out loud. I reread the paragraph, then read it aloud to Caleb. At the last sentence he stared at me with such disbelief I had to yank the wheel to keep us on the highway. He shook his head, "Who does that bitch think she is?"

Funny, I was thinking the same thing.

Chapter 44

We pulled up to the bluffs at 9:00 a.m. on the dot. It was the first time I'd seen them in the daylight. They looked so innocent and serene, nothing like the bluffs that dominated my nightmares for the past year.

There was a small congregation of about ten police vehicles, three with "Canine Unit" stamped on the side. This made me think that I should have brought Baxter.

I pulled up the utility compartment to toss in my cell phone and, I'll be, I had brought Baxter. I gave the pet rock a shake and he looked up with his big brown eyes and yelped three times.

Yeah, buddy, I hope we find her eyes too.

~

Caleb and I joined a group of twenty men at the bluff's edge. Caleb looked down into the cove and said, "I can't believe you made me jump off this last night."

I had to admit it was intimidating, close to a fifty-foot plunge by daylight. Take twenty feet off for the tide and it was a burly thirty-foot vault. Conner, Gregory, and Gleason sidled up beside us. Gleason looked down and shook his head, "If I'd known it was this far down, I sure as shit wouldn't have jumped."

Everyone knew Gleason would have jumped if it'd been a hundred feet. I looked at Gregory and envisioned him on the diving board with orange floaties on his arms. The only way Gregory would have jumped is if George Clooney was mooning him from below. I turned my gaze to Conner. Conner would jump right now if someone dared him. I grabbed his neatly pressed blue shirt, ruffling it, and said, "And where exactly were you last night? Aren't you supposed to be attached to Gregory's dick?"

Conner flipped me off, "I was on a date. Remember? Your sister dumped me." He gave Caleb a sideways glance who—at the present moment—was staring out on the water contemplating a quick death as opposed to Conner's wrath.

I edged between the two of them and said, "All right, we have some eyes to find."

~

Caitlin assembled her army and said, "Here's the deal. We have reason to believe last night's victim's eyes are in the general area and carry monumental weight in our case. Half of us will be searching the top of the bluffs and the rest of you will be searching below. There are plenty of nooks and crannies for a serial killer to hide a pair or eyes, or even a singular eye." Ready. Break.

I made quick eye contact with Caitlin and she threw an uncomfortable smile my way. It reminded me that she might be smiling because I was fathering her child. My stomach filled with another two ounces of bile as I went to put on my harness. Come to think of it, I was excited about my balls being crushed into my Adam's apple. It would take my mind off the four women in my life who had been murdered and my—roll of the dice—impending fatherhood.

~

Four hours passed and no flares were shot. No flares meant no eyes. No eyes meant no clue. No clue meant—well, I didn't want to think what it meant.

At 1:30 a box was lowered to the ten of us at the lower camp, and I was pleased to see Caitlin had arranged for Angelini to cater the event. Caleb, Gleason, and I plopped down in the shade of the steep cliff, unraveling our sandwiches. (I'd made the recommendation to Conner that he, Caitlin, and Gregory stay up top to minimize conflict.)

I'd taken down half my sandwich when Baxter appeared, which was peculiar because I'd locked him in the car with all the windows up. I rustled his small head and gave him a meatball to munch on. Gleason cracked a Coke, took a swig, and said, "I've been racking my brain as to how Tristen knows all our moves. He has to have a source at the force or with the Bureau."

I contemplated this and said, "You're right. He knows too much. You should have heard him when he was impersonating an agent from the Bureau, it was scary."

I asked, "Whatever happened with your missing agent?"

"To the FBI, he's dead. They're having his procession tomorrow. Todd and I are flying back for it in the morning. We'll be back up here Saturday."

That reminded me, Kellon's funeral was on Friday. I lost my appetite and gave the rest of my sandwich to Baxter.

~

No one stumbled on the eyes and the search group punched out when the sun did. The more I thought about Kim's eyes, the less concerned I became. I hadn't had to go on any treasure hunts for the past victim's eyes. The eyes had been blatant, handed to me. I was confident the eyes would surface, and if they didn't Tristen would throw me another bone. And he would know about the eyes. He knew my next bowel movement, my next sneeze, and probably knew if I were the next father-to-be.

Chapter 45

I slept like a rock. It seemed like the theme, seeing as I'd been walking on them, scavenging between them, and spelunking down them all afternoon.

I spent the day at the gallery with Lacy and Caleb going over the small details of the following night's gala. Lacy's lighthouse landscape had been professionally framed and hung beautifully on the wall with about twenty-five other paintings.

I looked around and saw two Bangor Police officers milling about. I'd taken Caitlin up on her offer and there were now three full-time BPD officers posted. Lacy put me to work setting up tables, draping tablecloths, and arranging centerpieces. There were tables for 130 people, and at $150 a head, Lacy had made close to $20,000 for the Multiple Sclerosis Society before the night's festivities kicked off.

Lacy and I left the gallery around 9:30 p.m. and were home for the second round of SportsCenter. I ate three waffles with butter and powdered sugar before snagging a beer from the fridge. On the way to the couch, I passed my answering machine and saw I had five messages. I went through the caller ID, four calls were from Alex and the other was Charles Mangrove. I wasn't in the mood to hear Alex's ranting apologies nor Mangrove's lame excuse for flaking on my sister's fund-raiser, and erased them all.

~

Kellon's funeral was at noon at the St. Michael's Episcopal Church in Newcastle, a small town about forty miles south of Bangor. I pulled into the parking lot and grabbed the kite I'd bought for

Kellon off the passenger seat. St. Michael's was a modern, gray brick church set in an immense grass courtyard.

I made my way up the ten steep concrete steps and through the open cast iron doors. The inside of the church was narrow, a red carpet splitting the bleacher-style pews. Eighty feet below the octagon vaulted ceiling, sparsely indexed, were fifteen adults and close to thirty kids. My esophagus attempted to trade positions with my large intestines as I took a seat in the far back right corner. The memorial service took close to an hour and I only choked up eleven times.

I needed to say my good-byes and made my way to a small group huddled near the casket. Kellon's father was in the front row, his eyes puffy, his suit disheveled. We made eye contact and held it. I tried halfheartedly but couldn't muster an ounce of animosity toward the man. I'd lost a friend, he'd lost a daughter. All the death I'd felt in the past two weeks was nothing compared with what this man felt.

After two or three minutes I was on deck. The coffin was empty; they'd cremated Kellon's crippled body, and each person was placing something special inside. I put the kite and a letter I'd written amid the roses and carnations then left the church biting my lip.

~

As formidable as Kellon's funeral had been—and it had been—I was dreading the second leg of my catastrophe biathlon more than the first. The doors opened at the Germaine Galleria at 5:30 p.m., and I was penciled in to pick Caitlin up at 5:00.

Before I hopped in the shower I did something I hadn't done in more than ten days: I shaved. The scruff had to go. The guy with the scruff let women close to him die, not the close-shaven man before me. On the surface, I did look a whole lot better clean-shaven. But it went deeper: it was a metamorphosis, a new beginning, a fucking renaissance.

I put on the second suit I'd bought from Armani, a pricey charcoal pinstriped number that fit immaculately and coordinated nicely with my slate gray undershirt. I snagged my favorite tie, diagonally striped charcoal on enamel white, and laced up my shiny black Armani boots. I looked in the mirror and cringed. How was I supposed to expect Caitlin to get over me when I looked this good?

~

I pulled up to Caitlin's house at 5:00 on the dot and had my hand on the horn when I decided better of it and hopped out of the car. Caitlin opened the door and my tongue landed on my left boot. She had on a teal dress, cut short. Her hair was straight and hung down onto her bare shoulders. Her glossy lips formed into a smile, and her piercing blue eyes danced in the moonlight.

Yowza.

I fell into step behind her on the way to the car and I had a flashback to the first time I'd met her: *there was an ulterior motive for my hesitation which paid off when I fell into stride behind Dr. Caitlin Dodds. To say the view was spectacular would be an understatement, her professional skirt unable to shroud the well-maintained, grade-A caboose housed beneath the fabric. Thomas Dodds, I could deal with that.*

Maybe I could marry this woman. Maybe Caitlin should be the mother of my children. I didn't like the direction my thought process was headed, nor did I like the direction Paddington was headed. I adjusted my belt, did a little shimmy, and caught up with Caitlin at the passenger side door. She had yet to say a word, and when I was uncomfortably in the driver's seat I said, "You're quiet."

She smiled, "There's not much to say."

I agreed. There wasn't.

~

There were two Bangor police officers stationed at the entrance to the Germaine Galleria. Caitlin knew both by name, and they both told her in their own words how spectacular she looked. She smiled a wee bit too long at the better looking of the two, and if I didn't know better I would have thought I felt a twinge of jealousy.

I wonder if I can kill him with my cuff link.

We walked through the doors and Caitlin slipped her arm through mine. There were maybe a hundred people, the majority permeating at the edge of the many hallways flanked with paintings. Caitlin said she needed to use the ladies' room and veered off, unhooking her arm, at which point I saw my friend Jack in the corner, some asshole holding him by the neck. I practically ran over to the two of them and yelled, "Double Jack and Coke."

The bartender poured me a stiff drink, and I ordered two flutes of champagne for the road. He asked for three drink tickets and handed me two flutes of Korbel.

I shook my head and said, "These look like clarinets."

He displayed no emotion to my witticism, and I was set to ask him if he had Multiple Sclerosis but I didn't want him to get stingy with my drinks—I only had two more tickets.

Caitlin sidled up next to me and I handed her a flute of champagne. We made our way toward the display area and were intercepted by Caleb and Lacy. Caleb fell under the classification "debonair." In his tan suit, black undershirt, and ivory tie, he looked like he belonged on the cover of GQ. As for my sister, she had on a tiny red dress, her hair professionally wrapped, and a single pearl necklace of my mother's draped around her neck.

Caitlin covered her mouth and said, "Oh, Lacy, you look wonderful. Absolutely darling."

I concurred.

Lacy asked, "Tell me the truth, does the place look riveting."

I brushed a single strand of hair from her eyes. "It looks amazing, Lace. Not a thing out of place. And the centerpieces, don't get me started on them. They're just so centered in the tables. Seriously, they're perfectly centered."

She rolled her eyes and said to Caitlin, "I have him do one stupid thing, and he won't shut up about it for weeks."

I grabbed Caleb by the shoulder and said to an arbitrary point between Lacy and Caitlin, "I need to steal Caleb for quick second. Will you ladies excuse us?"

I directed Caleb to a remote area near the entrance. He asked, "What's up?"

"I forgot to ask you a question last night"

His eyes cut over my left shoulder. "Uh-oh."

I turned around. Uh-oh was an understatement. Alex Tooms had just walked in on the arm of Todd Gregory.

Chapter 46

I surveyed the two arm in arm. Alex had on a tiny black dress cut up the side until, well, until her fun parts started. The dress was low-cut, and what little cleavage Alex did have was attracting every alpha male within a three-block radius.

Caleb leaned into me and said, "Holy shit. TKO. Tooms is a knockout."

Alex and Gregory angled off and I was granted a half second glimmer of Alex's kushy tushy. Caleb made a move back to the masses, and I would have followed had my paintbrush not been poking through the canvas.

I did a lap around the outskirts of the gallery, until my paintbrush restored to its flaccid, weary, despondent self. I wanted to be sure Paddington remained comatose and zigzagged my way through the crowd to the bar. Alex and Gregory were nowhere to be seen, and I used up my last two tickets on tequila shots, then wrote the guy an I.O.U. for a tall glass of Chardonnay. I scanned the masses but didn't see the celebrity couple anywhere. Maybe they were in the bathroom. Together.

I could strangle him with my shoelace.

I offered the bartender my Tag Heuer if he'd just hand over the whole damn bottle of wine, but he refused. He was gentleman enough to top me off as I went in search of the mystery couple. I spotted their backs at the bar cattycorner to where I was. My jubilation was a toss-up between locating Alex and the discovery of a second bar on the premises.

I was about five steps away when I felt an arm slip through mine. Seems Ms. Dodds had intercepted me like a Brett Favre wounded duck. Alex and Gregory turned as Caitlin and I approached. I shifted my gaze from Alex's timid grin to Gregory's defiant sneer. Gregory took a sip of something pink, probably a Sex on the Beach, and said, "I came on Charles Mangrove's behalf. I've been instructed to buy a painting in his stead. I'm sure he explained everything to you over the phone."

Ah, so that's why Charles had called. That explained why Gregory was here, but I was still confused why he was arm in arm with the cold, calculating Queen of composition. I shifted my glare to Alex. Her beer bottle was flat empty and she said meekly, "Your, uh, sister, uh, Lacy, invited me. It, uh, came up when she was staying the night. We started talking about my Winslow Homer pieces, and she said that I should, uh, should stop by."

Okay, that explained why A and B were here, but for the life of me I could not *see* why the two of them were here together. Caitlin decided to clear up the matter, "I told Todd he should call Alex and the two of them should come together. They're both single. I mean, why not?"

These were not the words I wanted to hear, especially coming from Caitlin's mouth. I grabbed two shots of something brown off a waitress's outgoing tray and knocked them both back. But why did I care if Alex came with Todd? I didn't want anything to do with Alex Tooms. Did I?

I mentally and visually sized Alex up. She was a sneaky, *extremely attractive*, deceiving, *wow, that slit really goes up high, doesn't it?*, scum of the Earth, *is that Chanel she's wearing*?, back-stabbing, *I don't see any panty lines! I don't see any panty lines!* journalist.

I felt a jab in my ribs and snapped from my reverie. Caitlin said, "Let's go, Thomas, they're seating everyone at their tables."

I followed behind Caitlin, a bit confused, a smidgen jealous, a tad pissed off, and a hell of a lotta drunk.

~

We were only allowed one drink at dinner, and if Caleb hadn't been beside me I probably would have tried to slit my wrists with my butter knife. The waitress cleared our plates and Lacy said she had to go get ready for her pre-silent auction, fund-raiser speech. No cue cards for that one.

The liquor had run its course and was now sitting in my bladder like a ski racer atop the Super-G. I excused myself, stood up, and gazed over the crowd at Alex and Todd's table. Alex was hunched over, and I surmised she must be choking to death because Gregory saying something funny was not an option.

Choke, what do I care?

I walked into the corridor I'd seen Caitlin hit on the way in and saw the sign for the bathrooms against the far wall fifty yards away. A quarter of the way into my pee-lgrimage, I passed Lacy's lighthouse painting. The bidding didn't start for another half hour, but I wrote my name and an astronomical amount next to it. No one was outbidding me on this one, I can assure you of that much. I made it to the end of the corridor and saw the bathrooms were another thirty yards down a peripheral hall.

I reached the bathrooms with limited pre-tinkle and saw Lacy had put posters on the doors that read "Buoys" and "Gulls." Seeing as my inhibitions were lowered, I peeled the signs off the doors and quickly switched them. Then I pushed through the door marked "Gulls," beelined it to a urinal, and chipped off a couple pieces of linoleum.

Ninety seconds later, I walked to the sink, brushed the hair out of my eyes, and ambled out of the bathroom. I was curious if there was an officer stationed outside the side exit and headed in that direction. From behind me someone snickered, "Why did you just come out of the girl's bathroom?"

I turned. It was Alex.

I took a step toward her, "I wanted to bid on a painting hanging in stall number three."

She lifted the back of the "Gulls" poster to reveal the word "Mens," and said, "You're an idiot."

Guilty as charged. She switched the posters and said, "Are you always this immature?"

Yes. "No. But your date brings out the best in me."

"Who? Pea Pod Todd?"

"Is that your pet name for him?"

"No, it's his name because he's so boring I want to snap his neck like a pea pod."

"You looked like you were enjoying yourself. He must have said something funny to get you doubled over a minute ago."

"I was choking."

Thank God.

Alex put her hands on her hips and said, "And how are you and Mommy Dearest?"

Mommy Dearest? Did Alex know something I didn't? Maybe she'd seen Caitlin at the grocery store comparative pricing home pregnancy kits. "We aren't really on the best of terms right now."

Alex cocked her head, "And what about us? What kind of terms are we on?"

In hindsight, I'll blame it on the liquor. I walked the last two feet to her, pulled her to me, and gently kissed her on the lips. Neither of us said a word. We walked out the side exit, jumped into my car, drove to my house, went to the bedroom, and played the hokie-pokie all night long.

If you must know, two slices of cheesecake were involved.

Chapter 47

I opened my eyes and stared at the dark chocolate strands sprawled across my arm. Waking up with Alex in my arms felt better than not waking up with her in my arms. I guess that translates into love at some level, lust at another. I was in lovst.

Alex wiggled in my grip and said, "Make me breakfast."

Uh-oh, looks like the honeymoon's over.

She turned around to face me, and said, "Just kidding, I'll make you breakfast."

Close call.

I pulled the sheets off the bed revealing Alex's stark form. "Why don't you take a shower while I make breakfast? I have a surprise."

A thin grin formed on her face and she said, "Why don't we take a shower together then make breakfast together."

Hold the telegraph. Did she just use "together" twice in one sentence? First, I enjoy showering alone. And second, I was starving. "Sorry, I have a date with a box of Bisquick, some blueberries, and a skillet."

"You're making blueberry pancakes. My favorite."

How'd she crack that one? "It's good to know that if back-stabbing, yellow journalism ever falls through, you can always get a gig as a recipe code breaker."

Alex deflated like a punctured beach ball. She scurried into the bathroom, slammed the door and screamed, "Screw you!"

Again?

~

Alex walked down the stairs, her brown hair held back in a ponytail. She had taken the liberty of grabbing a pair of my sweats and her, change that, *my* Winnie the Pooh sweatshirt. I looked up from the skillet and said, "I hope you don't plan on taking the bear with you."

She rolled her eyes and I guess she thought I was kidding. I did the last flip on the pancakes and grabbed a gallon of OJ from the refrigerator. Alex grabbed two tall glasses from the cupboard and set them in front of me. She looked like she was set to speak, then swallowed the first syllable before her tongue flexed. I think she may have been a tad upset at my earlier remark. Maybe I should have said, "It's good to know that if back-stabbing, yellow journalism ever falls through, you can always get a gig as a recipe code breaker, *buttercup*."

I grabbed two plates from a small stack in the cupboard and flipped three beautifully crafted flapjacks onto each. The microwave dinged and I snatched the hot form of Mrs. Butterworth, setting her in the middle of the table. Alex buttered her pancakes, and after each one I thought I saw the swallowed syllable rise in her throat, but it never escaped.

The two of us ate our pancakes in complete silence and I had an eerie feeling we'd fast-forwarded our relationship thirty years. I smiled at the notion and Alex said, "What?"

I'm not sure if I would have said the words, "Oh, nothing, I was just thinking about the two of us eating pancakes thirty years from now," if Tristen Grayer was tied to the tree in my front yard.

I shook my head. "Nothing."

Alex took down her last syrup dredged, triple layer blueberry bite, and gulped it down. Her emerald eyes moistened and she said meekly, "If you really think of me as a back-stabbing, yellow journalist then why did you sleep with me last night?"

Good question, take your time answering. "Good question."

F.

I was quite certain by the look on her face this was not the response she was seeking. I swallowed my last bite of pancakes—not to mention a large chunk of my pride—and added, "Because somehow, through your back-stabbing, and sensationalism, and runarounds, I fell in love with you." I wasn't lying and I wasn't in the mood to play any more games with Alex Tooms.

~

After a lengthy post-sex coma, Alex and I saddled up in the Range Rover and headed in the direction of her house. She asked me, "So what are your plans for the day"

"We still haven't found Kim's eyes and—" I stopped. "Sorry, I can't tell you."

Love did not bridge the gap between our professions. Speaking of which, I don't remember Alex heaving any declarations of "I love you" my way. I put this in the recesses of my brain and, while I was there, extracted a question that'd been hibernating for the last couple days. "I have to know who told you about the Kim Welding murder. There were only six people there. It was that little shit Gregory, wasn't it?"

"It was—" She drowned off. "Sorry, I can't tell you."

"This isn't a two-way street, missy. Whoever told you jeopardized our entire case."

"Sorry. My source demanded he remain unnamed. I can't renege on my promise. Journalists and their sources fall under a doctor-patient relationship."

What, the Dr. Seuss-English Patient relationship? *He got sick. He did not get sick quick.*

It didn't matter. I knew it was Gregory. They'd obviously collaborated at some point for them to have shown up at Lacy's fundraiser together. Gregory knew how steamed I would get at seeing Alex on his arm and traded the details of Kim's murder for her escort services. Damn, I was a good fucking detective.

I pulled through Alex's gate and dropped her at her doorstep. She planted one on my cheek before opening the passenger door. Then she slipped the Pooh sweatshirt off, threw it in the car, and raced into the house. Now, if that isn't love, I don't know what is.

Chapter 48

Back on the freeway, my cellphone chirped. I looked at the phone number—it was Caleb. I flipped the phone open to him biting my ear off, "Where did you go last night? Lacy's going to kill you."

"Don't worry, I'll buy her off." I had a check for twenty-five hundred dollars written out to the MS Society in my pocket. "Hey, listen, I was going to ask you last night before we were sidetracked by Alex and Agent Dickhead, you didn't talk to Tooms after we left the bluffs did you?"

"Hell no. I got home and slept like a rock."

"Sorry, but I had to ask. Someone talked to her, and it had to be either you, me, Gleason, Gregory, or Caitlin."

"Then it was Gregory."

I was starting to have my doubts. "Yeah, I guess you're right."

"Now tell me, where did you go last night?"

I told him the story and he giggled like a tenth grader after each detail. When I was finished, I asked him, "Where's Lace?"

"At the gallery. They have to get the silent auction winners finalized and fill out all the proper paperwork. I dropped her and Baxter off about an hour ago."

We hung up and I headed for the Germaine Galleria, parking near the side entrance. I wound through the corridors and into the main hallway where I'd bid earlier on Lacy's lighthouse painting. I read my bid for twenty-five hundred dollars, and saw just below it: "$2501-Todd Gregory."

Of all the paintings to bid on for Charles Mangrove, he'd picked Lacy's lighthouse landscape. I took ten deep breaths and excavated a simple solution buried deep: I would simply call Charles Mangrove and tell him he was outbid on everything. He wasn't here. What the hell did he know?

I heard Lacy's voice in the main ballroom and walked into the large void. All the tables were gone and the place was hovering around immaculate. Lacy was at a table with an older gent and I stealthily approached their table. Baxter stirred from his slumber, yelping at me twice. Busted.

I stood still, but I couldn't fool either of them. Lacy stood and screeched, "Where the hell did you go last night? You better have a damn good excuse, buddy."

"I had my appendix removed. I was discharged from the hospital about ten minutes ago. Incision's a little sore, but they gave me some pills for the pain—"

She cut me off, "Did you see that you were outbid on my lighthouse painting? If you would have stayed around and not abandoned me and Caitlin, you could have topped Turd Gregory's bid."

I stopped listening at the word Caitlin, then zoned it just in time to hear Lacy refer to Todd as Turd. Priceless, it must run in the family. I said, "I forgot about Caitlin. What happened to her?"

"Caleb said she asked him where you ran off to a couple times, then must have left."

Boy, was I going to pay for this one. Or girl.

I decided I might as well get it over with and whipped out my phone. I tried her twice and received her voice mail twice. I left a message the second time telling her I needed to talk and to call me back. I wasn't sure if the message was in regards to screwing her over once again or pursuant to borrowing her copy of *Children out of Wedlock for Dummies*. I tried Conner but he didn't answer his phone either.

The Dodds were both missing, and I had a bad feeling in the pit of my stomach.

Chapter 49

Today was Saturday, October 13th. The next hot date was on Sunday at 8:41 p.m. I looked at my watch, it was a little after two in the afternoon. Thirty hours until game time and Kim Welding's eyes still hadn't surfaced.

I called Gleason but he didn't know any more than when we'd talked on Wednesday. He asked if I'd conversed with either of the Dodds in the last twenty-four hours. I told him I hadn't and that I would swing by and do a spot check on both their "cribs."

I went by Caitlin's first. Her car was gone, but I rang the bell anyway. No one came to the door and I used the key Caitlin had given me earlier to let myself in. Unless she was hiding under the bed, Caitlin wasn't there. I went by Conner's next, same drill. I'd probably see them both later and they'd be all, "We were under the bed, you idiot."

I called Ali and Holly, my two female students who hadn't been turned into science experiments. Both had flown back to be with their parents at their request. One of your students gets killed, it's a freak incident and everybody wants to stay and help. Two of your students get killed and your students are harder to find than a Stick Bug in Sticks Abundant, Stick Island.

Driving home I started to think, what if this is no longer a game to Tristen? What if I'd gotten too close and now it was every man for himself? The last four bodies would be saved or lost within the next fifty-six hours. Tristen Grayer liked to go out with a bang. Would this year be any different? In fifty-six hours would Alex, Caitlin, and Lacy all be dead?

Not a chance. I would keep the castle safe from the inside and let the FBI ward off any attack from the street.

~

Alex, Lacy, and Caleb started cooking dinner and I spent a half hour on the phone with Gleason. I informed him I searched both Caitlin's and Conner's and both were vacant. He couldn't hide the fear in his voice. We went through every possible scenario and by the end of the phone call I was sick to my stomach. Gleason and Gregory would be stationed outside in the next couple hours and this did nothing to pacify any of my fears. I wasn't scared for the four of us. I was scared for Caitlin.

Chapter 50

I woke up with my head on the kitchen table, my finger white against the trigger of my .45. I scanned the kitchen for bullet holes, but it appeared I hadn't suffered a single body jerk during REM.

Lacy and Caleb were still sleeping when I peeked in Lacy's bedroom, and Alex was sawing logs next to Baxter in my bed. I checked the clock, 8:55 a.m., less than twelve hours until the next woman was killed. I was no longer thinking in terms of a generic woman, I was thinking in terms of Caitlin.

I peered through the bedroom window and saw the overcast sky steadily weeping a light drizzle. I grabbed my running shoes, some sweats, my University of Washington hoodie, and walked out into the crisp morning air. A tightly formed unit of geese flew overhead, the cold arctic Canadian air stowed in their down feathers.

Gleason and Gregory were parked across the street and I jogged over to their black Caprice. Gleason rolled down the driver side window and asked, "What's up?"

"I was going to ask you the same question. You get hold of Caitlin or Conner?"

He shook his head grimly, "No luck. I've tried calling them every fifteen minutes for the last eight hours."

I made eye contact with Gregory and, yes, we did nauseate one other, but we were still in this heaping pile of shit together. "What do you think?"

He shook his head, "I think we need to find those eyes."

For the first time since I'd met the little shit, we were on the same page. I told them I'd be back in an hour and set out in a steady pace toward town, contemplating my playmate Todd Gregory. It hurts to say this, but he wasn't as bad as I make him out. He's quasi-bad. After looking into his eyes, I knew he hadn't given the story to Alex Tooms. He wanted Tristen Grayer brought down and divulging inside information was not an option. Now, with Gregory's name scratched from the list, I didn't have a name.

On the other side of the coin, Alex had the name. Soon as would I.

~

I was drenched by the time I made it to town. But I was glad to see I hadn't made the trip in vain; Benny was open for business. Gleason and Gregory weren't in the car when I returned and I hoped they were both taking bowel movements and not moving bowels.

I pushed through the front door and saw Caleb, Lacy, Gleason, and Gregory milling around the kitchen with coffee mugs in hand. I handed everyone a burrito, and even received a "Gee thanks, Thomas" from my comrade Todd.

I took a bite, savoring the delicious sausage, egg, potato and green chili, and asked, "Is Alex still sleeping?"

Caleb looked up, "Nope. She's gone."

I ran upstairs and checked the bed, but it appeared as though Alex had flown the coop. I tried her cell, house, and *Waterville Tribune* extension, but didn't get an answer. Great, now Caitlin *and* Alex were missing.

Gleason made some calls and issued an APB on Alex's plates while I saddled up in the Range Rover and headed toward her house.

~

I pulled through the gate and saw her Jeep parked in her usual spot. I knocked three times and nothing happened. I tried the door. Locked. Then I ran around back and climbed over the small brick wall enclosing her terrace. I tried the back door. Again, locked. I pulled out my credit card and held it between my left thumb and forefinger, then kicked the door violently with my right foot. The wood splintered and I left a note for Alex to buy a new door with my credit card.

I canvassed the house quickly for Alex's body. I entered Alex's study last. The room looked like a stage set for Act III rather than a tame study. Two rows of books were overturned on the wooden floor, a love seat was on its back, and there was a small puddle of blood between the desk and the front door.

I touched the blood with my fingertip, it had just began to harden and had presumably been there less than an hour. How stupid had Alex been? Why had she come back here? She knew the danger. *Whap.*

I went behind her desk and opened the bottom drawer, which played home to envelopes and stamps. I tried the top drawer and was rewarded with a stack of computer paper. I checked all the other drawers and didn't come across it. Wait, Alex had done something odd the first time she'd retrieved it. I pulled open the top drawer and felt around underneath the wood. Bingo.

There was a false level and I slid out Alex's tape recorder.

I hopped on her desk and hit the play button with my thumb. A male's voice said a half syllable and the tape ceased spinning. The lone syllable sent chills up my spine and I noticed tall goose bumps had formed on my forearms. I let the tape rewind then pushed play. The tape rolled in silence, then began:

Alex: *Take your time. Detail is the key.*

John Doe: *At around 9:30 or so Thomas Prescott made a huge break. He figured out the victims' eyes from each previous murder were actually seeing where the next murder would occur.*

Alex: *What do you mean "were actually seeing where the next murder would occur"? Can you elaborate?*

John Doe: *The first victim's eyes were nailed to the wall of Lacy Prescott's room. The eyes were positioned directly at a wall mirror hanging near Lacy's bed. The eyes would see the reflected image of a lighthouse painting hanging on her wall. So in a sense Jennifer Pepper's eyes saw Ashley Andrews would be killed at a lighthouse.*

Alex: *(Gasp) You're right. Then the eyes on the lens of the lighthouse saw Kellon would be killed on Thomas's boat.*

John Doe: *Exactly. Then Kellon's eyes were found attached to the two fishing poles at the back of Thomas' boat cast into the Atlantic. They saw Kim Welding would be killed where the Atlantic meets Thomas Prescott which, sadly, is the bluff he plummeted off almost exactly one year ago.*

I hit the stop button.

I hadn't told anyone about Kellon's other eye. Only that her one eye had been baited on my one fishing pole. The only way John Doe would have known both of Kellon's eyes had been on separate poles was if he was the one who'd baited the hooks. I leaned my head back and thought back to when I'd showed them the eye on the boat and he'd asked, "Where's the other one?"

I hadn't thought it strange at the time.

John Doe was Conner Dodds.

Chapter 51

I wasn't sure what role Conner played in the killings, but I knew he was an active participant. He hadn't even been at the scene of Kim Welding's murder. He hadn't been briefed of our eye theory. Conner may not be the killer but he was unquestionably in contact with Tristen Grayer. This would explain why Tristen knew our every move. I popped the tape out of the recorder and read the date and time penciled in Alex's cursive, "Oct. 9, 11:30 PM."

So, that's why Conner hadn't been at the crime scene; he'd been sitting down with Alex over a cup of tea. Conner had given his testimony before the first cop car had appeared at the Rogue Bluffs. This explained the laughter we'd heard coming from the walkie-talkie at the edge of the cliff. This also explained Ashley Andrews's eyes on the lighthouse lens, and how they'd been present one minute and gone the next. It also explained why the person I'd chased at the lighthouse hadn't limped, while Tristen obviously suffered from the injury I'd inflicted upon him a year earlier. This had been a tandem effort from the beginning, Tristen and Conner. But why?

I listened to the remainder of the interview. Conner's last statement stopped me in my tracks. I listened to it a third time:

Conner: *Thomas was so close. At one point, he was only a couple feet away from Tristen. This must be a hard pill to swallow for him.*

There it was again, "Swallow." It'd also been in Alex's article. Goose bumps formed on my forearms a second time. But this time I knew why.

~

I took out my cell phone and dialed Gleason. He picked up and stated immediately, “I just got hold of Caitlin.”

Thank God. “Where was she?”

“She wouldn’t tell me. She said she needed some time to herself to sort some things out.”

I was relieved Caitlin was alive but I had more important fish to fry. I told him about Alex’s house and how it appeared Caitlin was in the clear but Alex was in deep trouble. Then I asked him, “Did they do an autopsy on Kim Welding’s body?”

He scoffed, “How could they? They do an autopsy to see how people die. You don’t do an autopsy when the body is in thirty pieces. The person died because they’re in thirty pieces.”

Good point. “Where would her body be?”

“At the Bangor County morgue. Last I heard her parents hadn’t made a decision whether to cremate.”

“Meet me at the morgue in thirty minutes. No questions. Bring Caleb.”

I dialed Caitlin next. I apologized for abandoning her at the benefit and she simply admitted it’d been a mistake for the two of us to have gone together in the first place. I kept the information about Conner and Alex to myself and asked her to meet me at the morgue.

~

I drove into the parking lot of the Bangor County morgue and saw the FBI Caprice illegally parked near the entrance. The building was large, gray, and projected a cadence of death. Good location though. I pulled the heavy iron door open and was immediately struck by the stench of stale formaldehyde.

There were two gentlemen leaning against the wall of the barren main lobby. Caleb was one, Todd Gregory was the other. I asked, “Where’s Gleason?”

Gregory said flatly, “He didn’t think you’d want me alone with your sister.”

Good thinking. Although to be fair, Lacy was blind and would not be susceptible to Gregory’s likeness to a Ken doll, same hair, same eyes, same height. I was set to pass along this insight when the front door opened and Caitlin pushed through. She looked at me and said, "What's up?" I couldn't help notice Caitlin was wearing a generous amount of Mary Kay's "Tough Front" foundation.

I couldn't help myself and asked, "When's the last time you talked to Conner?"

She shook her head. "Not since the benefit."

Bad news. I let this slip and Gregory said, "You want to tell us why we're here?"

I confided to the group, "I need to take a look at Kim Welding's body."

Caitlin threw me an awkward glance, "Why? There isn't much, and what there is isn't pretty."

"Just take me to her body."

She shrugged and unlocked the steel cage door leading into a long beige corridor. Caleb quickened his step parallel to mine and asked, "What did you find out? What are you looking for?"

What I was about to do was a shot in the dark. I ignored Caleb's question and said a quick prayer.

~

Kim's cadaver was in slot 121. Caitlin pulled the handle and the pastel blue drawer exhaled. She unzipped the body bag and you could almost witness death try to escape. Caitlin said modestly, "I tried to piece her back together as best I could."

The sight was repulsive. Kim Welding's body was by no means complete. I looked at Caitlin and asked, "Where are her insides?"

"They're all there. I shoved them back in the cavity before I sewed it up." She pointed to a long section from her neck to just above her navel. "A bit of her long intestines is unaccounted for, but other than that, all her hardware is in there."

She gave me an inquisitive glance as if to say, "Why?"

I looked her sternly in the eye and said, "I need you to cut into her stomach."

Gregory threw his hands up, "I have to step in here. Will you listen to yourself? You want to cut into this poor girl—listen to what you're saying. Deface her body further so you can see what she ate before she was killed. Why? Why, would you do this?"

Caleb looked up from Kim's cadaver and said, "Because Kim's eyes are in there."

Chapter 52

Caitlin, Caleb, and I wheeled the gurney to the autopsy room and helped get Kim's cadaver situated on the cold steel table. The four of us put on surgical gloves and Caitlin extracted a scalpel from an array of tools resting on what looked to be a cafeteria-issued lunch tray. As she touched the tip of the scalpel to Kim's flesh, Caleb and I gave each other a strained glance. I wasn't apprehensive of being wrong about the eyes being in Kim's stomach, so much as I was the idea that if the eyes weren't there, all hope was lost for Alex.

Gregory was at the foot of the table, mentally and literally biting his inner lip. I wasn't altogether sure what was going through his mind as Caitlin flexed her wrist and the scalpel slid into the hardened flesh. Caitlin made a long incision, then administered two pairs of clips to hold back the thick area of fat tissue directly above the stomach.

I peered into the human crevasse; the stomach was beige, the color of Silly Putty, and smaller than I would have imagined. Caitlin applied a generous amount of force to the tissue and it folded open like a TV turkey.

Caleb looked up stupefied, "How? How did you know?"

Sitting amid a pile of gray mass were two large protuberances. They were cragged and yellow, but there was no denying the lumps of tissue were once eyes.

Caitlin looked up in disbelief, "Well, I'll be."

Gregory had made his way over for a good angle and shook his head in what I surmised was absolute awe at my deductive capabilities. The four of us stood in silence, taking in the implications of the sight.

Caleb broke the silence, "So what exactly are her eyes seeing?"

~

Caitlin said she would run every test imaginable and get back to us by 5:00 p.m. Caleb rode back with me, and once safely in the car he repeated his earlier question, "How did you know?"

I told him about the tape recorder and Conner's involvement. He played Devil's Advocate, but was unable to convince me of Conner's innocence. There were a few inadequacies, and I tried Conner's cell to have them pacified, but he wasn't taking my calls.

Once back at 14 Surry Woods Drive, Caleb and I hopped out of the Range Rover and I whispered on the way up the steps, "Keep a lid on the Conner bug. I don't want these idiots doing anything stupid. Best to keep them in the dark."

He nodded and we pushed through the front door. Gleason was sitting at the table and said, "Gregory filled me in on most of the details. I can't believe this shit. When and where did you get the hunch Kim's eyes were hiding in her stomach?"

"I'm not sure. I started thinking maybe one of those fifty thousand birds had gotten hold of them. Bird—eat—stomach, I'm not sure. From there, it just popped in my head."

He did a half shrug which either meant he bought my lie, or he didn't really care in the first place. Gleason stood, "Do we have any leads on what her eyes may have been seeing? They were sitting in her stomach, there had to be something else in there."

I think Gleason was expecting a key and some magical, indigestible map of sorts. I said, "Unfortunately, everything else was digested and a different shade of gray. Caitlin is doing some tests on the contents as we speak. Hopefully, something jumps out at her and we can get moving on this."

I didn't want to ask, but a driving force propelled to bad news brought about the question, "Heard anything from Conner?"

He shook his head and said, "There's a good possibility we may never hear from Conner again."

If only that were true.

Gregory walked through the door thirty minutes later with two pizza boxes. I guess he wanted to even the score for the breakfast burrito I'd bought him ASAP. Lacy came down the stairs and was into her second slice before I'd handed out paper towel squares. She took a third slice and retired to the living room to listen to the Mariners-Indians game seven playoff.

I was tinkering with the idea of having a quick chat with her, but I didn't think she would take the news of having slept with a serial killer—or a serial killer's secretary—lightly. I checked the clock, it was ten to five. Four hours until Alex's date with death.

We couldn't do much until we heard back from Caitlin, and I had a nut to crack with Gregory. I took a bite of sausage, leaned back in my chair and said, "I have a proposition for you, Toddy. How's this sound? I'll cut you a check for three grand right now for Lacy's lighthouse painting. You tell Charles Mangrove you were outbid, give him his twenty-five hundred back, and walk with five hundred for yourself."

Gregory shook his head, "That's not the painting I bid on for Director Mangrove."

Then who? No, he wouldn't. I choked on my bite of pizza for a few unpleasant seconds, before stammering, "You mean to tell me you bid on that painting for yourself?"

He took a bite of pizza to hide his smirk and said, "We must have the same taste in art."

It was lucky for Gregory my cell phone rang or he would have eaten his next slice of pizza through a straw. I grabbed my cell off the table and flipped it open, "Prescott."

"It's Caitlin."

Caleb mouthed, "Put it on speaker."

I hit the speaker button and set the phone atop the two pizza boxes. "All right, shoot."

Caitlin started, "I did some preliminary tests and it appears the remnants in Kim's stomach had been sitting there for about an hour before she was killed. Looks like some peanut butter crackers and milk or some other dairy."

Caleb bowed his head and murmured, "Kim always brought a pack of crackers and two lemon yogurts to the library when she studied."

Caitlin continued, "I did a molecular scan and everything checks out as amino-acid based. Nothing alien. No dirt, rocks, anything of that sort."

Sorry, Glease. No ring, no key, no map.

I asked, "Did you do a blood test?"

"Yep. Glucose levels were stable. No poisons. No alcohol. No barbiturates. Blood work's clean as a whistle."

"So what you're telling me is, you didn't find anything abnormal, nothing seemed tainted by a second party, and that we are royally and totally fucked."

"Not exactly."

The four of us froze.

Caitlin said passively, "There was one thing."

The refrigerator's incessant humming resembled a firing jet engine as Caitlin started back in, "I was arranging Kim's corpse into the body bag and was forced to move one of her hands to make room for her abdomen. As I was moving it, I noticed a cyanosis of the nail bed I hadn't caught at first glance. It appeared as though Kim suffered from peripheral vasoconstriction."

Gleason stole the words out of my mouth, "What's that translate to in laymen's terms?"

"I'm getting to that. It means that Kim Welding's fingernails were blue, which is consistent with death by asphyxia."

Gregory stated, "So you're saying Kim Welding was strangled."

Caitlin said flatly, "No, I'm saying Kim Welding was drowned."

Chapter 53

Drowned? Why the sudden change in MO? The four of us looked to one another for answers, but when there's no Scantron, it's hard to fill in a bubble.

Caitlin continued, "The nails started me thinking, and I did some backtracking. Kim's body appeared to undergo a blood shift. A blood shift is the shifting of blood to the thoracic cavity, the chest between the diaphragm and the neck, to avoid the collapse of the lungs under higher pressure during drowning."

Gregory said, "Big deal. So Tristen drowned her before he killed her. That doesn't change much."

Caitlin said, "There's more."

More? My stomach clenched. The four of us inched as close to the phone as possible without smashing our heads together.

"In most victims, the larynx relaxes sometime after unconsciousness and water fills the lungs. This is what we call a wet drowning. Water, regardless of freshwater or saltwater, will damage the inside surface of the lungs, collapse the alveoli, and cause a hardening of the lungs with a reduced ability to exchange air. Freshwater contains less salt than blood and will therefore be absorbed by the bloodstream due to osmosis. Saltwater is much saltier than blood and, due to osmosis, water will leave the bloodstream and enter the lungs."

Gregory beat me to the punch, "So what?"

"So there was no evidence of water in Kim's lungs."

Gregory again beat me to the stupid button, "Meaning?"

Caleb cleared up the matter for the three idiots sitting next to him, "Meaning Kim was drowned in a fresh body of water and not in the Atlantic."

"Precisely," Caitlin replied.

~

We terminated the call with Caitlin and stared blankly at one another. I felt like I was riding the short bus with two of my even more handicapped friends. Let me get this straight, Tristen and/or Conner made Kim swallow her eyes, drowned her in a freshwater body of water, transported her to the Roque Bluffs, dismembered her, and stuffed her in a lobster cage all in a time span of one hour. This was a lot of information to absorb.

We'd ended the call with Caitlin at 5:15 p.m. It was now almost six and we hadn't made a lick of sense of any of the new information. Gleason offered, "There are 2,000 lakes in Maine and about the same number of rivers. This would be in relation to you, Thomas. You got a fishing hole somewhere?"

"Nope, not here. I did in Washington." I was more talking to myself than the other three. I said to the three of them, "He started this in Maine and he's going to finish it in Maine."

We were all interrupted by Lacy hopping around in the living room screaming, "Oh my God. They came back."

Her beloved Mariners had apparently made a game of it. Caleb shook his head at Lacy and then straightened up, "What about the lake Alex's house is built on?"

Gregory and Gleason's eyes widened, and Gleason said, "That could be something."

~

By 8:00 p.m., Alex's house and Lake Wesserunett was our best bet. Lacy was all smiles and seemed disappointed I made her ride with Gleason and Gregory. I didn't want her to overhear Caleb and I talk about Conner's involvement just yet.

We were rocketing westbound along I-95 in the Range Rover two car lengths behind the Caprice when Caleb shook his head and said, "This isn't right. It's too vague. Have you seen the lake? It's enormous. How are we going to know where to look? From the beginning, this thing hasn't been a treasure hunt, it's been a dead giveaway."

I agreed with the kid. The lake was about six miles around and we were flying on the loose connection between Alex and myself. The Caprice signaled to get off the highway at the Route 2 junction.

I eased the SUV into the exit lane behind the Caprice. The Range Rover had two wheels down the ramp when Caleb yanked the wheel vaulting us back onto the highway.

I slammed on the brakes and we came to a skidding halt. Caleb said serenely, "Turn around."

I floored the Range Rover through the grass dividing the traffic and headed east on the freeway. "Are you going to tell me what's going on?"

"All the murder sites have been boat accessible. Your house, the lighthouse, your boat, and the bluff. Why would this time be any different?"

He was right. All the sites had been boat accessible and the lake Alex's house backed up to was landlocked. I felt Caleb raise himself an inch off his seat with his fingertips and waited for him to apprise me of Alex's death site. He said, "You row with Conner at the Verona Rowing Club, correct?"

I nodded.

"Did you know until about two years ago it was called the Penobscot Bay-River Rowing Club?"

I'd never read about this in the newsletter. "What? Penobscot Bay-River?"

"The club is positioned where the Penobscot River runs into the Penobscot Bay. Haven't you ever wondered why the water is so calm in that area. It's because the two currents flow against each other to create relative equilibrium."

"So then it would be half river water, half Atlantic ocean."

"I said relative equilibrium. Think how the water flows. And the fish you see."

The water flowed out to sea. The fish were all freshwater. It all fit. We would find Alex on the grounds of the Verona Rowing Club.

I looked at the dash. It was 8:26 p.m. If we found her in the next fifteen minutes she would be alive. Sixteen and she would be dead.

Chapter 54

We were barreling along the freeway at 110 mph when the fatal minute flickered on the dash, 8:41 p.m.

Seven minutes later, we pulled into the barren Verona Rowing Club parking lot. The wind had picked up considerably and the last of the scullers had called it quits hours earlier. My phone rang for the sixth time in twelve minutes and I flipped it open, stating, "Alex is at the Verona Rowing Club."

Gleason didn't ask how I knew this, "We'll be there in twenty minutes."

"Stay in the parking lot. I don't want Lacy leaving the car."

"You're the boss."

You're the boss? If I hadn't been in a dead sprint to the club entrance, I would have stopped to shit my pants. The place shut down at 6:00 on Sundays and the entrance doors were locked. I peered through the glass but didn't see a janitor vacuuming with headphones on like in the movies. Alex wasn't going to be inside, and Caleb and I went to work on the eight-foot terra-cotta wall enclosing the club.

The wind was whipping the glass water out to sea and I squinted into the horizon. I tapped Caleb on the shoulder and pointed straight out. "Do you see anything out there?"

He didn't, but I could have sworn I glimmered the salient shadow of a stern amid the high waves. I gave the ocean a hard stare, but didn't see the mirage again. Caleb and I were protected from the gusting wind, but it was still remarkably loud and Caleb yelled, "Where do you think she is?"

I could think of only one place we would find Alex's body and started running.

~

They kept the shells in a long brick storage shelter across the bridge. Caleb followed behind me as I did a steady jog across the football field-length bridge.

We came to the wrought iron door locked with thick cable and a rotund Masterlock. I pulled my automatic from my waistband and fired off three shots in quick succession. The third round did the trick and the broken cable shuttered against the steel door. Caleb pulled the cables aside as I wrenched the heavy door open. The long room was musty and darkly lit with overhanging garage lighting.

The shells were held in wooden mounting much like submarine barracks, four high and twenty five long on each side. Conner's shell was in L7C, the third slot of the seventh row on the left side. I placed my hand on the hard wood as if I could tell if death had visited the shell simply by its temperature. I lolled the shell on its side and pieces of Alex's body didn't come tumbling out.

Caleb asked, "Should we check them all real quick?"

Checking 200 shells real quick still translated into one big, slow, sloppy chore. If Alex's body wasn't stuffed in Conner's shell, then it wasn't here. It's not like I had a shell here.

Whap.

But I did have a locker.

We hightailed it back across the bridge and to the outdoor lockers facing the bay. The lockers were thirty feet from where Caleb and I had first found our bearings after hopping the outer wall. It wasn't hard to pinpoint my locker. It was the only one leaking blood.

~

Caleb and I stood motionless in front of locker 81. I straddled the blossoming puddle in front of the locker as I lifted the light combination lock in my left hand. I turned the dial right to 7, left to 32, then right to 6. Unfortunately, the combination was 6-34-5. On the fourth attempt, I unlatched the lock and tossed it to Caleb. The wind was fierce and as I looked at Caleb one last time, he yelled, "What are you waiting for?"

I'm sorry, but I was little weary about finding the woman I'd fallen in love with just forty-eight hours prior in forty-eight pieces.

I lifted the lock mechanism and eased the locker door open against the prevailing wind. My fingers slipped from the door and the locker slammed shut. I only saw the ravaged body for an instant but—there was no mistaking it—the body was that of Conner Ellis Dodds.

Chapter 55

My head flooded with different components of anguish. Conner was dead. But he deserved it, didn't he? By default, was Alex still alive? And if so, for how long?

I reeled four or five steps backward and Caleb moved in to take my spot. He opened the locker door and stepped to the side. I numbly took in the sight. The locker was a bloody mess; Conner's limbs were in a pile at the bottom of the locker, his midsection hung in limbo—I'm guessing from one of the clothing hooks—where his initials, CED, were visibly tattooed across his ripped abdominals.

His head sat in the top cubby lolled to the left, pinning a splintered walkie-talkie against the inner wall. Conner's face was unrecognizable, only his bright blue eyes remained. They'd somehow escaped the massacre unscathed.

I took two steps forward and Caleb yelled, "Why didn't Tristen take his eyes?"

I heard myself say, "He wants me to know the game is over. No more clues. No more help. I lost. And I'm next."

~

I called Caitlin and informed her about Conner. The conversation was one-sided and I wasn't sure if she would be playing Chief Medical Examiner on this one. Caleb and I made a pact to keep the Conner information to ourselves; nothing could be gained by defaming him at this point. I still wanted to know why. Why had he helped Tristen? And how had the two come to find each other?

The only person with the answers was laughing at me right now, and there was a good chance he would tell me about Conner's involvement seconds before he took my life.

Caleb and I hopped back over the wall and strolled toward the Range Rover. The back bumper of the FBI Caprice was barely visible parked parallel with the SUV. Caleb and I passed the front end of the Range Rover and froze.

Caleb said uniformly, "Looks like Gregory won't be needing Lacy's painting after all."

The windshield of the Caprice was covered in blood and brains. Gregory and Gleason were dead. Lacy was gone.

~

I channeled my anger, uneasiness, and misgivings into all-out rage. At who, I'm not sure. At myself? At Gregory? At Gleason? At Conner? At Tristen? It was a combination of all of them and it wasn't digesting well. Speaking of which, my sausage pizza from three hours earlier was now part of the Verona Rowing Club montage.

I wrenched the driver side door open and surveyed Gregory's limp body. The bullet had entered through the back of his skull and sent the better part of his brain and chiseled features onto the dash. Gleason had taken one in the right temple, and needless to say, his left temple was decorating the driver side window.

I couldn't understand it. How had this happened? Whoever had accomplished the feat had obviously been sitting in the backseat. And it sure as hell wasn't Tristen Grayer. As naïve and incompetent as the FBI was—and trust me they were—I couldn't see them inviting Tristen Grayer into the backseat for an invigorating game of 21 Questions. There must be a third party involved.

Caitlin arrived on the scene and I had to console her for ten minutes before she muscled out a word.

I gave her a quick rundown on the carnage, then explained the most pressing detail, "Tristen and whoever else is involved in this nightmare has both Alex and Lacy. I need you to autopsy Conner and see what exactly Tristen is up to. There has to be a clue here somewhere. This is crunch time. I need you to be strong."

I'm not sure if she saw through my lie. I had little hope for Alex and Lacy at this point. Tristen had thrown in the towel with the clues. His legacy would continue and he would come back next year and turn someone else's life upside down.

Chapter 56

I don't remember falling asleep. Caleb and I had gone through two pots of coffee, but neither of us had an inkling who the third party might be. The more I thought about it, the more I was convinced Tristen could have pulled off the stunt. He could have crept up on the Caprice, pulled the back door open, blown both Gregory and Gleason's brains out, and then snatched up Lacy. This is all assuming the backdoor had been unlocked, which wasn't consistent with FBI protocol. But then again, it was FBI protocol. I knew preschools that ran tighter ships.

I peered across the table at Caleb asleep in a pile of spilled coffee. I grabbed the pot off the table and went to work on a fresh batch. Caleb stirred and wiped the dripping coffee from his nose, "What time is it?"

I looked up at the clock, it was 2:00 in the afternoon. "We have eight hours. We shouldn't have slept."

He nodded, but the both of us knew we needed the catnap. By the end of our brainstorming session last night, one of us had broached the possibility Tristen was a triplet. Could there be three of them, Tristen, Geoffrey, and Bernard?

I checked my cell phone and saw I had five missed calls, three from Caitlin and two from Charles Mangrove. My answering machine was blinking and I knew I would have the same five calls. Charles' were first and I skipped them both. The last three were indeed from Caitlin. All three messages were fairly similar: she didn't find any clues, but had something important to tell me and to stop by the morgue.

Terrific. Alex and Lacy were both missing and soon to be of the deceased variety, and Caitlin wanted to drop the bomb on me that I needed to set aside the month of May for Lamaze class. Can you get cyanide over the counter or do you need a prescription? No, killing myself was option F. Option A-E would bring me close, but I'd probably survive.

Caleb poured two large mugs full of dark Colombian brew and the two of us hopped in the Range Rover. I chugged the coffee down in three gulps, and if I hadn't killed off all my taste buds with last night's load, I might have thought the coffee hot. My brain started working again around mile marker 203, and was in full tilt when I parked the Range Rover next to Caitlin's red Pathfinder in the Bangor County morgue lot.

Caleb and I walked through the front entrance and into the waiting area. My eyes found the thick steel cage door leading to the corridor. The lock was bent inward and the door ajar. The work appeared to be at the diligence of a large, heavy ax.

I crashed through the gate and sprinted down the long corridor, slamming into the door leading to the surgical annex. Caitlin was nowhere to be found. Caleb disappeared into the storage area to search the body bags for Caitlin, but we both knew he would come up empty. I tried Caitlin's cell and seconds later heard her distinctive ring coming from behind me. I picked her cell off the counter and stared at it long and hard, as if in some way it symbolized Caitlin's death.

I fought the image off. She wasn't dead. Death would come for Caitlin, Alex, and Lacy at 10:10 p.m. tonight. Caleb and I had five hours.

~

Caleb came back into the autopsy room and shook his head. I hadn't noticed the surgical table in the center of the room where Conner's body had been laid out and an attempt at reconstruction made.

I looked at Conner's tattoo, his bulging muscular body, his almost buzzed blond hair, his revered blue eyes, and his fairy tale wanger. Then I looked up at Caleb and said, "The game isn't over. It's just begun."

~

I explained everything to Caleb on the way to the Verona Rowing Club. He shook his head in disbelief. Hell, I almost couldn't believe it. But it all fit. The puzzle was complete.

There was quite a scene at the Verona Rowing Club and I had to find one of Caitlin's higher-ranking men before Caleb and I were let through the masses to the crime scene. The weather had gone from bad to worse, and the day seemed three hours ahead of schedule. The wind was howling in from the ocean and the small waves were running up onto the deck near the lockers. I stood near the cordoned-off locker and faced out to sea.

I'd yet to disclose one facet to Caleb and forged the last wrinkle in our little shit pot, "Tristen and Conner were working together on this so I think it's safe to say they'd worked out a plan from day one. I'd gone rowing with Conner the day before the first murder. We'd chatted it up about what we would do to Alex Tooms if we ever got our hands on him. Of course, I thought it was a *him*. Conner must have known Alex was a woman, and always referred to her simply as Tooms. Conner said he would take Tooms to an island where he would make Tooms rewrite the book. He said he would torture and starve Tooms until Tooms wrote the truth."

Caleb added the gloss, "The eyes in the locker weren't looking at you, they were seeing the next murder site. They were seeing the island."

I placed it in the kiln, "Tristen has Alex, Caitlin, and Lacy on Matinicus Island."

Chapter 57

The rain whipped against the windshield and my wipers fought a losing battle. It was ten after seven when Caleb and I pulled into the muddy Bayside Harbor parking lot. There were only two other cars, a by-product of the seven to ten foot swells smashing against the harbor pier.

Caleb ran to the *Backstern* and I ducked headlong into the wind toward the manager's hut. I pushed through the door and evidentially Kellon's deadbeat dad thought I was there to kill him. He had on a yellow slicker and shot his hands up in the air. Imagine a high school referee signaling a field goal in a typhoon. That's what he looked like.

The deadbeat screamed, "Don't shoot!"

I shoved my .45 in my waistband and said, "I'm not here to kill you. I need your help."

DBD slowly put his arms down and started breathing again. I said, "This concerns your daughter's killer. He's on Matinicus Island and I need to get there so I can kill him."

DBD nodded like this was a run-of-the-mill demand at the Bayside Harbor manager hut. He grabbed a map off the wall and laid it on the counter. Smoothing it out, he said, "We're here. Matinicus Island is thirty miles directly south. It's pretty small. It's going to be a shot in the dark finding it in this weather."

I asked, "How long by boat?"

"Two hours in a good sea, four in this storm. I just got off the radio with the coast guard, says it's even worse the farther you get out. Tropical Storm Fernando or something."

Speaking of the Coast Guard, I wish I had my FBI sidekicks to pull some strings. Unfortunately, the only strings Gleason and Gregory would be pulling would be on their *Welcome to Heaven* harps. I could get Charles Mangrove on the phone and see what he could do, but I had a feeling when all the strings had been pulled, the sand in the hourglass would be glass itself.

Kellon's dad must have seen I was contemplating the odds of a Tropical Storm Prescott and walked to a wall safe. He had his back to me for twenty seconds and then turned around with a pair of keys dangling from his fingertips. His eyes were moist and he said, "This boat should get you there in under three hours, it has GPS so you won't be able to miss Matinicus. Doesn't seem right for me to hang onto the boat now that she's dead."

I took the keys from him and asked him which slot the boat was parked. He said he'd show me, then disappeared into a backroom, emerging seconds later with a double-barrel shotgun. For a moment I thought he might be coming with, but after he loaded the gun he slammed five extra shells into my hand and said, "Put one in him for me."

~

Caleb and I were in the big Formula 500 speedboat getting a crash course, which was fitting, from Kellon's father. On a side note, the 360-horsepower vessel was named *The Kellon*. That is when Kellon's deadbeat dad became Frank, Kellon's father.

The crash course lasted a little under three minutes whereby Frank programmed the exact coordinates for Matinicus Island into the GPS console. I shook Frank's hand and promised to inflict as much pain as possible on his daughter's killer before I released him to the fiery pits of hell.

I eased the throttle forward, the rudder caught, and we began overtaking the crashing waves. The GPS computer read a distance of thirty-two miles, and at an estimated speed of thirty knots, that would put us at Matinicus Island at approximately 9:30 p.m.

~

An hour into the trip, Caleb and I were soaked with seawater down to our drawers. There were three or four times the boat would have flipped had it not been for the added weight of the water, which was coming in faster than the bilge could pump it out.

Caleb retreated to the small cabin and came up with two life preservers. These particular life preservers were made of a space-age aluminum, and the only life they preserved were those of the hop and the barley. I cracked open the can of Pig's Eye and had never tasted anything so abhorrently satisfying. It appeared as though Frank was not a connoisseur of fine beer.

Caleb took the helm and I went in search of some actual life preservers. I found them under a cushioned seat, and both Caleb and I began strapping on the bright orange vests. As I was pulling the life vest on, I stifled a laugh. What was I doing? If I didn't make it to the island and fell at the hands of the Atlantic, then so be it. I'd read the script and it was simple: either Tristen Grayer or Thomas Prescott was penciled in to die on this night. Tonight's fate was not unforeseen.

Caleb had apparently drawn on the same conclusions and the both of us tossed the life jackets over the side of the boat. Drowning was supposedly the Queen of Spades in the deck of death, and I had the ingenious idea to tie the shotgun to my ankle using fishing line. I had the image of trying to pull the trigger on the shotgun with my big toe while attempting not to drown. I thought about the irony while finishing off my Pig's Eye.

~

If it wasn't for the GPS satellite, there would be no telling which direction the boat was headed. All manual operation had concluded when I'd pushed the throttle to full bore seconds after we'd escaped the harbor walls. The navigation screen began to beep loudly, and Caleb informed me it was the five-mile alert. I checked my watch. It was 9:13 p.m.

The ocean raged for the next ten minutes and I thought for certain we'd high-sided on several different occasions. But each time we went up, we eventually came down.

~

By 9:35 p.m. I still hadn't seen a speck of land.

Caleb grabbed my arm and yelled, "The current is changing!"

He was right, it appeared we were now riding over the top of the waves, rather than running up them. Caleb stuck his arm out and screamed, "Look out."

In hindsight, I'd assume he was pointing to the small rock bed thirty yards in front of us, not the island looming in the distance.

I yanked the wheel hard to the right, but it wasn't nearly in time, and the Formula 500 hit the rock formation hard. For an instant I thought I'd hit the rocks, but I was wet, salty, and hypothermic, which is consistent with a mid-Atlantic drowning.

I kept my head above water and craned my neck for any sign of Caleb. I screamed his name a couple times, but the howling wind and raging seas made for a futile effort. My eyes and ears might have well been painted on. I was engulfed in blackness. I couldn't help but think that this blackness, this was Lacy's life. I was enraged by the thought. Lacy would die before she would again see the beauty of this world.

I turned over on my back. Not if I could help it.

Chapter 58

At first I thought a great white had attacked me. It took me a moment to register the bites were at the hands of a jagged rock shore. I smashed against the rocks three times before I was able to grip a stationary rock and heave myself from the surf. I tried not to think about Caleb, but I subconsciously clicked the death toll from seven to eight.

The faceplate on the Tag Heuer was shattered, but it appeared to be functioning. It showed 9:52 p.m. I'd been in the water for exactly fifteen minutes. Funny, I'd done the same thing one year ago, almost to the minute. Of course after my swim last year, I'd taken a 483-hour nap. Tonight would not be the case. I was probably borderline hypothermic and my moving was the only thing that would save my life, not to mention Alex, Caitlin, and Lacy's.

I took a step up the black rock, my right leg snagged, and I heard a definitive metallic clank. The shotgun. The fishing line had somehow held throughout the ordeal.

Was I smart shit or what?

I pulled on the fishing line and the shotgun emerged from behind a large rock. I had two shots at glory. I would have to be perfect.

~

The island was less than a mile at its widest and its longest. According to Frank, there was an unmanned lighthouse and abandoned living quarters on the northeastern tip.

I quickly shed all my clothes, keeping only my boxer briefs and shoes on. My extremities were starting to get feeling back, and the pins and needles had started. If it hadn't been pitch-black, I might not have noticed the faintest change in blackness at the far right edge of the island. I held the shotgun to my chest like I was a minuteman in the Revolution and did the steeplechase until I was a hundred or so yards from a dilapidated lighthouse. The lighthouse was simply a concrete column sitting on a large concrete foundation. Picture an old man with glasses taking the last shit of his life; that's what the lighthouse looked like.

There was a small cottage, which I deduced was the lighthouse quarters, less than thirty feet from the lighthouse. It was safe to assume no one had slept a night in the windswept structure in more than twenty years. This was not a homey bungalow; this was a could-fall-over-in-a-heap-of-dust-at-any-second carriage house.

There were two small windows on the western edge, out of which a slight glow emanated into the darkness. I didn't want to risk being overheard and found my way back to the water's edge. It took me a little over a minute to navigate the short distance to the base of the lighthouse. The lighthouse door was breathing in the wind and I slipped in the narrow, musty staircase between exhales. A flaxen glow from the light above seeped through the many cracks in the cylindrical concrete stairwell.

I twisted up the stairs and sidestepped into the small chamber. A large form blocked the light against a far wall, and I could tell by the shadow it cast it was a body. As I neared, I noticed the dark chocolate hair carried auburn highlights under the red glow.

I ambled toward Alex. Her naked body began squirming, the metallic cuffs around her wrists slinking through the glistening steel railing. With the duct tape over her eyes, she reasonably mistook my footsteps for Tristen Grayer's. I gingerly pulled the tape from her eyes and covered her mouth. Her scream heated my palm, and I whispered in her trembling ear, "It's me, everything will be okay."

It would take ten minutes for her eyes to adjust, but she relaxed at the sound of my voice. She whimpered, "Get me out of here."

I couldn't waste a bullet on the handcuffs. I had no choice but to leave Alex's side and come back for her later. My gut, right down near my gallbladder, told me that she wasn't in danger. At least not the immediate peril that faced Caitlin and Lacy.

I checked my watch, 10:01 p.m. I had nine minutes.

I kissed Alex on the lips softly and promised her I'd be back for her. I could hear her faint whimpering as I quickly descended the lighthouse steps and slipped past the inhaling door.

Chapter 59

I sprinted the thirty feet to the back corner of the guest quarters in a low crouch. I pressed up against the soft wood, a billowing paint chip brushing against my cheek. The red paint was weather beaten, the flailing chips trying feverishly to catch a nor'easter and drown their sorrows in the Atlantic.

There was light rustling behind me and I whipped around. Nothing. It was the lighthouse door changing rhythm in the wind. I took five or six deep breaths then edged around to the west wall, my back continuously in contact with the tender siding.

I came to the first of two windows and peeked inside. My eyes had adjusted, my pupils surely the size of a buffalo nickel, and I could make out the shadow of an old toilet and a small sink, chipped, drooping, and breathing asthmatically through rusted pipes. There were two doors: one appeared to open to a small closet, the other serving to separate the small outhouse from the main quarters. From this door, I caught the residue of flickering flames cascading through a hole where a doorknob once rested.

The window was once a four-pane and only the wooden cross and one pane remained. I reached my arm through the frame and pushed hard on the glass with my open palm. The glass bent slightly and popped from beneath the wood's edge.

I pulled the piece of glass out and silently laid it on the rocky earth. Now for the window's skeleton. The horizontal piece was only connected peripherally through its vertical better half and slipped off without much fray. The vertical piece ran up into the frame of the window and would be more of a hassle. If I had an hour to kill and my Boy Scout survival knife, I may have been able to remove the twenty-four inch casing without a peep. Unfortunately, I would have to peep. The key would be to peep at the right moment.

It would have been easier to push than to pull, but if I pushed I risked dropping the casing inside. I dug my right knee into the softness of the beaten timber and grasped the casing with both hands. The door of the lighthouse was banking viciously in the foreground and I started moving my body slowly with the rhythm. *Whip, whip, clack.* Forward, forward, back. *Whip, whip, clack.* Forward, forward, back. *Whip, whip, cla—*

I pulled with all the strength I could muster and I thought I felt the entire structure move when *snap.*

Even with my front row seat I was unable to hear the wood splinter beneath the door's cry. I leaned the shotgun against the outer wall where I could reach it from inside, pulled my shoes off, and bellied up to the window. My plan was to go in hands first, then use my leverage to crawl down the inner wall with my feet. I checked my watch. Seven minutes.

I had the strange feeling Tristen was on the other side of the door doing precisely the same thing.

~

I wiggled my torso through the window and leaned forward until my hands pet the dusty floor. Pushing hard backward against the inner wall I used my feet to climb down. Then as soon as I'd begun, I was lying on the mold riddled floor staring under the tiny crack separating the rooms.

I cocked my head. In the silence I thought I could hear Alex's hushed whimper resonating from the lighthouse chamber. Then I heard a fingernail bend, a knuckle crack, the door scratch its head, carbon dioxide levels rise. Then blackness.

Chapter 60

I blinked my eyes and stood up gingerly. Standing made me nauseous and I threw up, which is when I noticed my hands were handcuffed behind a steel pipe running from the ground to the ceiling, one of the guest quarter's hurricane poles.

A voice ingrained in my nightmares resounded from behind me, "Relax, I hit you with the handle. You'll live. For another few minutes at least."

I took a step around the pole and saw, leaning against a four-foot ax, his hell-orange eyes shimmering in the candlelight, Tristen Grayer. To the right of me, standing naked, duct tape over her eyes and mouth, attached to a second pole, was Caitlin. She mumbled something, and thrashed about, before succumbing to her tangible restraints.

I canvassed the room for any sign of Lacy. Tristen took heed of this and said, "Looking for your whore sister?"

I didn't answer and Tristen took a couple paces toward me. He said apathetically, "She's dead. You would have been proud though, Thomas. She took a blind dive into the Atlantic about five miles out. But I have you in her stead. I wanted to keep you around for next year, but it appears I'll have to find a new victim after all."

All the will I had left to live seemed to drain from my body. My brain and heart ceased activity, as if they'd both sent conscripts to the other about surrendering. I wanted one answer before I died and asked, "Tell me about Conner."

Tristen smiled. "Oh, Conner. Shame about him, wasn't it. And him saving my life and all."

"He what?"

"Last year when the two of us, you and I, plummeted over the cliff, Conner was the one who dragged me from the surf. I told him about this island and he took me here. He kept me much like you are now. He would come by a couple times a week to give me food and water. Eventually we got to talking, and I even started considering him a friend."

I mentally gagged at the idea of Tristen and Conner as friends. Tristen did a circle around Caitlin and I noticed his laggard left leg drag on the earthy floor. He continued, "Then one day, about a month ago, Conner tells me he has this idea, a game. He wants me to help him get his revenge against you, Thomas Prescott, for reaping his benefits. Can you believe my luck? He said he didn't have it in him to rape and kill and that I would be his tool."

I interrupted him, "Then why did you kill him?"

He acted like I'd asked why lions and tigers don't mate. "When I'd served my purpose he was going to lock me up again, or kill me. I got to him before he got to me, simple as that."

It was closing in on that fateful minute and I went into stall mode, "How'd you know about this place?"

He did a tight spin on the toe of his right foot, then said, "This is where I brought Geoffrey."

I nodded like this was common knowledge. He laughed to himself and continued, "I couldn't believe it. I go back three years later just to see what the dump looks like and I walk in on the two of them fucking like dogs."

I shook my head in disgust. "Were you mad or jealous?"

He seemed to ponder the question and walked behind me. "A little of both I guess. I didn't like the fact my family had been screwing for the last hundred years, but I would have liked to think Ingrid would have picked me over him. But when I found out Ingrid was pregnant with Geoffrey's child, I lost it."

"I'm sorry, but "lost it" is not the correct term for chopping your sister and the child she was carrying into fifty pieces. It's called going psycho." I laughed, which in hindsight I would have tried harder to hold back. The ax struck me in my right midsection and the sound of cracking ribs filled the room.

I fell to my knees and Tristen continued as if nothing had happened, "I made love to Ingrid before releasing her to the beyond. It was an ecstasy I'd never felt before. Geoffrey was a different story, he would need to suffer, to know he'd caused Ingrid's demise. I left him slightly alive. That night we stole a boat and drifted for a day before coming to shore here on this very island."

He wiggled the ax at me, "I kept Geoffrey much like you are now."

He snickered to himself, and said, "Do you know what I did? After each murder I would bring the girl's eyes back here and nail them to the wall."

I was having trouble breathing, but was able to lift my head a couple inches. A deluge of black masses protruded from the walls. A shiver ran up my spine as I conjured up the image of Geoffrey handcuffed to this pole, ten beady eyes penetrating his soul. Tristen was in front of me again and said, "Do you know why I killed those three girls on the same day last year? This exact date one year ago to be precise."

He didn't wait for my answer, "Geoffrey said he was sorry. He said he was sorry for screwing Ingrid when he knew I loved her, and begged me to kill him. He was my brother, so I finished it that night. I called Conner Dodds and told him where to find the bodies."

I helped him along, "Then you dumped Geoffrey's body off the bluffs to make it look like a suicide, then hacked the girls into chicken feed." They'd found the women's bodies almost pureed together.

He lifted my chin with the blunt side of the ax, "I knew it would be the last of my killings for a stint and couldn't stop. But then you came along and ruined everything. That however will be rectified here in a matter of minutes."

I felt the floorboard directly beneath me tense. I stood up holding my ribs and said, "You know the guy you stuffed in my locker?"

His smile faded as mine began to form. I enlightened him, "That wasn't Conner."

Tristen didn't have time to answer before his head exploded.

Chapter 61

I turned in time to see the mouth of a pistol snake from within the vacant doorknob aperture. The door swept inward and a familiar voice rang out, "How did you know?"

A mild scream erupted from behind me, and I wasn't sure if Caitlin was frightened or elated to hear her brother's voice. I answered his question, "The first thing I noticed was the size of his dick, then I started to see the other inconsistencies."

He laughed, "I shouldn't have used an agent. Everyone knows you have to have a five-inch dick to get into the Bureau."

Had Conner not been minutes from killing me, I would have laughed. I said, "So how did you get Tristen to believe the agent was you?"

Conner snapped on a pair of thin surgical gloves. "I knew he would strike at night with a quick blow to the head, rendering the face unrecognizable, so I kept the guy drugged face down in my bed at all hours of the day. I picked out the guy who most closely resembled me. I knew the guy had to be close but not perfect. I needed to fool Tristen, but at the same time I needed you to figure it out. I needed you to come here to be killed."

Touché.

He continued, "Anyway, I had the agent follow me to my apartment, told him I had an extra pair of night goggles he could try out, and juiced him with a mild sedative. Then I met Tristen and handed over the car."

"When did you get the tattoo?"

"I drove down to Vermont and paid a guy a hefty sum to do it while the guy was passed out. I told him it was a fraternity prank, but I don't think he gave half a shit."

I'd pieced most of this together already. I straightened up, light-headed from the pain and the anguish. "How long have you been planning this little endeavor?"

He looked at Caitlin who was shaking her head and whimpering, then settled his eyes back on me. "Truthfully, when I pulled Tristen from the water, I thought it was you. When I saw that it was him, a light went off. Not everything all at once, but enough where I knew I wanted to keep him around."

"So after you talked to him last year, you sent us on a wild goose chase, then drove to the true site of the murders?"

He laughed, "Only you fucked everything up. You sealed your own fate a year ago."

"I should have known when I followed you that night. Were you meeting Tristen there or were you just supposed to pick up his groceries for him?"

"I figured that when Tristen called, he'd already committed the act. I had no idea he would be there that night. When I got to the bluffs, I had second thoughts about sending you and the rest of the task force on a red herring. That reminds me, I never asked you, why did you decide to follow me in the first place?"

"Dumb luck. I was supposed to ride with your sister to the site, but I was real gassy and decided to drive myself. I floored it out of the lot and saw you headed in the opposite direction and decided to ride your coattails. I remember thinking it odd at the time that you would send us to a destination and not accompany us."

He furrowed his brow, "Why didn't you ever tell anyone this?"

"I figured you wanted the limelight of finding the bodies. Big whoop. Like you said, you didn't think Tristen would be there, you just thought you were taking out someone else's dirty laundry."

He nodded then said, "I was so nervous when I reached the bluffs. Hell, I'd never seen one dead body, let alone three. I was getting my nerve up when I saw you in my rearview mirror with a flashlight straddling over the guardrail. The light started bounding toward the bluff's edge and I figured you saw something."

I nodded. I'd seen Tristen's ax glimmer in the moonlight as he raised it for a severing blow. Conner continued, "I jumped out of the car and followed in the direction you'd gone. I saw a figure holding an ax and fired twice. Then another figure appeared and both went careening off the bluff."

Un—fucking—believable. Conner had been the one who'd shot me. I'd shot Tristen in the knee, then picked up his ax to finish him off. I'd taken a step forward when I took a bullet in the left shoulder and right thigh. I'd always figured Tristen had a gun on him and had shot me from where he lay on the ground. After I'd been shot, I'd staggered backward, and Tristen had picked himself off the rocks and jetted forward. I remember clawing at his face, then weightlessness, then icy Atlantic.

Conner continued, "You have to believe me, Thomas, I thought it was Tristen who I'd shot. When I saw the two of you go over, I ran to the edge, and jumped myself. You have to believe me. When I pulled Tristen from the water, I thought it was you."

I found it ironic Conner was so adamant of my believing his innocence, just seconds before he took my life. "So what did you do after you pulled out Tristen?"

"There was a boat anchored there. I pulled Tristen out and just started sailing out to sea."

"Why didn't you just take him in? You still would've been the hero."

"I thought about that. But I felt there was a good chance Tristen would tell the cops what he'd told me and everyone would see what I'd done, see how selfish I'd been. Actually, after about an hour, Tristen started talking. He told me everything. Ingrid. Geoffrey. Matinicus. That's when it clicked. I figured I could make up some crap about Tristen getting me on his boat. Taking me to the island, where I would escape, killing Tristen, and come out the hero. I mean, shit, I would've been on fucking Regis. But early the next morning I was listening to the radio to see if anything had been reported. Apparently, someone heard the gunshots and called it in. You were reported as alive, but in critical condition. Then the guy says how they found Tristen Grayer's remains splattered on the rock bed. That's when I knew I was screwed. If you just would have died, I could have done anything. But I wasn't sure what you knew. So I just kept him at the island."

"So that's why your name never showed up in the book. You didn't want it to."

He nodded. "I get a call from Alex Tooms three days later wanting to interview me. I gave all credit to you, told her if my name so much as showed up in the book, I'd sue her ass."

I helped him out, "So now what's your plan? You're going to kill the two of us, make it look like Tristen did it, then rescue Alex and no one will know the wiser. Have her write a sequel to *Eight in October* where you, Conner Ellis Dodds, are the hero."

He winked. "You have to admit, it's a beautiful story. Tristen back from the dead, the eyes seeing the next murder site, and the romance, don't get me started on the romance. Me and Lacy, you and Caitlin, you and Alex, and soon to be me and Alex. It's a far cry from last year's simplicity."

Conner made his way to Tristen's limp body, a pool of blood forming around his shaved head. He bent down, wrestled the ax from Tristen's grip, and said, "And what an ending the book will have."

~

He was right, it sounded like quite the tale. I helped him along, "Let me guess, Conner Dodds puts a bullet in Tristen Grayer's skull seconds after he's finished massacring his final victims."

He grinned wickedly. I pointed out, "Two problems. Lacy died at sea. The blind girl is the pinnacle of the story. And second, I already spoke to Alex and told her everything."

He scoffed, "Don't think I'm not pissed about Lacy. I mean, I go out of my way to nab her when I have the chance. You should have seen it. I stroll up on Gregory and Gleason, thinking you've spilled the beans about Tristen's and my relationship, but it turns out they didn't know squat. I hop in the backseat, plugged the two of them, and grabbed Lace. You should have seen the look on her face, total disbelief. If I didn't know better, I'd think she knew it was me.

"I taped her up and hand delivered her to Tristen's boat. He wouldn't have had another chance to get her. I mean, you weren't going to leave her side. Tristen must have thought I'd done this hours before he smashed my skull in with the ax."

He pointed to an earpiece, "As for Alex, you're a terrible bluffer. She doesn't know shit."

That explains why I thought I heard Alex whimpering, Conner had been behind the second door in the outhouse. Conner said, "I was thinking of raping Alex while she still thinks it's Tristen, but it's too risky. And look how she went after you once you were famous. She'll be my willing slave after I save her life."

He looked at his watch and said, "Sorry to have to say this, but I have a timetable to stick to." Conner picked up the ax and walked over to Caitlin. He brushed her hair back and she squirmed. He said softly, "I'm so sorry, Caitlin. I really am."

I used every ounce of strength I had remaining to break free of my restraints, the sensation of warm blood oozing from my wrists possibly the last my brain would register.

Conner waited for my tantrum to subside then said, "I won't torture you, Caitlin, not like what I'm going to do to Thomas. It'll be one quick strike. You won't feel a thing. I'll perform the defacement and slaughter after you're dead."

How brotherly.

He said, "Lay down and this will soon be over."

Caitlin was sobbing hysterically and her naked body involuntarily descended to the dusty floor. Conner pulled her legs out so she was flat on the ground, her hands above her head handcuffed around the pole. Her body was shaking violently and she may have been having an epileptic seizure from shock. Conner glanced at me as he pulled the ax skyward and said, "You don't know how hard this is."

He pulled the ax to its peak and smiled.

~

In hindsight, I found it fitting Conner's eyes would be the last to adhere to these forsaken walls.

The blast came from the second window. The shotgun shell exited the barrel at a speed of 1500 feet per second, shattering the brittle quarter-inch glass pane, cutting through sixteen feet of dusty coastal air, and nipping the first strands of close-cropped blond follicles a thousandth of a second later. The slowly expanding buckshot splintered Conner Ellis Dodd's skull, ripped through his brain, and splattered the majority of his brain and eyes against the far wall.

As the ax thudded to the ground and Conner's shell of a body fell to its knees then flopped forward in a heap, my first thought was that Caleb somehow survived the boat crash and washed up somewhere on the island.

I slowly turned my gaze from the pool of blood forming around what was left of Conner's head to the shotgun's fading echo. Framed within the shattered window, holding the smoking shotgun was not Caleb but a trembling, wet, and stoic Lacy.

I shook my head in complete awe. After a few seconds, I said, "I guess it's safe to assume you can see again."

Her heavy breathing slowly turned into a wry smile.

I returned the smile. "Mind if I ask when?"

She swallowed hard, then letting loose one of her infamous cackles, said, "During the baseball game. I yelled, 'Oh my God! They came back.' No one noticed."

Chapter 62

It's been two weeks and the four of us are drinking beers on the deck of the *Backstern*. Caitlin isn't with us. She relocated to a state that started with an A. She said she didn't want it to be too difficult if I did decide to seek her out. Oh, and she wasn't pregnant. Private Prescott hadn't slipped into Fort Dodds after all. At least that's what she told *moi*.

The first magazine came out yesterday. It was *Time*. Tristen and Conner's faces split the cover underneath the caption "The Maine Catch." This wasn't a coincidence. And, yes, the size of my hook has grown into something of a legend. The details of the story were rough and dry, the four of us were keeping the juicy stuff confidential, only to come out in Alex's sequel later in the year.

Alex still wanted to call it *Encore in October*. I was rallying for *The Thomas Prescott Apology*. Lacy was lobbying for some stupid play on words about her blindness, like *Unforeseen*. And Caleb (yes, Caleb had somehow clung to life and scrambled onto the rock formation we'd collided with. We found him the next day asleep with a certain pug, don't ask), Caleb was in favor of *Autumntrocity* which, after everyone heard, decided to second. Well, everyone but me. I thought *The Thomas Prescott Apology* had a nice ring to it, but Lacy made the point that it sounded like I was the one doing the apologizing. I guess it still needed some tweaking.

The four of us clinked beers to being alive, Tristen and Conner being dead, and the beautiful autumn day. I descended to the cabin and grabbed a second cooler of beer. I had the boat cleaned, $2,000 worth to be exact, and a monument of sorts erected in Kellon's honor. I figured if I live in a house that has dealt with death, I can *notsail* in a boat that has done the same. The monument was a bench seat much like the one before with a cushion enshrined with Kellon's name and the quote "Sailing's the best thing in the wool-wide-wuld."

I flipped the cushion up and pulled out one of about fifteen kites. I decided I would hand out the kites to the kid who successfully docked Captain Dipshit's schooner.

That tradition, however, would start next year.

Author's Note

Well, I hope you enjoyed the read. I can't believe this book has been out for ten years already. I feel like I was just a kid when I wrote it. I know it's a bit crass and the ending is a bit rushed, but I wouldn't change a single word. This is my baby. That being said, I have come a long way in the past decade. I've attached a teaser for the second Thomas Prescott thriller, *Gray Matter*, which is my favorite book I've ever written.

You can learn more about me and see some embarrassing pictures of me and my dogs at www.nickthriller.com.

Thanks for reading,

Nick

GRAY MATTER

Chapter 1

The phone rang. It rang again. It rang a third time. The answering machine kicked in halfway into the fourth ring.

Click.

"*Hello, caller. I'm going to be gone for the next couple weeks. I've set out to find the guy who coined the phrase 'It is better to have loved and lost than never to have loved at all' and blow his brains all over the sidewalk. You can leave a message if you want, but odds are I'm either in jail or dead. Happy Holidays. Live long and prosper. Jesus loves you. The pen is mightier than the sword. Vote yes on 3B. Always compare to the placebo. Seat belts save lives. Freedom.*"

Beep.

A voice gave an exasperated sigh, then started. "Nice message, Thomas. Very eloquent. I would tell you that you're an idiot, but you already know that. I know you're home. In fact, I know you're lying on the couch with your blue comforter. There's probably a jar of peanut butter, the jelly, a loaf of two-week-old bread, and about ten juice boxes sitting on the coffee table."

I lolled my head to the left and peeked at the glass coffee table. Skippy Extra Creamy. Welch's raspberry preserves. Sara Lee Golden Honey Wheat. And six boxes of Tree Top apple juice.

I guess Lacy knew me pretty well.

"Do me a favor and get off your pathetic ass and pick up the phone." She was silent for a second then started back in. "Fine. If you want to self-destruct, isolate yourself from the world, then that's your problem. Have fun."

I will. Thank you.

"Just remember there are those of us who still love you. Even when you're acting like a huge baby."

Ouch.

"Well, I just wanted to call and wish you a happy Thanksgiving. Sorry I couldn't be there for you. I hope you find your way to some pumpkin pie."

A Pumpkin Spice latte from Starbucks would suffice. I hoped they delivered.

"I know I've said it a hundred times already, Thomas, but she doesn't deserve you. You're too good for her. It's been almost six weeks. It's time to get on with your life."

Wrong. I didn't deserve *her.* She was too good *for me.* It'd only been *41 days.* And it was time *to wallow.*

"Bye. I love you."

I hit my head backwards on the pillow three times, then threw off the comforter. I snagged the remote from under the couch and blindly turned on the television. The parade filled the screen and I mentally gagged. This had the potential to be the most depressing day in the history of time.

On-screen, a giant Snoopy floated by. Followed by a giant Charlie Brown. I waited for Woodstock, but he never came. An overly joyous woman commented on the procession, each affected syllable steaming the cold New York air as it left her mouth.

I pulled on my bear paw slippers and padded to the window.

If it was cold in New York then it was *freezing* in Maine. The sky was a dark gray and the earth looked frozen, the dew brittle, tundra-like, the land preparing itself for the long onslaught of winter. The first big snowstorm of the year was expected to start in the late afternoon, early evening. Then everything would be white for the next five months. At least until late April. Old Man Winter wasn't very friendly in the Northeast. In fact, he was one mean old sumbitch.

I made my way to the sliding glass door and peered out on the bay. By bay, I refer to the Penobscot. The last body of water before the Pond, silent *e*'s, and bad teeth.

Anyhow, it was early, around 8:00 a.m., but even so there were a couple brave souls in their sailboats getting one last ride in before the snow began to fall. The water was three shades darker than the sky and lapped idly against the rocky shore. Just off-center was the Surry Woods Lighthouse. The old, tattered lighthouse's light was still visible, a reflective coin on the drab horizon.

Sort of made you want to catch the red-eye to the Bahamas.

On that note, I went into the kitchen, cranked the heat to Bahamian, and opened the freezer. There were five boxes of waffles: Regular, Buttermilk, Cinnamon Toast, Blueberry, and Strawberry. I know, I have a problem. *Hi, my name is Thomas and I'm addicted to waffles. Hey, leggo my Eggo.*

As my waffles toasted, I started a cup of water heating in the microwave. I opened the front door and scampered the ten steps to the paper. It was already half drizzling, half snowing, and I had a feeling the storm was six hours ahead of schedule.

I sat down to the waffles and a cup of steaming apple cider and read the paper. You can tell a lot about a person by the way they read the paper. I was a comics, sports, weather, front page, Dow Jones, Jumble kind of guy. Alex had been a front-to-back kind of gal. Maybe that's why it hadn't worked out.

I retired back to the couch and turned on football. Detroit and Minnesota. One of them was winning. I was looking forward to John Madden's Turkey Leg awards, but it turns out he wasn't doing the game this year. Shucks.

I picked up a different remote and hit the stereo. Some stupid Shania Twain song was playing (you know the one, "The One I Want for Life"), and I couldn't move. I couldn't even think. I almost—I stress *almost*—started crying. And I'm fairly certain if there had been a gun in the house, I would have shot myself through the heart. I turned the stereo off.

So there I was, about an hour into my thirty-third Thanksgiving and it had already proven to be the worst yet. Well, the first one after my parents' death was awful, but this one was giving it a run for its money.

I packed a bag, turned the heat off, hit all the lights, and recorded a new phone message. When I pulled the front door open, I was hit by a wall of cold. It was officially snowing now, and everything that wasn't made of concrete was white. I took two steps, then froze. I pressed my ear to the door. The phone rang three more times before the answering machine picked up.

"*If this is Lacy, I'll call you in a couple days. If this isn't Lacy, stick the phone in your mouth and swallow it.*"

"Hi Thomas. It's me. Listen—"

It was Alex.

I panicked. I couldn't find my keys. Then I couldn't find the *right* key. By the time I got the door open, Alex was long gone.

I made my way to the answering machine and peered down at the blinking red light. Time for a real gut check. I took a deep breath, picked up the machine, and threw it against the wall. I'd clean it up when I got back. If I *ever* got back.

Two hours later, I was at 37,000 feet.

Headed for Seattle.

Chapter 2

The cross-country journey from Bangor International to Chicago O'Hare and on to SeaTac took about seven and change. But I gained three hours during the flight, so when I landed the local time was just after 3:00 in the afternoon.

The weather was typical Seattle November: overcast, gloomy, with a light drizzle. No blizzard in these parts. Old Man Winter in the Northwest had Alzheimer's. He got lost a lot. Mostly in Canada.

I hailed a taxi for the eighteen-mile trip north to Magnolia. A bit of Magnolia lore here: in 1856, Captain George Davidson of the US Coast Survey named the southern bluff overlooking Puget Sound for the magnolia trees growing along it. Had he been a better botanist, he would have clearly recognized the red-barked trees as madrones. The madrone is a shiny, dark green-leafed evergreen species that thrives on west-facing bluffs. The trees, which can reach heights of ninety feet, usually have a twisted, windblown shape. Anyhow, the surrounding community preferred the name Magnolia to Madrone and decided to keep Magnolia to identify the affluent, well-ordered, waterfront properties.

My parents' house—I still had a problem calling it "my house"—was built on the westernmost bluff overlooking Puget Sound. It was too steep to build anywhere near the house so there wasn't anything within a quarter mile in either direction. The main concern was landslides, the wet soil building up over time, the vegetation slowly losing its tenacity in the soft earth. It was a miracle the house hadn't slipped into the Sound years ago as many of its brethren had.

The house was built in 1964. It was a monolith then, a work of art. But then, so once was the Coliseum. When my parents bought it, they began a slow overhaul, gutting it from the inside out. There had been plans for a total facelift, a new kitchen, hardwood floors, upgraded plumbing. But my parents never got around to it. Then it was too late.

The cabbie pulled up alongside the expansive wrought iron fence surrounding the large estate. He wished me a happy Thanksgiving, and I tipped him an extra twenty. When I said I'd packed a bag, I failed to mention I'd packed only a small carry-on of the essentials: contact solution, shampoo, conditioner, mouthwash, and a couple other things, all of which had been red-flagged at airport security because some science wizard had decided three ounces was the magic number. Apparently, three ounces of acid, anthrax, or whatever these zealots make in their caves wasn't going to harm anyone. But four ounces…

So basically, I had the clothes on my back—my favorite pair of jeans and a black T-shirt over a long-sleeve thermal—a rarely-used cell phone, and my wallet.

I pushed through the rusted gate and ambled up the long drive. The once neatly-manicured yard was overgrown with weeds and other debris. Dark vegetation sprung from every crack and fissure of the dilapidated drive. As for the house, the wet Pacific climate and harsh ocean air hadn't been kind in my absence. The five thousand-square-foot Victorian was a combination of rust and sodium-lime deposits. Brown meets green. Almost as if some pesky kids had unloaded on the house with a barrage of aged avocados. Thick foliage had attacked the house from every angle, crawling up, around, and through the gray brick.

Vines spider-webbed across the front door like organic crime scene tape. I cut these away with my keys. The door had warped to the frame so I had to literally kick it in. It gave on the second try, and a wave of musty air washed over me.

I took a step inside the foyer and stopped. I hadn't touched anything in the wake of my parents' deaths. I'd just left. Fled. Denial isn't just a river in Egypt where people wash their clothes, get sick from drinking the water, get bitten by snakes, get eaten by hippos, contract malaria, West Nile, or worse.

There was a small table to my immediate left. A pink vase was at its center, the remnants of a paper-thin stem silently listing over the porcelain edge. I ran my finger over the table, the years of dust coloring my finger a thick black.

I left the front door open and entered a small hallway. I took two steps, my shoes sinking into the inch-long shag. Lowering down to my haunches, I dug my fingers into the long green tendrils. The carpet was reminiscent of the second cut at Augusta, and when I was young, my father and I would take turns setting up golf holes throughout the house. We'd grab our nine irons, a putter, and a couple of those white plastic golf balls and proceed to drive my mom about insane. I stood up, the popping of my knees masking my deep exhale.

Walking forward, I traced my fingers against the eggshell brown walls which had been an eggshell white last I remembered. I came to a set of two doors: one leading to the basement, the other to a bathroom. I poked my head into the bathroom and flipped the light. The two seventy-watt bulbs were clouded with dust and barely illuminated the small room. Evidently, someone—or some financial entity—was keeping up on the bills. The floral wallpaper had begun to peel in many places, its glue well into its late thirties. I heard a soft noise and peered down at the small sink. Water slowly beaded around the head of the faucet before giving way to a single tear.

I shook my head. Those tears could have filled a swimming pool over the course of the last eight years.

I turned the faucet on. After five seconds, a loud rattle shook the foundation of the large house. The pipes screamed and the house shuddered. I held on to the door frame.

It would be slightly ironic if I'd left for eight years, come back for less than an hour, and the house slid into Puget Sound. Or would that just be a terrible coincidence? Or just unfortunate?

The rattling slowly began to subside, and after what seemed

like a full minute, water spurted from the faucet. It was brown. I turned the water off.

I spent the next half hour reacquainting myself with the old house. Pick your cliché. *I took a ride down memory lane. Home is where you hang your hat. Absence makes the heart grow fonder. You can't put toothpaste back in the tube. Even a blind squirrel finds an acorn every once in a while. Too many chiefs and not enough Indians.*

Okay, so maybe those last few weren't exactly relevant, but you get my drift.

I made my way into the kitchen. There were a couple cardboard boxes strewn about the linoleum. A roll of packaging tape and a black Sharpie rested on the island centering the small kitchen. Just above the stove was a round clock. I'd bought it for my parents for Christmas three years before they'd died. It was from Brookstone. Kinetic. The hour hand was halfway between the four and the five. Let's see here, plane landed at just after three, half hour drive, hour or so poking around. Yep, I'd say that was the best thirty bucks I ever spent.

I pulled open the refrigerator, picked up the milk, and read the expiration date: 13APR02. It was green and it said, "Where ya been, Thomas?"

I'm lying, of course. The fridge was empty.

I rummaged through the cabinets. There was a lot of canned stuff, lots of nonperishables, and lots of other things you see in those Thanksgiving donation barrels. I picked up a can of beets and pondered the irony of the situation.

Anyhow, I pulled my cell phone from my pocket and turned it on. There were only a handful of people—and by handful, I mean less than five—who had my cell phone number. I believe the last call I'd made was to my dean at the university telling him I wouldn't be returning to work the following semester. That call had been sometime in early June. In the months since, I'd had all of five missed calls and three voice mails. I scrolled through the five calls. They were all from Alex. Two calls were in October, two in early November, and the last just hours earlier. Being that I was once a detective—albeit a second-rate one—I deduced the messages were also from Alex.

Still got it.

As for Alex, I wasn't sure if I wanted to hear what she had to say. As much as I loved her—and I still did—I could never take a girl back who'd dumped me. It's a pride thing. But maybe that isn't why she'd called. Maybe she wanted her *Fried Green Tomatoes* DVD back.

I picked up the black marker off the center island and wrote on my palm, "She dumped you for a fucking stockbroker." Underneath this I scribbled "toothpaste" and "contact solution."

I located one of the old phone books and, after a couple unsuccessful attempts, found a pizza joint still in service. I inquired if I was the only person to order a pizza on Thanksgiving. The guy informed me that there were a couple others.

At five the pizza came. I grabbed a slice and headed out to the narrow balcony off the kitchen. The sky was a deep gray from which a light drizzle steadily dripped. The sun was preparing for its descent in my right viewfinder, undressing layers of pinks and oranges behind the clouds' satin curtain. A distant island was thinly traced into the horizon on the far left, and I remember my father telling me it was Japan. I'm still not sure if it was or wasn't. Straight down from the balcony was a thicket of tall, windswept madrones, then black rock, then rippling Sound. It was all very melancholy if you ask me.

I rested my elbows on the railing, ate pizza, and watched the sun lower its landing gear. There was a port a half mile south and I watched as a colossal freighter made its lackluster final stretch. It rode high on the black water, inching across the gray horizon. The ship had traveled thousands of miles and here I was witnessing its last steps. Such is life. I spent the next couple minutes thinking deep philosophical thoughts brought on by a stupid boat, the *SS Aristotle.* I thought about where the *SS Prescott* was in its voyage. And what freight it would carry. How it got here and where it was going. I thought about Alex. Was she cargo? Or was she one of these rogue waves I kept hearing about?

A vibration in my pocket startled me out of my rumination. Staring at the screen, I fought the urge to flip the phone open. It pulsed four times then relaxed, then pulsed again two minutes later notifying me I had a new message. Must be some message. But then again, Alex *loved* Kathy Bates.

I stared at the phone for a solid minute, then reared back

and hucked it at the setting sun. For a brief moment I thought it would reach the rippling black water. But it lost velocity, splattering against the rocky shore, its ashes quickly swept away by the incoming tide.

Bye, Alex.

I rubbed my right shoulder and peered over the edge of the balcony then I leaned down and squinted hard. Something was floating in the water. It would hit the black rocks then be sucked back into the channel with each ebb and flow. The white water receded into the black rocks, and I was granted a quick glimpse of arms and long black hair.

It was a woman.

Made in the USA
San Bernardino, CA
30 March 2018